# Of Love and Other Wars

## SOPHIE HARDACH

HEAD
ZEUS

*An Apollo Book*

First published by Simon & Schuster in 2013
This paperback edition first published by Head of Zeus in 2021
An Apollo book

9 7 5 3 1 2 4 6 8

A catalogue record for this book is available from the British Library.

ISBN (PBO): 9781838939212
ISBN (E): 9781838939205

Typeset by M Rules
Printed and bound by CPI Group (UK) Ltd, Croydon, CR0 4YY

Head of Zeus Ltd
First Floor East
5–8 Hardwick Street
London EC1R 4RG

WWW.HEADOFZEUS.COM

*For my dear Dan, who first listened to this story
outside a mountain hut in Georgia and
encouraged me to write it down.*

When after a victorious battle, all London sparkles with illuminations, when the sky is ablaze with fireworks, when the air is filled with the noise of thanks-giving, bells, organs, cannons; we wail in silence over the murders that caused the public rejoicing.

Voltaire, quoting the Quaker Andrew Pitt
in *Premiére Lettre sur les Quakers*, 1734

# 7 MAY 1945

There was a tremendous noise outside, as if the four winds had come together and blown upon the dead. Mr Lamb put his finger between the chapters of Ezekiel he had been reading and pushed back the curtain. Instead of an army of bones, he saw only a brass band trailed by cheering women and children.

His wife called from the hallway and he shuffled towards her, still holding his Bible with the index finger between the pages. In the bright rectangle of the doorway there stood a young man, an airman. His feet were respectfully planted outside the threshold, which no uniformed man had ever crossed.

The Bible slipped from Mr Lamb's grasp. It landed on the carpet with a soft thud. His visitor stepped inside, reached out, steadied him with a strong arm just as the brass band passed their front garden. Mr Lamb tried to say something, but the drums and tubas drowned him out with their triumphant song.

Mrs Morningstar watched the fireworks from her office at Bentham College in Bloomsbury. She switched off the Anglepoise, tore the old blackout paper from the windows and leaned out. Cheers and shouts drifted up from the streets. A green flare travelled across the sky and erupted in a shower of green and yellow light.

It was time, then. She pulled back into the room and walked to a shelf crammed with lab tools, where she carefully retrieved an opaque jar from the very back.

Outside, a golden chrysanthemum covered the fading green sparkles.

In a hospital in northern Germany, a British Army medic drew aside a curtain and asked: 'Mrs Hoffnung, are you quite sure this is your husband?'

She nodded.

'Well, he's lucky you recognized him. Under the circumstances.'

She cupped her hands around her husband's brittle fingers. Out in the corridor, some of the soldiers broke into song.

'I didn't,' she said. 'He recognized me.'

The boys in Paul Lamb's unit were peeling potatoes and singing. There was going to be a feast. A bottle was going round and Paul already felt slightly drunk. The sergeant cook was chopping onions to the rhythm of the song, and when they got to the end he punctuated it by driving his blade into a whole bulb. Paul put down his knife and mumbled that he needed some air. Outside the tent, with the hoarse singing voices behind him, he kneeled down and wiped his hands on the damp grass.

# PART ONE

# Of a Slow Tongue

# The Peculiar People

# 1

When Paul was a boy, he loved murder as much as any other healthy child. In the 1920s, during one of those cold winters when the ponds froze over so quickly that they trapped several ducks, he roamed across Hampstead Heath with his brother, Charlie, and a gang of local boys. They stabbed sticks into potato sacks and howled with pleasure when another German soldier spilled scraps of wool and paper under the assault. On the real battlefield, the bayonet was more of a nuisance because it often jammed; he learned this from a reliable source. One had to use a foot to lever away the body, which was a waste of effort, and some men solved this problem by switching their rifles for sharp-edged shovels.

'Like so,' Mr Boddington, the grocer, said, and halved a cabbage with a spade, sending one half flying across the shop. He scooped up the scattered cabbage leaves, pulled his collar to one side and patted the pale fleshy patch between his neck and shoulder. 'Here. Splits your chap right down to the lung.'

Mr Boddington wore short trousers like a boy, even in winter.

Paul's parents were unaware of the bayonets and the potato sacks until his mother caught the boys frogging by the pond in the back garden. Paul, for once a leader rather than a follower, had invited them. He had been the one to smash the ice on the surface and dig the frog out of the mud at the bottom, easily overwhelming it in its wintery stupor. He had been the one to deliver it to the chief torturers, who placed it between two wooden planks and counted down to the great jump, all of them together, just as the kitchen door opened and his mother stepped out in her brown dress. The boys scattered like fruit flies.

'Oh, Paul.' She lifted the top plank. 'And I was so fond of that frog.'

They continued their rampage. Ants under a magnifying glass angled cleverly in the winter sun. Bee-on-a-string, in which a hibernating bee was dislodged from its bed of moss, dextrously belted, then released and warmed in a room or a shed until it spread its translucent wings and took to the air, one end of the string knotted around its waist, the other pinched between the grubby fingers of a boy, who reeled and steered it like a kite.

Perhaps Paul and Charlie would have continued on that path; perhaps they would have joined the Cadets and the Officer Training Corps and all those other organizations for energetic boys and young men, had not their father walked into the grocery shop one warm spring morning just as Mr Boddington was showing them how to trap a bee in his icebox, where it had to be cooled before it could be safely lassoed.

'Mr Boddington,' his father said. 'Bullying defenceless insects again?'

'Mr Lamb.' Mr Boddington scratched his bare knee with the sharpened stick he used for bayonet practice. 'Being a God-bothering pain in the neck again?'

Paul's father calmly walked over, took the stick from the grocer and broke it in two.

With that, the games came to an end.

Opposition to bayonet games was not unusual then; there were several fathers in the street, some with missing limbs or persistent tremors, who could not bear to see a potato sack stabbed. But who could object to a robust and hearty game like frogging? Who could object to bee-on-a-string, which did not even result in the destruction of the bee, at least not always? It was this aspect of Paul's family and their mysterious religious society, this readiness to detect malice in an innocent, traditional English game, that would later lead to a rumour, sowed by boys within minutes and nurtured by adults over many years, that the meek, mild Lambs at number nine were spies.

The Lambs were used to such accusations. Their ancestors had gathered on storm-swept northern moors to rail against the

King's Church and its priests, had crept into remote farmhouses, hands cupped around candles, to worship in the spirit of the early Christians. In the seventeenth century Lambs in bonnets and wide-brimmed hats had prayed in silent circles, waiting for the sound of galloping hoofs, for armed men who would jump off their foaming horses and yank down the reins with one leather-gloved hand while the other already pounded against the wooden door. In the wilting old books on Paul's shelves, martyred Lambs were dragged across the Morecambe sands, branded with hot irons, gaoled on charges of treason; and when they defiantly told their judges to quake at the word of the Lord, they were mocked as Quakers.

The Lambs on Swains Lane in Highgate merely smiled at their suspicious neighbours, took their sons out of the local school and sent them to one run by their own people, the Religious Society of Friends, as the Quakers called themselves. It was a school where sticks were used to toast bread over a fire and Germans were pen friends who wrote postcards from Bad Pyrmont: 'Dear Paul! How are you? I am fine thank you. The weather here is fine. Visit us soon! Yours, Ludwig.'

Unlike Paul, Charlie insisted on writing all his letters to Bad Pyrmont in the persona of a seventeenth-century elder striving to convert the fictional town of Snotsborough.

'Upon the fifth day of the second month, the Lord called on me once more to spread his word to Snotsborough. Lo! No sooner had I entered the steeple-house than the harlots of Snotsborough fell upon me and beat me exceedingly, and bruised my face with a Bible, and strangulated my neck with

10

their foul underthings. Woe is me, Brother Friedrich, for I truly believe the devil has besmeared the people of Snotsborough with his filth . . .'

In response to which Friedrich would write: 'Dear Charles! Thank you for your letter. I did not understand all of it. Apparently you got into a 'scrap'! Visit us soon. Yours, Friedrich.'

It was at the Quaker school that Charlie's creative energy found a purpose. He smuggled boiled sausages into the vegetarian dining hall; switched the Temperance Society's jugs of apple juice for cider; scattered itching powder on the pews where the entire school gathered in the morning for silent worship.

Paul played the delighted, terrified assistant to his brother's pranks, stealing sausages from their parents' pantry and crates of cider from the back of the pub. At dinner he gripped his knife and fork with the panic of a boy sliding down a coal chute as he waited for the nightly battle to begin, for Charlie to launch the first attack disguised as an innocent remark.

'Father, I do often wonder why we call it First Day Meeting instead of Sunday worship.'

'Because we believe in plain speech and simplicity.'

'Thank thee.' Charlie thoughtfully twirled his fork. 'But I reckon it would be even better if we simply said "Day". For simplicity. Or perhaps we could do away with speaking altogether. Perhaps we ought to simply grunt?'

Mother rapped her plate with her knife. 'Charlie!'

11

'Mother!'

Father frowned liplessly. 'Don't speak to your mother in that tone.'

'I called her mother. Isn't she my mother? Fine. Next time, I shall grunt.'

He pretended to be the Elder of Snotsborough until he was sent up to his room. Climbing the stairs, he laughed and shouted: 'Woe! Woe to the people of Lichfield!'

Through the cheap thin walls they could hear him singing bawdy Georgian ditties. Paul had found the lyrics in a shop on Charing Cross Road, in a tea-stained pamphlet titled 'The Quaker's Opera'.

> Oh how thy Beauty warms!
> Good now, resign thy Charms
> Into the glowing Arms
> Of a stiff Quaker.

Their mother tossed her fork aside and went upstairs.

'Charlie!'

'Mother!'

'That song ...'

'It's for school.'

And he ran past her, down the stairs, out the front door, down the dark street, singing at the top of his voice:

> Oh how thy Beauty warms!
> Good now, resign thy Charms ...

They could hear Mr Boddington chuckle as Charlie passed his house. Paul's mother stood in the glowing rectangle of the door and waited for her errant son to come home.

Paul waited with her for a while. Then he went to bed because it was Seventh Day, and in the morning they would have to get up early for Meeting.

# 2

By the 1930s, Paul no longer bayoneted potato sacks and understood why his parents disapproved of the game. He had learned to wish his fellow worshippers a pleasant Third Month, though when he bought a bag of apples from the corner shop, where the now rather bald Mr Boddington still sat wearing his short trousers, he would mutter that it was sodding cold for March. He was happy to admit, when asked directly, that his family were Quakers, yet he cringed when he stood by the cricket field in the Highgate Woods, as some elderly lady from Meeting rustled up to greet him in her grey skirts and bonnet, and one chap could be heard whispering to another: 'I say, is that his mother?'

His people had once deliberately referred to themselves as peculiar, the Peculiar People, peculiar in the sense of chosen. As a boy, Paul had wished over and over again that they were less peculiar – in the sense of queer and ridiculous – and more like other people. But years later, when he sat in a trembling bathtub and listened out for the sound of raiders overhead, he would wonder whether certain decisions might have been easier for him had the Friends in fact been *more* peculiar. Certain choices might have been clearer had they still shut themselves off from the world and lived in a community of people who cut all their clothes from the same pattern and spoke in their own language; where a cup of tea was accepted with a smile and a 'thank thee', and worship was always on First Day. In such a community it would perhaps not have been possible to muddle right and wrong, because everything was plainly named.

'You're a hopeless old sentimentalist,' Miriam Morningstar would then say, and trail her hand through the cold soapy water in the bathtub. 'And whenever you talk about those grey dresses I always picture that lady ... Mary ... Mary Rye?'

'Mary Pye. She was actually not all that particular about plain dress. It's just that grey was her favourite colour.' He caught her fingers underwater. 'She once told me I reminded her of Moses.'

'Slow of speech, and of a slow tongue.' Mary Pye smoothed her grey skirt. 'Exodus chapter four. Moses said he was not eloquent, but slow of speech, yet the Lord chose him as his messenger. Thee might take comfort in that.'

'Thank you.'

Mary Pye was an elderly aunt who had been hauled out of her cottage near Preston and brought south to live in the Lambs' attic; for her own health, Paul's parents said. Paul suspected it was because they needed the moral reinforcement.

'There are Friends who run pubs,' Charlie muttered on the way home after Silent Meeting. 'There are Friends who give lectures on birth control. And then there's us, forced into Bible study with Mary Pye. We're troglodytes, Paul! It is nineteen thirty-seven and we are the last of the troglodytes!'

Not troglodytes, thought Paul. We're frogs in the lake of darkness. Which was another of Mary Pye's little sayings.

That afternoon they bunked off Bible study. Charlie hopped on his bike and said he was going somewhere important, Paul could follow him or stay with the troglodytes, it was up to him. Paul overtook him on the Heath. Charlie overtook him on the road down to Camden. Paul overtook him in Regent's Park. When he looked over his shoulder, Charlie had disappeared. He came at him out of nowhere just before Harley Street and they crossed Hyde Park side by side, colliding dangerously, laughing at the thought of their parents' frowning faces.

Charlie was seventeen then. Paul was sixteen. It was a warm July day in 1937, with just enough rain to keep the roses happy. Pale girls in trousers sat on park benches, bit their fingernails and smoked. German refugees in long coats clustered around a thin young man on Speakers' Corner.

That was what Paul and Charlie could see on that day in Hyde Park, but there was so much they couldn't even imagine.

In an office in Whitehall, a man in a sweat-soaked shirt drew three lines across a map of Europe, rubbed one of them out, then covered his face with both hands.

At Friends' House on Euston Road, Paul's cousin, Grace, wrote a name next to the number 136, looked up and asked: 'Is there really no space for one more?'

In her house on Rose Walk, Hampstead, Mrs Morningstar handed her daughter, Miriam, a pair of scissors and said: 'From ear to ear, as usual.'

Under the high stuccoed ceilings of a living room in a leafy suburb of Berlin, Mrs Hoffnung wrote on a piece of paper: 'Esther Morningstar, Rose Walk, London. Or: Bentham College, London'. She handed the piece of paper to her son, Max, and said: 'In case.'

But in Hyde Park, Charlie raced past Paul, skidded to a halt just behind a hideous gilded monument and cried out: 'I've got something for you!'

He tossed a cloth-wrapped package at Paul, who failed to catch it and bent awkwardly over his bike to pick it up, not wanting to look too excited, unsure whether to expect a present or a joke.

He remained unsure even after he undid the bundle. Inside was a wooden figurine, about a foot high, with limbs carved from cherrywood, held together by rusty metal joints.

'You do know what it is, don't you?'

'Of course,' lied Paul.

Charlie sighed. 'It's an artist's model. I bought it from the watercolour chap who lives next to Boddington. Look.' He pointed at some dark stains on the red wood. 'Those are genuine wine stains from Paris.'

Paul felt a spasm travel up his spine, a sensation of wanting to retract his head, arms and legs like a tortoise, roll up in a ball, and disappear.

'And what would I do with that?' he said casually.

'Improve those sketches you've been hiding under the brown rug for the past five years,' said Charlie. 'It's not that they're all bad. The fruit bowls are good. The socks and our garden, too. All those drawings of weeds and tools. When it comes to the human form, however ... I know they say people come in all shapes and sizes. But actually, they don't come in *that* many shapes.'

Paul forced himself to look at Charlie.

'They'll never let me study art,' he said feebly. 'It's going to be accountancy, isn't it? And then the soap shop. I'll be smelling of lavender all my life.'

'The shop?' Charlie spat in the direction of a gilded ornament. 'That's what I think of the shop. Now put that away, we've already missed the first speech.'

Charlie swung his arms and legs as he walked, in the natural assumption that everyone would step out of his way. He cleared a path through a crowd of men outside the Royal Albert Hall. Paul followed close behind, an explorer hurrying after his machete-wielding guide.

There were more men inside, thousands of them, some old and embittered by the Great War, others young and filled with the conviction that everything could be solved by

17

Esperanto. Here and there a chap recognized Charlie and greeted him with a clenched fist, and he returned the salutes and called the young men comrades.

It was a pacifist meeting, Charlie explained, but not the sort of meek, tedious pacifism their parents embraced. No, this was a meeting of the Peace Pledge Union, a gathering of men who knew what they wanted, and what they wanted was a new world – which was what Charlie wanted, too. What Paul had to understand, he said, was that Quakerism was all very well, but it was an awfully passive way of being, wasn't it? It was a shopkeeper's religion really, ideal for someone who liked to stand behind a ledger and count his pennies and soap bars.

'Some men don't mind smelling of lavender,' Charlie said, 'but I prefer the smell of adventure. Tobacco, sweat, mud – that's what men are made of.' He raised two fists before his chest and for a moment looked ready to challenge the men around him to a fight. Then he relaxed and put his hands on Paul's shoulders. 'That's what peace means. It means believing in the brotherhood of man. Workers united in sweat and mud. Now listen to what these chaps have to say.'

Paul crossed his arms and planted his feet wide apart. This, then, was what it felt like to be a man: to wear a cloth cap and stand there with his arms crossed, to nod grimly when he agreed with the speaker and push his chin into his chest when he didn't.

'Wasn't the last war meant to end all wars?' the speaker

bellowed. 'Look at us! Here we are again, rearming and readying ourselves for the next one!"

'This one's a trifle tedious,' Charlie whispered in Paul's ear.

'No!' Paul stared at him. 'No, he's incredible.'

'Shush,' said a chap with a black beard.

'Warfare is as primitive as witchcraft, as primitive as cannibalism,' cried the speaker on the stage. 'And soon it will be as outdated!'

They cheered. It was a stirring argument, but even more stirring was the feeling of being in this mass of men, of being addressed as a man who could choose between supporting war and opposing it; whose choice would shape the future of the country. The thought came to Paul that his old pen friend, Ludwig, might be standing in a concert hall in Bad Pyrmont and listening to exactly the same sort of speech, might in fact be thinking of Paul standing in a concert hall in London. His parents had always said that killing was wrong because even one's worst enemy carried an inner light that must not be squashed: it was a concept that had never meant much to Paul because it was too abstract, too metaphorical. It occurred to him now that war was wrong precisely because it was *not* metaphorical. It was not about snuffing out an inner light, or bayoneting potato sacks, or splitting cabbages: it was about learning to operate a weapon, and then going out and using that knowledge to kill his pen friend, Ludwig. It was madness that chaps who had for years exchanged dutiful letters of 'visit us soon!' should suddenly be enemies.

This feeling of personal insight and importance moved

Paul more than any Quaker meeting ever had. When the speaker shouted: 'Sign the peace pledge, comrades! Sign the pledge! Send me a million men like you and then any government must look out!' Paul knew it was time to act, and it was he, ever so placid Paul, who gripped Charlie's arm tightly enough to make him wince, and whispered, 'Let's sign the pledge! Let's do it right now.'

Charlie grew suddenly hesitant. 'Why should we? We know where we stand, don't we?' he muttered.

But Paul, seized by sudden fervour, pressed Charlie until he agreed, then badgered the men around him until he had procured four postcards, two to send off to the Peace Pledge Union, and a copy for each of themselves. The brothers squatted down, laid the cards on their thighs and signed beneath the statement they bore.

'I renounce war, and never again, directly or indirectly, will I sanction or support another.'

## 3

A year later, Charlie found a job as a clerk for the *Peace News* newspaper and Paul enrolled for an accountancy degree at Bentham College in Bloomsbury.

'There's no shame in running a soap business,' his father said, and patted his back. 'There is freedom in running a soap business, genuine spiritual freedom. If you have a soap shop, you'll never have to compromise on your beliefs.

When I came out of prison during the Great War, no one would employ me. What did I do? I sold soap out of a wheelbarrow. Then out of a tiny shop in Clerkenwell. Now we've got a nice shop front in Highgate, suppliers in the south of France, customers as far north as Manchester. There's freedom in shopkeeping, and I wish your brother, Charlie, would understand that.'

He left Paul at the college gates and walked back towards the bus stop, trailing a faint cloud of lavender.

A gravel path led from the wrought-iron gates to a vast quad planted with chestnut trees. Squirrels and magpies rustled through the fallen leaves, observed by the utilitarian stare of Jeremy Bentham cast in bronze. On the far side of the quad loomed a mock Doric portico that inhaled a choppy flow of students. Stone columns, thick and tall, guided the gaze up towards a dome, a giant cranium holding the brain of the world.

From the moment he shuffled through this entrance to the realm of reason, Paul knew he would never live up to it. Even the stone columns were more enlightened than he would ever be. None of his fellow accountants aspired to be shopkeepers or clerks. No, they saw themselves as guardians of mathematical beauty and balance, wrote treatises that they prefaced with quotations from Luca Pacioli, the Tuscan monk who invented double-entry bookkeeping: '*Ubi non est ordo, ibi est confusio.*' Where there is no order, there is confusion.

The enlightened accountants forced the university to let them study statistics with the natural scientists. Everyone except Paul thought this was a wonderful privilege. Paul wished they had their own statistics course, perhaps taught by some placid shopkeeper who expected no great leaps from the minds of men. Instead, they were taught by Mrs Morningstar, a short, slender, terrifying woman scientist from the physics department. Her brilliance burned right through Paul and left him as parched and exhausted as a man in the desert. Numbers, letters, brackets converged in a dazzling beam of knowledge that blinded him for an hour and a half every Monday morning. By the end of every lecture, when the professor collected her notes and walked out, he blinked at his empty notepad, a desert traveller wondering what had happened to the oasis on the horizon.

'Pretty clever for a woman,' the man behind him remarked.

'They do say she studied under the Wizard,' another replied.

A third chap said something in Latin, and they all laughed.

'Would anyone like to buy a copy of *Peace News*?' Paul asked nervously.

No one replied.

He fled to the one place that provided a refuge: a studio in a shabby part of Bloomsbury, where an acquaintance of Charlie's ran a drawing course.

*

22

On a table outside the studio, wooden models were lined up, to be borrowed and used in class. Paul clutched his own scratched and wine-stained figure in gratitude. The communal models had suffered far worse abuse: some prankster had switched around their limbs so that their arms grew out of their necks and their heads were grafted to their armpits. Paul pitied the students who would have to use them for the first part of the course, 'The Human Form'.

He picked up one of the mutilated wooden dummies, put it down again, picked up another. He arranged them in a circle, a pyramid, made them walk in line, dance in pairs. He circled the table and looked at them from different angles, and was so absorbed in this idea for a new painting, or even a sculpture, that he almost missed his class.

He followed the eager scratching of charcoal on paper and the nutty smell of oils and turpentine into the studio, found a free paint-splattered easel by the door and clipped his sheets into place.

Only then did he notice that the students were not drawing wooden dolls.

There, on a pedestal in the middle of the room, sat a naked girl.

She was resting her elbow on one raised knee, with her torso slightly twisted, her face turned away and her sizeable breasts in full view. Two silver clips held back her black hair, and it was those two silver clips that emphasized her nakedness.

The teacher clapped his hands.

'Two minutes for every pose now, chaps, to loosen up!'

The girl turned round and Paul saw her face. He blushed and backed away, but she stared right past him. The teacher approached his easel and, in his panic, Paul picked up a piece of charcoal and began to draw her.

Long afternoons spent drawing the wooden dummy now stood him in good stead. He held out the charcoal and squinted, measuring her head with his thumb on the stub. Miraculously, her head fitted seven times into the zigzagged length of her seated body. He began with a stick figure to get the tilt and twist right, then built her legs and torso in simple triangles and trapezes. Her breasts were somehow lost in the process.

She stood up and tilted her head back. No time to squint and measure now. With one confident stroke Paul captured her spine dipping into the small of her back and then the curve of her bottom. Another standing pose, this time with her feet together and her arms crossed behind her neck, like a human vase. Paul's fingers flew over the paper and soon the stub was gone and he picked up another. His right hand was smudged and so was his left from dwelling a little too long on the cross-hatching where her thighs met.

Only during the final, long posture did he capture her face, though he overdid her large brown eyes and the lecturer muttered that she looked a trifle toadish. He picked up a piece of charcoal and tossed it in the palm of his broad hand. 'The eyes, by the way, should be in the middle of the head, equidistant from chin and crown. You don't learn that kind of stuff from a dummy, do you?' He walked on, whistling and tossing the charcoal in his palm.

After three hours, the girl threw on a yellow silk kimono and disappeared behind a screen to get dressed.

Paul unclipped his drawings, rolled them up, ran out of the door, and, in a flash of inspiration, pulled the dog-eared stack of newspapers from his bag. When she came out, he was still slightly out of breath. The excitement and running emboldened him and he thrust the newspapers under her chin.

'*Peace News! Peace News!*'

She drew back.

'*Peace News!*'

He had not developed a strategy beyond the initial approach, and was unsure what else he could say. There had been a vague expectation she would be intrigued and quite naturally strike up a conversation, but this didn't seem to be the case.

'*Peace News*,' he repeated once more, a little less certainly. 'Would you like to buy a copy?'

She frowned and craned her neck to see the front page.

'*Peace News*,' she read out slowly, and suddenly the name of the paper, to which he had never given much thought, sounded daft.

'It's only . . .' he caught himself. 'I mean, it's free. For you. Here, have one. We're going to have a debate on the German situation at Bentham College tonight. In fact, well, I'm going to be representing the Peace Society.' He paused. 'There's going to be biscuits. All proceeds to go to good causes.'

'*Good causes*?' She arched one eyebrow, looking impossibly mature and sophisticated. The paper shrunk to a shabby loud rag in her hands. But suddenly she smiled, said, 'I'll see you tonight, then,' and walked away.

Paul remained by the door for a long time, clutching his stack of newspapers, wondering if he had heard right. When he finally walked back across the quad, he realized that not only had he heard right, he also had in his possession four nude drawings of this girl. The thought made him so happy that he laughed out loud.

The debate was held in the student union lounge, an airy room with high, arched windows that overlooked the quad with its statue of Bentham. It was furnished with a billiard table, a few sunken leather armchairs, a bookshelf stocked with leather-bound collections of humorous university anecdotes and old student magazines. Women students were not usually permitted to enter the room. They had their own small lounge at the bottom of the hallway, and their own Women's Union Society, whose members were known as Wussites.

Paul lived in fear of the Wussites, who wrote sharp letters to the student newspaper and rarely, if ever, smiled back at him. Yet he had bravely asked for the student union to be opened to women for the night of the debate, arguing that in this time of national emergency both sexes must be addressed. He regretted the move when he saw the stern female faces in the front row: the type who could not wait to go to work in munitions factories.

The lectern provided a shield of sorts, and he began to feel more comfortable. Mistrustful of his rhetorical skills, he had asked Charlie to help him draft a speech, which he now read from the pages before him.

'Warfare,' he read, 'is as primitive as witchcraft!' He shook his fist for emphasis. 'As primitive as cannibalism! And soon,' he shook his fist again, 'soon it will be as outdated!'

There were a few cries of 'Hear, hear!' and a few of 'Nonsense!'. He decided against shaking his fist a third time, and instead read a few more paragraphs. This time the cries of 'Hear, hear' drowned out the heckles. With a note of triumph, he read on: 'Wasn't the last war meant to end all wars? And now – look at us! Here we are again, rearming and readying ourselves for the next one! Well, what can I say, sign the peace pledge, chaps!'

Half the room burst into applause. Paul looked up and shouted again: 'Sign the pledge!' then moved to the seats at the side of the makeshift stage to make room for his opponent.

Just then, one of the girls in the second row stood up and walked towards him.

It was the nude model, now dressed in a blue cotton dress printed with yellow squares.

'Our next speaker will be Mrs Morningstar,' the chairman of the student union called out. 'Tonight's delegate from the Women's Union.'

Paul scanned the crowd for his diabolically intelligent maths lecturer but the girl in the cotton dress climbed onto the stage and suddenly he realized that he had misheard. His opponent would not be Mrs Morningstar, but *Miss* Morningstar: the nude model, who was now calmly taking her place behind the lectern. Without the slightest display of nerves, she thanked the chairman, thanked Paul for his 'interesting contribution', thanked the audience for coming. Her brown duffel bag remained closed: she did not need notes.

The man next to Paul put his mouth close to his ear and hissed: 'Miriam Morningstar. She's *fierce.*'

'Is she the daughter of . . .?'

'The physics dragon? Yes.' And it was impossible to ignore the pity in the chap's voice.

Miriam Morningstar placed both hands on the lectern and began.

'I always grow a little emotional when I hear a pacifist speak,' she said with fluent confidence. 'And before you say that it's because I'm a woman, well, may I just point out that I saw a few men in this room pull out their handker-chiefs. And why not? After all, our friend here used some terribly stirring phrases: "Young men sent to the slaughter! Think of the weeping mothers!"' She leaned forward and smiled at her audience. 'It sounds heartfelt, doesn't it? And so innocent.' She paused. 'But therein lies the danger. We hear the word "appeasement" every day. We hear it from innocent-looking chaps like the one right here. But what, I ask you, lies behind the rhetoric? Well, as it happens, this morning I was given a publication that paints a rather different picture.' She opened her bag, took out the copy of *Peace News* and waved it over her head. 'Has any of you ever read this rag? It gives the most interesting insight into what really goes on in those cosy pacifist clubs. Let me read you an extract from the following article, written in response to Mr Churchill's speech on Hitler. Mr Churchill, you see, called Hitler a cornered maniac. The author of this article, a certain John Middleton Murry, politely disagrees, and offers the alternative opinion that Hitler has instead a "touch of genius".'

Paul considered dashing out into the corridor, but his entire body seemed to be welded to his armchair.

'So how was this "touch of genius" acquired, in Mr Murry's opinion?' Miriam cleared her throat and began to read in an artificial baritone: '"His decisive experiences were gained as a down-and-out in the lowest stratum of modern capitalist society … Hitler knows the depths of contemporary despair. And he has it in for the Churchills of this world. He knows them and hates them: rather than see them still in the seats of the mighty he would pull the whole world down in ruins. The world has had great destroyers before now, and has appeared to need them. Hitler knows a good many things that Mr Churchill has never dreamed of. He knows that this is, in the fullest sense of the word, a lousy world; he will de-louse it and damn the consequences!"'

She paused and took a deep breath. Then she gripped the

paper with both hands, tore it apart and flung the scraps at Paul.

'Mr Lamb, this is the most disgusting nonsense I have ever read, and I can hardly believe that you would dare to sell something like this at Bentham College, our one beacon of tolerance and liberalism in this darkening world!'

The sinking sensation stopped. Paul jumped to his feet.

'It's an opinion piece, Miss Morningstar. One piece! And it was low of you to quote that single piece out of all the rich content of that newspaper.'

'Which one would you rather have me quote, then?'

Unfortunately, Paul had not yet read that particular edition of *Peace News*. He had not quite got round to reading the previous edition, either.

'Well . . . there are many important advertisements in the paper, for example.'

The room burst into howls of laughter.

'Yes,' Miriam said drily. 'I noticed. Vegetarian hotel in the Lake District, conscientious objectors welcome. That does balance it out somewhat, I admit.'

There was more laughter.

Paul was no longer in a debate about pacifism and politics. He sensed his very core being attacked. All he could think of was that he must somehow defend himself in a battle only one of them could win. With high-pitched desperation, he cried: 'And the bit about de-lousing, that was . . . that was a metaphor for ridding the world of poverty and evil!'

'Ridding the world of poverty and evil?' Miss Morningstar let out a scornful laugh. 'I can tell you exactly what Mr Hitler would like to rid the world of. He does want to de-louse the world, quite right, and the people he sees as lice – the people he has described as vermin – are the German Jews.'

'Well, that is just ... now you are just ...' Paul stooped, picked up one of the scraps of paper and waved it in her face. The audience sat silent and spellbound. He picked up more scraps and frantically pieced them together. 'He doesn't mention Jews anywhere. Those may be Mr Hitler's views, but you cannot in all fairness ascribe them to Mr Murry, the author of this article, now can you?'

He looked up. Her calmness had given way to a tight smile.

'Unfortunately, I have met all too many people with views like Mr Murry's. I know that even in this country, there are enough people who would favour a spot of *de-lousing*.'

'In all fairness, Miss Morningstar, this is not something for you and me to decide. In all fairness, this is something to discuss in a different event with a representative of the Jewish students' union.'

She gave him a very curious look. Some people in the audience began to laugh again.

'Well,' she said, and then laughed as well, a surprisingly high and girlish laugh. 'The thing is, Mr Lamb, I'm not sure if you realize, but I *am* Jewish.'

*

31

'In all fairness,' Charlie said, and chuckled. He put his arm around Paul's shoulder. 'Sorry, old chap. No, really, in all fairness, she *is* called Miriam Morningstar.'

'And so? That's a Jewish name, is it?'

Charlie rolled his eyes. Paul shook off his arm.

'How would I know? I'm not sure I've even met a Jewish person before.'

'You must have come to some of Grace's fund-raising events.'

'Which one? Self-Denial for Spain? That was for Basque persons.'

'You're such a troglodyte.'

'Troglodyte yourself.' Paul kicked a stone at the statue of Bentham.

'The worst thing is, her mother teaches my statistics course. I'm going to fail.'

'Because you argued with her daughter?'

'Because I can't count.'

They were out in the street now. Paul walked with his head bowed, his hands angrily stuffed into his pockets, and tried to understand why the mood had so suddenly swung against him. Hadn't they all felt relieved just two months ago when the Munich Crisis had ended, when the Prime Minister had promised 'peace for our time'? Certainly, people were learning about air-raid preparations, Bentham College had converted its vaults into bomb shelters, the chemistry department was printing leaflets about different gases the Germans might use in their attacks. But at the same time, the Peace Pledge Union was receiving sacks full of signed postcards from all over the country, and there was a march against conscription every other week. Uniforms and gas masks had been tried on and stored away again, and even the most bellicose hecklers in the student lounge, even Miss Morningstar herself, could not seriously be wishing to unpack them once more.

'Think of this as a test,' Charlie said. 'It's hard defending the sort of views we hold, and it's going to be even harder.' Walking past a pub, they heard the garbled sound of drunks arguing, then a glass smashing on the floor. Charlie stopped, listened, turned to Paul. 'You do realize there's going to be a war, don't you? Even Father says so.'

# 4

Paul completed more than fifty nude drawings over the next year. Not one of them depicted Miriam. She never posed for them again, but he began to spot her at Bentham College, leaving the arts wing in a pair of paint-splattered dungarees, chatting to lecturers in the quad, and decided she must be an art student. It took him a while to realize that she was not at all angry with him, but rather seemed to see their clash as a bracing bout of wrestling she had won. She smiled at him with familiar ease, as if there was a special camaraderie in having publicly fought over politics. He stood next to her in the luncheon queue, chatted with her on the steps leading up to the portico, and eventually had to admit to himself that these meetings were not coincidences, that he waited for the bus with her even though he always took the tube, that he persuaded the art department to let him use a corner of the studio with the sole intention of watching her stretch her canvases.

In late spring 1939, Paul failed his statistics course but finally plucked up the courage to submit his masterpiece, *The Homecoming*, for the Bentham College summer show. *The Homecoming* was a thin, almost milky oil painting of a forest of ghostly, scorched trees against a grey-white sky. A group of ragged creatures dragged themselves through the forest in single file, backs bent, limbs strangely mutilated. One of them had two arms where the legs should have been. Another, a second head growing out of his armpit. They were the distorted wooden models from the Bloomsbury studio, which Paul had scooped up, set up on a windowsill and painted as if they were nightmarish soldiers returning from a battlefield of ghouls. Lagging behind was his own model, intact but for the wine stains, which he had turned into open wounds in the painting.

From his new friends in the art department he heard that there was some discussion over whether *The Homecoming* quite fitted the spirit of the show, or indeed of Bentham College. Some found it implied a criticism of the military, and of rearmament, that was inappropriate at this time of heightened tension. Others argued that it was precisely the point of art to provoke and unsettle. In the end the work was accepted but given a space at the very back of the exhibition hall.

Two days before the summer show, when Paul was certain no one would dare take out his painting at the last minute, he sneaked into the hall and wrote along the bottom of *The Homecoming* in red paint: 'War will stop when men refuse to fight. What are you going to do about it?'

On the morning before the show, Paul passed a shop window of tiered velvet shelves covered in earrings, bracelets, watches. One item caught his eye. He stopped and examined it through the glass, shook his head and walked on.

The shopkeeper scurried after him. His trained eye had spotted the telltale look on Paul's face: the look of a sensible man secretly wishing to be seduced.

'I believe these are the ones you were interested in, sir?'

The cuff links winked at him from their bed of blue velvet. He would have to buy a new shirt, too, if he wanted to wear them that night. He angled the velvet box in the light. Plain silver cuff links with an inlaid graphic pattern of black jet. Rather nice, really. Very modern.

'You have an excellent eye, sir. Superb craftsmanship but not at all flashy.' The shopkeeper lowered his voice and switched to confidential chumminess: 'Tell you what, I'll give them to you for half. My boy was called up today; suppose you'll all be out there before the year's up. The least I can do is make you chaps look half decent.'

*

Paul's father wore his best suit; his mother, a cream-coloured silk blouse and a dark green skirt that she had bought for the occasion. She nervously fingered the single string of pearls around her neck. Mary Pye had enlivened her grey dress with a silver brooch. Charlie turned up late, but surprised Paul by wearing a smart jacket.

The relentlessly earnest spirit of Bentham College had softened for the summer show. Lanterns swayed in the chestnut trees. A few couples danced on the lawn. Paul's father smiled and tapped his fingers to the rhythm of the swing band, and his mother bought a raffle ticket even though it was gambling. The mildness of early summer gave the night a tender and almost Mediterranean spirit; surely no one could even think of going to war in such lovely weather. For a moment, Paul wished he had created something decorative and inoffensive to exhibit: bright lino prints, or perhaps portraits of musicians and dancers.

Under the pretence of looking for the organizers of the show, he made his way through the crowd. He found Miriam talking to some fellow Wussites. She was wearing a midnight-blue silk gown with silver webbing over the shoulders and stood with her back to him. Her hair was swept up and secured by a silver comb, and when she turned around to greet him, a few curls came loose and fell across her cheek.

The spirit of the night infected him and he held out his hand with a strange new confidence and led her towards the dancers. He spun her around, placed his hand flat on the cool silk between her shoulder blades, guided her through the steps he had practised with Charlie; and it seemed to him that no one in the whole world had ever danced this well. The band played 'The Flat Foot Floozie with the Floy Floy'.

'I've always wondered what a Floy Floy might be,' he said, and repeated 'Floy Floy!' because it sounded so jolly and matched his festive mood.

'It's slang for venereal disease,' said Miriam, perfectly poised in her silk gown.

He laughed. 'I don't think I've ever heard a girl say those words before. Then again, I've never danced with a nude model before.'

She stiffened under his hand.

'Who told you that?'

'I was there, remember? You must have seen me.'

'No!'

She stopped and pulled away. The band struck up a new song and Paul and Miriam began to move again but could not find the lightness of their first dance. They kept looking at their feet like bad and uncertain dancers, fell out of step, had to start again.

Miriam clicked her tongue in frustration.

'I only posed that one time,' she said defensively.

'Only once?' He looked straight into her eyes. 'You're clearly a natural.'

For a moment he feared that he might have made things worse, that he might have offended her. But then she laughed and looked grateful to him for having popped the taut awkwardness.

They danced well after that. Another song, and another. He caught sight of his parents standing forlornly at the edge of the party, ignored them for one more song, then murmured to Miriam that he would quickly show them his painting.

She flinched. 'You haven't seen it yet?'

'Not tonight. Why?'

'Nothing ... I assumed you'd seen it and didn't mind.'

'Didn't mind what?'

Before she could reply, he left the dance floor and elbowed his way through the crowd. He ignored the curious glances, the muffled asides. His parents and Charlie joined him at the studio entrance and asked him if anything was the matter, but he continued walking past the sculptures and lino prints, right to the very back of the room.

When he reached the corner, he heard his mother let out a gasp. Someone held his arm.

*The Homecoming* had been ripped open by a long diagonal gash.

Next to the painting, on a column, sat Paul's wooden model, its arms outstretched and pleading: *Look what they did to me*. Someone had dipped it first in glue, then in white feathers.

# Adamantine Lustre

'When light meets a diamond, a small part of it is reflected, while the remainder penetrates and passes through the transparent stone. The reflected light produces what is known as adamantine lustre.'
*A Theory of Diamond-Cutting*

# 1

Visitors often assumed delicate Mrs Morningstar to be flighty and artistic, and her sturdy daughter, Miriam, to be robust and practical. It had become a family joke that the opposite was the case.

Mrs Morningstar took an interest in the arts, certainly, the way other people were interested in the weather or the changing seasons: they were beautiful enough, and with two artists in the family, she liked to make sure she was well informed. Ultimately, however, aesthetics mattered little to Mrs Morningstar. She had no time for fashion or beauty parlours. Once a month, she had her hair cut by Miriam in a straight line from earlobe to earlobe, in what was not so much a hairstyle as a safety measure. When, during a visit to a Moore and Hepworth exhibition in a local gallery, her husband and her daughter asked her what she considered the most beautiful thing in the world, she said: the structure of benzene.

It was therefore not surprising that she spent the opening night of the summer show in her office. Down in the quad, one of her students played the saxophone and her daughter danced under lanterns that swayed in the breeze. Up at her desk, Esther Morningstar sat in the light of the Anglepoise and marked end-of-term essays from the statistics students. What a tremendously useful occupation for a trained crystallographer, she thought: teaching accountants the probability of finding the one pea in a jar of dried beans.

Footsteps crunched across the gravel under her open window. The voice of a young man drifted up, followed by a cry of protest or outrage. Another voice joined it, clearer and louder.

'What did you expect? Everyone knows that the Bentham art department is ruled by troglodytes.'

It seemed rather fitting that this comment should seal the term. It chimed with her dissatisfaction, with her sense that a long slow slide had brought her to this desk with its Anglepoise, which nodded sleepily because one of the springs that held the head was missing.

In the top drawer of the scratched desk lay a medal cast of

solid gold, a Nobel medal, and when Mrs Morningstar was in a certain mood she liked to take the medal out of the drawer and weigh it in her hand.

A remnant from another life, this habit of falling into a certain melancholy at the end of the academic year; to tally up what had been achieved, what had been missed, and in the warmth of summer mourn the losses of the past. Mrs Morningstar did not believe in judgement season, did not believe in the judge. She walked past crowded synagogues as the first caveman walked past a group of apes; she never enjoyed a bacon bagel more than on Yom Kippur. Yet there was a deep hidden part of her that refused to admit reason and modernity, a deep dark hollow where low voices mingled with the smell of bread, where a woman covered her eyes with her hands and recited a blessing.

The gold lay pleasantly heavy in her palm. She traced the Latin inscription with her fingers. Her Latin was dry and functional, and she would have translated the phrase literally: 'Inventions enhance life, which is beautified through art.'

It was the Wizard who had quoted Virgil in the lab, had taught them a looser, more poetic meaning: 'And they who bettered life on earth by their newly found mastery.'

She placed her other hand over the medal and thought how satisfying it would be if the name engraved in the gold were her own.

# 2

Esther Morningstar, née Adler, had never posed naked on a plinth. Nor had she ever ripped a newspaper to shreds in a student union lounge. And yet, there had been a time when, in her own bowl-haired way, she had lived with a hot pulse, an intensity that left all those around her looking rather limp and lifeless.

She often told her daughter about her early research, about the days when she ran to the lab every morning because she could not wait to get her hands on her spectrometer. Porridge, bathroom, shoes, coat, were meaningless items on a list that must be checked off before one could begin one's daily task of living life, the real life that was there in the shape of a crystal waiting for a young woman scientist to extract its secrets.

The lab was a wonderland. Hand-welded instruments blew up in the middle of the room. Men in white coats crawled around on all fours searching for a dropped crystal the size of a crumb. Her supervisor was none other than Herbert Littlewood, whom everyone called the Wizard. He taught her that to be a scientist meant to be fearless, to love surprises, accidents and explosions, because that way lay discovery. And all of them, the Wizard and his fellow sorcerers, all of them predicted a bright future for young Esther Adler.

'And then what happened?' Miriam would ask (innocently

when she was small, more provocatively as she got older).

'Then I married your father and we moved into this big house and had you. Isn't that wonderful?' She ruffled Miriam's hair. 'It's important to appreciate the present.'

Once, when Miriam was small, she cried: 'Like my birthday present!'

'Just like that,' her mother said, and added silently: just like a birthday present; one that is not exactly what one had wished for.

Esther was the youngest of eight, and the only one of the siblings to display an extraordinary mathematical talent. As a child, she had loved the story of Joseph, who dreamed that his older brothers bowed down to him as slaves. She thought Joseph a fool, though, for telling his brothers about it; no wonder they sold him to a passing Ishmaelite.

To her teachers, it was obvious that she had inherited her brilliance from her father, a diamond cutter, especially since she had early on displayed a passion for geometry. The wonder girl alone knew that her gift had nothing to do with her father, despite their shared interest in crystals. He was an able cutter, but he did not have the inquisitive mind of a scientist, nor a sense of how things fit together.

She remembered very clearly the first time she beheld the beauty of smaller shapes arranged within a larger shape. She had been about five years old, and had watched trapezes and triangles being fitted into a larger rectangle by a person with a most extraordinary sense of space and geometry: her mother, who was expertly laying out a dress pattern on a stretch of fabric.

Esther never shared this memory with anyone. She would have been mocked by her colleagues had she cited her mother's dressmaking as an influence. Her mother would have been embarrassed. But Esther continued to watch her mother lay out dress patterns, and imagined that she was quietly aware of her talent, or at least proud that she ended up with less scrap material than any other woman in Hatton Garden.

Old Mr Adler showed Esther around like a particularly well-cut gem whose perfection reflected his own skill. Her success was his reward for all he had sacrificed, for his tenacity in teaching his children the craft, even the girls, even though his friends and neighbours thought this eccentric.

'It'll make it hard to find a match,' they warned him. 'Who wants a wife who coughs like an old cutter?'

In the evenings, he would gather his children in his workshop. Two high wooden tables pressed into a hot, dark, dirty attic, a nightmarish doll's house that had followed them from Antwerp to London. Three cutters hunched over their spinning scaifes on one side, their calloused hands gripping wooden tangs that held the stone against the disc. Esther's three gangly brothers crammed into the narrow aisle behind the cutters' backs, kindling braziers and softening lead balls over hissing gas flames: Nathan and Simon, and Solly, whom they called the rabbi when their parents were out of earshot. Sticky, greasy black dust crept up their noses and stuck to their fingertips. Esther would wipe her face and then that was blackened too. The white bows around her sisters' braids had long turned grey. Her thick brown wool stockings and the patched flannel dress tied high under her chin itched with trapped heat and dust.

Then one of the cutters would stop his wheel, smear a slick of oil across it, sprinkle it with diamond dust and lower his stone again. Fifty-seven times. Fifty-seven facets for a sparkling full cut, eight facets for a cheap splinter.

The men sang over the hissing gas flames, folk songs in strange tongues when it was a good day, a fifty-seven-facet day. When it was an eight-facet day, you could hear only the hissing gas flames and the clanging metal and another, deeper hiss, the hiss of diamond grinding diamond.

Esther and her sisters kneeled in a corner in their thick flannel dresses, folding paper into rectangles that would later be labelled with dates and names.

The door opened and her father hurried in. He untied the big leather wallet with the stock, carefully placed it on his desk and gathered his children around him to show them a large cut stone he had just brought in. It was tucked away in a folded piece of paper like a humble splinter, but he unwrapped it with reverence. 'Look, if the cut is perfect every ray of light will follow the best path. It goes into the stone and bounces round and round, then shoots straight back into your eye. It's not that hard to understand, is it?'

But they all found it very hard to understand. All of them, except Esther.

He was speaking to them now in the formal German and

French he used to flatter clients. When he scolded the children or gave them orders, he mixed Yiddish with Flemish. English hardly ever made it up the steep staircase and into the dirty workshop. It usually waited on the street like a patient English gentleman, and when the children went home at night they picked it up and spoke it among themselves.

'Just look. Take this loupe – Nathan, give your sister your loupe – and look. This one's perfectly clear. Now think about the light. First there's the light reflected off the surface, what we call the adamantine lustre. Then there's the light that enters the stone, and which we mustn't let out the back. And finally we have what we call the fire of the diamond, which I won't bother explaining to you, since Esther appears to be the only one here who is following me. Esther, do you happen to have any brains to spare for your brothers?'

There was a knock on the door and her father slipped the stone into his pocket. He whistled once to send the boys back to their braziers. The girls followed, except for Esther, who pretended to tie her shoelaces so she could stay and watch. A heavy-set man came blundering in, steadying himself on the doorframe to catch his breath. He held a parcel under his arm: a roll of newspaper tied with string. It smelled of fish and she already disliked this man for bringing a fish with him that would spread its smell in the workshop.

The men moved to the desk by the door. Her father pulled an envelope from a drawer and unfolded it. He held the loupe in his right hand and his left sorted through the tiny splinters on the paper, pushing some to the left, some to the right.

'Forget this one, and this one. Four or five are worth the trouble,' her father said in Flemish. 'Take the rest back to Café Flora. Tell your client they're not worth my time.'

The man murmured something.

'You could have saved yourself the climb,' Esther's father said.

The man reached for his own leather pouch but her father shook his head. His voice grew angry and he used a word Esther had never heard before.

After the visitor left, her father stayed at his desk and rolled the loupe between his fingers, as if he regretted having sent him away. He had forgotten all about the lesson, and with that look on his face none of the children dared remind him.

Esther quietly repeated the words that had enchanted her: 'Adamantine lustre.' She picked up a piece of chalk and drew the shape of a diamond on the table, gave it different facets the way a cutter would before getting to work. Then she wiped it away with the ball of her hand.

'If the diamond is so clear,' Esther asked Shimon, who had stopped his wheel to apply a new coat of dust, 'then why are we all covered in soot?'

'Because diamond is coal,' he said without looking up from his loupe. 'You know how a diamond is made, don't you? By a great weight pressing down on coal.'

He ran his finger over the scaife and dabbed a black dot on Esther's nose.

She turned her smudged hands. It was true. They looked as if she had been playing in the coal cellar. Her brother Nathan tugged at one of her braids and told her to stop pestering the cutters.

'Help me with this if you're bored.'

He passed her a metal cylinder containing diamond splinters and debris swept off the worktop, and a metal pestle and a hammer. 'Just clobber it until it's really fine, all right?'

And she clobbered. And clobbered. And clobbered.

It was dark outside, night-dark, when the diamonds had finally turned into dust. She did not mind because it was dark outside even during the day, fog-dark. Nathan called the country Fogland. Every day English people stood in the street and agreed that it was awfully foggy, gosh yes, terribly foggy, as if it was an astonishing novelty. Esther's mother never mentioned the fog, though sometimes when they hung up the laundry she told the girls about the gardens of Antwerp, where lines and lines of washing flashed white like teeth in the sun.

That evening the fog was so thick that Esther let her fingertips trail along the walls to make sure she was still on the pavement. With the other hand she grabbed Nathan's sleeve and asked him what that man had tried to sell their father.

'An emerald.'

'And why didn't we want it?'

Nathan stopped and waited until the others were out of

earshot. He gave her a minty humbug, which she clicked against her teeth with her tongue. Then he explained to her that a lot of emeralds were cracked but he'd learned to uncrack them. All you needed was a tub full of oil and a pipe with a vacuum. Take a pile of cracked stones and make them flawless. No one would ever know the difference, until some lady wore her big green ring to a ball and, eek, it leaked oil all over her silk dress. But by then the emerald would long be sold and Nathan would have made a packet. What was one soiled dress compared to a lifetime in an attic?

If he had his own way, he said, he wouldn't mind experimenting. Mix a bit of lead and water, make a nice crystal. With a proper cut it's as pretty as a brilliant. Mount it on a fine ring, sell it to the lady who just threw away her emerald because it spoiled her dearest dress. Give a cut to the jeweller and pocket the rest. That was his idea, but it was secret, did she understand? Their father was strict about that sort of thing, and if Esther breathed a single word, Nathan would hang her up by her braids.

She knew he did not really mean that.

'What's a shlemiel?' she asked.

'Someone who's not as stupid as our father thinks he is.'

That night, her mother came into the kitchen and screeched.

'Esther Louisa Jeannette Adler, what on earth do you think you are doing in the middle of my kitchen, filthy as a scrapheap, and ...' she looked at Esther's feet, '... standing on a lump of coal!'

'Making diamonds.'

And her mother sat down on the big carved trunk in the corner, put her head in her hands and laughed and laughed.

'Adler,' she called, 'come and see what your daughter has come up with now.'

Esther put down the metal weight she had been holding with both hands and stepped off the lump of coal. Her face was hot with tears and anger.

'But if we make diamonds we'll never have to go to the workshop again!' she cried. 'We'll never cough again, and we'll never have to clobber diamonds again, ever.'

She thought: and Nathan won't make filthy forgeries.

Her mother stopped calling for Adler to come and watch the spectacle. Instead, she took a soapy cloth and wiped Esther's face. Esther had expected to be slapped for cursing the workshop. But her mother merely continued cleaning her face.

Many years later, Esther would think about what had been on her mother's mind that night. Perhaps her mother had been recalling the delight of Esther's teachers, her little girl's curiosity, her facility with weights and numbers; perhaps she had thought, why not give this one a little more time away from the workshop, a little more time to sit at the kitchen table and learn her grammar and arithmetic? Perhaps she thought: we have four other girls who can help me scrub pots. We have three boys who can rub two diamonds against each other for hours until they are perfectly round and ready to be cut. Why not let this one, the smallest, spend more time with her neat exercise books?

The older girls were born in Antwerp, where the neighbours peered into your tureens and the community's only matchmaker hurried from door to door with his black notebook. Esther was born after they moved to Hatton Garden: a spring child for a new beginning.

The next day, Esther was told that she did not have to come straight to the workshop after school. She would still have to help with some of the tasks, but she could sit in her mother's clean kitchen where she would not be breathing black air. And she would never again be told to make diamond dust.

3

Esther won a scholarship to a women's college at sixteen, an award for best master's thesis at twenty-one, a research post in the Wizard's lab at twenty-two. And then she was suddenly in a great rush to marry. The family could not understand why; unlike her sisters, she had not been under any pressure. Perhaps, they thought, it was only natural for a woman ultimately to prefer a warm home over a cold laboratory. With the help of friends and relations, a suitable young man was found. An architect. His leg was in a plaster cast and he walked with a strong limp. Something to do with steep crooked steps and a pail of soapy water.

Before the leg was healed, Esther became Mrs Morningstar. On their wedding day, she circled him seven times under the chuppah and thought: what an utterly primitive and superstitious thing to do; I might as well be poking a stick at the sky to make it rain.

After the ceremony, she muttered to him: 'It's all a lot of mumbo jumbo, isn't it? Isn't it?' And he stared at her with an expression of astonished hurt.

They moved into a Victorian pile in Hampstead left to Esther by an aunt, a confirmed spinster, with the recommendation that she turn it into 'an academy for scientifically-minded young ladies'. Esther ignored the recommendation. She prepared to pull the cloth cover over her spectrometer for good and fill the big empty house with children.

'I didn't marry you to turn you into a cook and a maid,' her new husband said gruffly. 'You might as well keep your work until we have a child for every room.'

'And then you *will* turn me into a cook and a maid?'

No amount of ambition would make her return to the Wizard's lab, but she found a modest, quiet teaching post at Bentham College, which she imagined would lead to greater things.

The leg never quite healed under the plaster cast. Some nerve had been squashed, some vein compressed for too long, some bone rejoined incorrectly. The calf withered and Mrs Morningstar grew used to her husband's limping shuffle echoing through the many empty rooms of the house.

# 4

Down in the quad, students were unstringing the dead lanterns and stacking empty cups. The Bentham College show, Mrs Morningstar supposed, had been a success. She weighed the medal in her hand again, opened the drawer, but on an impulse slid it into her coat pocket instead of locking it away.

'Gottfried von der Weide' read the name on the medal. It was a name made for being engraved in gold, a name that evoked images of old-world aristocracy and stiff-backed gentlemen dancing in ballrooms. Neither the medal nor the name quite fit the awkward young foreigner who had always been lonely in the Wizard's lab. She remembered how he had once fought desperately with his white coat until he realized someone had sewn up the sleeves. As pale and pudgy as a flour dumpling, he spoke with a stammer and wiped his sweaty palm on his coat before shaking hands. The chaps never asked him to the pub after work. They did not ask her, either. The two of them would work in the lab long after the others had left, but their enforced company was shy and awkward. Later, when the men decided that they liked and even admired her, Gottfried had already returned to Heidelberg. They wrote to each other once or twice; questions of recruitment, equipment. Yet two years ago he had sent her his Nobel medal, smuggled to London from Heidelberg in the double-walled suitcases and thickly lined jackets of men who knew well that the German government had imposed a ban on the export of gold. Why me? she had asked the man who knocked on her office door one day with the medal in a small blue case. Why not the Wizard? And it alarmed her that people should have such trust in her, that a persecuted scientist should send her his Nobel medal, while a cousin she barely knew had sent her her only son, whom she had taken in as a lodger. If she was considered the most trustworthy person these people knew, what did that say about the state of the world?

With her hand in the sagging coat pocket, she crossed the quad. Her daughter must have gone home. She took the train up to Hampstead, where the horrid old house awaited her, its empty rooms now gradually filling up: not with laughing children, but with relatives from the Continent waiting for a passage to America.

'Is that you, Essie?' her husband called from upstairs when she turned the key in the lock. She rummaged through the envelopes on the silver tray by the door before she replied. Bills, subscriptions, and then, a thin envelope stamped with an address she had not read since her marriage.

Glancing at the staircase to make sure no one was watching, she tore open the envelope with uncharacteristic nervousness.

It was a letter from the Wizard, or rather, a few formal lines typed out by his secretary. A tap on the shoulder, the call to a research mission of national importance. It would not be particularly glamorous: she would probably sit in a field and watch test persons fire projectiles into mattresses, or work on the theoretical side, calculating trajectories and scatter fields. But she would be working with the Wizard's set again, with bright lights who illuminated each other's work.

It was the letter she had been expecting for two decades: the letter asking her to return. And yet her trembling fingers were tearing the envelope into tiny pieces.

Her answer must be no. She had rehearsed it for so long, the politely withering refusal. But as her hands continued to tear the paper, her mind was already digging up the ancient burial ground and opening the well-sealed graves. She dipped a piece of film into a tub of developer and watched it darken until a pattern of scattered white dots emerged and made the invisible visible. She heard herself breathlessly tell Gottfried about the Wizard's praise for their project, and Gottfried reply in his German accent, 'And to think I used to sell shoes in Passau!' She felt the metallic taste of anxiety at the start of an experiment and the sweet rush of triumph at its conclusion. And even the memory of the Wizard's green armchair, and the rough cold fabric pressing against her bare back while his sick wife's muffled coughs seeped in through the walls, could not quite dispel that rush of triumph.

That night Mrs Morningstar fell asleep as soon as her head touched the pillow. Her husband, who knew the signs, studied her fearfully twitching face with concern. Around midnight, he was woken by low hisses and murmurs. His wife, the respected scientist, was sitting up with her back against the headboard, her white nightdress dark and translucent with sweat. She was rocking back and forth and muttering to herself with the aimless fury of a tramp in the gutter.

'Oh, Essie,' he sighed. 'It's been a long time, hasn't it?'

He moved the heavy bed away from the wall, which was more difficult than it used to be. And then he began slowly, slowly circling the bed, not unlike the way his sceptical young bride had circled him so many years ago on their wedding day.

# Worship

'I'm not going,' Charlie said.

But Paul needed him to come. Everyone knew what was going to happen, everyone was resigned to it. The fire was lit and they were walking towards it, and now suddenly Charlie was leaving him to pass through it alone. He patted Paul's shoulder, ignored his stammered protest and grabbed his coat.

'That's bloody unfair,' Paul shouted after Charlie when he was already half-way down the street. 'You can't just leave me to go by myself.'

Charlie turned around, walked backwards for a few steps and waved at him.

'You won't be by yourself. All the chief troglodytes will be there.'

Church Square in Highgate was just large enough to accommodate two houses of worship and a pub. On the first Sunday in September 1939, the pub was closed and the most impressive building on the square, St Matthew's Church, received only a trickle of faithful. Paul cycled past the open doors, then stopped to watch the worshippers. Usually they lingered outside and traded gossip between the notice board and the saviour on his crucifix. Today, they crunched briskly across the wet gravel and hurried through the entrance, ushered in by the bells like serfs into a fortress.

A wall of sandbags shielded the portal. The tall stained-glass windows were latticed with strips of sticky paper. Someone clever had remarked that Britain was reverting to the Norman style of architecture, sacrificing comfort for security. Walls were fortified, windows covered. All those vast glass panels, the pride of the modern movement, now looked vulnerable and foolish.

Paul tucked his scarf tightly around his neck and pushed his bicycle across the square towards a small brick cottage with plain, low windows and a white porch. Nothing distinguished it from the residential cottages around it except for the fact that it was entirely unprotected. No sandbags blocked the doors, no blast-proof tape secured the windows. A white banner hung from the fence, probably imprinted with some soothing psalm, but the previous night's thunderstorm had drenched the fabric and blurred the letters.

He leaned his bicycle against a discreet sign that said 'Highgate Meeting House', rubbed his hands together and looked back at St Matthew's, tall and dignified between the lime trees. The square was strewn with leaves and fallen branches. There was a chill in the air; the year had not fulfilled the promise of its May.

The two bell-ringers of St Matthew's, local boys who many years ago had played bee-on-a-string on the Heath, yanked their ropes in rhythmic alternation. One pair of feet lightly left the stone floor just as the other pair touched down.

'Sixpence says they're going to sing "Onward, Christian Soldiers",' said one of them.

'Sixpence says "For Those in Peril on the Sea",' said the other.

One pair of feet touched the floor; the other was gently pulled towards Heaven.

In Highgate Meeting House, the Friends had already gathered on their bare wooden chairs, hands folded, heads bowed in silence. When Paul slipped through the door, they broke their circle to let him in. He leaned forward and crossed his forearms over his thighs. Mary Pye was there, of course, and his parents. His father in a worn tweed jacket, his mother in a brown skirt suit. His cousin Grace, who preferred to worship separately from her parents and sisters, had joined them, and next to her sat a little girl whose ears barely poked out of her coat.

Paul caught Grace looking at her watch. She was good like that. Instilled order, made sure everyone was on time. Her pragmatic efficiency was wonderful, really, and it was quite unfair that Charlie had taken to calling her Major Spank.

They were breathing quietly now. The silence was so peaceful it might have been sleep. Some meetings were entirely silent, though Mary Pye could usually be relied on to say something appreciative about the dahlias in Tavistock Square. Grace, on the other hand, had lately developed a worrying tendency to aim her words directly at Paul, smiling at him while she spoke, not always with flattering results: '*And thou, faithful babe, though thou stutter and stammer forth a few words in the dread of the Lord, they are accepted*'. Paul, the faithful babe, had never spoken in Meeting. Every Sunday he waited for the spirit to move him. Every Sunday the spirit stayed silent, and then it was tea and biscuits and he had missed another chance to minister.

Through the low plain windows he could see the doors of St Matthew's swinging shut.

Today, he decided, he would speak. Yes, he was quite certain that on this strange and rather frightening day, he would finally speak.

'*Onward, Christian soldiers*,' the congregation sang under the red and blue windows of St Matthew's Church, '*Marching as to war! With the cross of Jeee-sus going on before!*'

Sixpence was passed from one sticky palm to another.

Paul tried to savour the presence of stillness rather than the absence of noise. His mother's stomach rumbled. For as long as he could remember, this had been her only contribution to meeting for worship. Oh, and once she had stood up and read out her favourite quotation: *'You will say, Christ saith this, and the apostles say this; but what canst thou say? Art thou a child of Light and hast walked in the Light . . .?'*

George Fox. An appropriate piece of ministry for today, perhaps.

'Is God on our side?' thundered the vicar of St Matthew's. He leaned out of his pulpit and shook his fist. 'I ask you again: is God on our side?' His flock cowered under his bushy grey glare. 'The answer is, only if we make ourselves worthy of his help! Only if, like the disciples on the Sea of Galilee, we pray *and* row. Only if every young man, every able-bodied young man in this parish, is willing to fight the enemies of God. Yes! The enemies of—'

—George Fox then. Paul took a deep breath, squeezed his hands together and in doing so glanced at his wristwatch. It was almost eleven o'clock. Charlie had been right. It was absurd to be sitting here when the whole world was waiting for that one voice on the wireless to seal their transition from a nervous peace to a catastrophic—

Grace stood up, opened a book on the table in the centre of the room and read: *'Art thou a child of Light and hast walked in the Light, and what thou speakest, is it inwardly from God?'*

She sat down again.

Paul was gripped by an urge to run into the pantry and switch on the blasted wireless. The bowed heads around him in their potent, worshipful silence looked to him like insects in a clear resin paperweight. And then he realized that he, too, was trapped in that resin and bound by that spirit. Even now with all his doubts and irritated impatience he would find it impossible to walk out.

*Art thou a child of Light?* Perhaps this, then, was the Lord's gift to the Children of Light. Everywhere on this island, men, women, families might be dashing this way and that, packing bags, seeking shelter, gathering up hideous gas masks, and the fellowship around him, stubbornly resisting the news, was the last remaining circle of peace.

It was then, as he settled against the backrest of his chair, that they heard the faint moan of the siren. Paul stood up.

'Well, Friends, it looks like that is that, then,' he stammered through the strangely mournful sound. 'We're at war with Germany.'

The vicar fell silent.

One of the bell-ringers thought of his brother, who was out at sea.

The other stared at the stained-glass window to his right and noticed for the first time that it depicted St Matthew writing the gospel.

The strips of sticky paper that crossed the pane were flimsy enough to let the weak September sunlight through. It was very unlikely, the bell-ringer thought, that they would hold even a third of the glass if it shattered.

\*

Paul sat down again. After a respectful pause, his mother got to her feet and slid her finger down the page of her Bible: *'Yea, though I walk through the valley of the shadow of death, I will fear no evil: for thou art with me ...'*

He closed his eyes. From the outside came the noise of the vicar of St Matthew's leading his congregation to the nearest shelter. A rhythmic knocking sound rose through his mother's voice.

*'... goodness and mercy shall follow me ...'*

It took Paul a few seconds to work out what it was.

*'... all the days of my life ...'*

Someone hammering on the front door.

*'... and I will dwell in the house of the Lord for ever.'*

Someone gave the door a determined push; it swung open and Miriam Morningstar walked in. She wore a pair of overalls, an air-raid precautions armband and, on her head, what looked like a battered saucepan.

'Oh!' She gave a little start when she saw Paul. 'I'm sorry, I didn't realize ...' They exchanged uncertain smiles. She collected herself, quickly turned to the rest of the group and introduced herself as the air-raid warden for the neighbourhood.

Paul's father put his hands on his knees and stood up in that heavy ponderous way of his. Miriam misunderstood the gesture.

'Thank you.' She smiled at him. 'If the others would kindly follow this gentleman, there's a shelter just underneath St Matthew's Church.'

Paul interceded before his father could respond. 'I suppose she does have a point. It may well be a false alarm, but it would be foolish to sit through it none the less. Just look at all these windows, all this glass!' He could see the Friends from Miriam's perspective now: a group of confused innocents huddling together in an impossible flimsy and vulnerable cottage.

No one spoke. For a moment, he thought they had not heard him. Then his father cleared his throat and addressed the others without looking at Paul: 'Our Friend is a little disturbed. We can easily understand his upset.'

He put his hand on Paul's back and applied gentle pressure to guide him out into the entrance hall. It ought not to have surprised Paul: this was how these things were handled. One did not stand up and start an argument in Meeting. One did not answer back. But the pressure of his father's hand combined with Miriam's confused gaze made him tingle with irritation.

'I'm not disturbed.' He tried to stand firmly. 'I may be breaking the spirit of worship, but I'm not disturbed. We all heard the signal.'

This time his father remained silent. The others sat with bowed heads. The thick resin enclosed them all and he knew that even if he were to shout and stomp his feet, he would not be able to stir them. Helplessly furious, he left the room.

Miriam followed them outside and whispered to his father: 'Sir, I don't mean to be disrespectful, but there's a penalty for refusing to cooperate.'

A single note sounded.

'That's the all clear,' Miriam cried out with relief. 'You may continue your worship now. There's no need to go to the shelter. All clear! All clear! Thank you for your co-operation.'

She tipped her saucepan-hat and hurried out of the door. Paul waited in the entrance hall until his mother shook Grace's hand, which was their own all-clear signal, the sign that Silent Meeting was over. Limbs were stretched, crumpled clothes patted down. No one mentioned the sudden intrusion, nor Paul's misplaced agitation.

Paul was the last to leave the cottage. He locked the wooden front door that he had entered in peace and exited at war.

# The Ladies' Pond

## 1

Ten days into the war, Liverpool Street Station was swarming with children: scrawny East End boys, stout girls like miniature fishwives. Mothers shouted last-minute instructions. Busy men in uniform blew whistles, waved children in and mothers out and dogs out of the way. Trains pulled into the station, scooped up a platform-load of boys and girls, then hurried off into the distance. Londoners waved handkerchiefs like the burghers of Hamelin. Grace handed over Inge, one of her little evacuees, to a relation who would take her to a country house in Hertfordshire. It was difficult to concentrate on the farewell, difficult to put sufficient warmth into the hug and the promise of visits in the near future. Her mind was on the other train.

She walked to the far side of the station, to a quiet platform where only a handful of people were waiting. One or two women greeted her with smiles and chatter. There was an elderly couple in Sunday clothes, their hands folded, faces set into pleasantness. Grace pictured them sitting by a black range, listening to one of the appeals on the wireless. The husband would have said: 'We're a bit too old for that kind of thing, don't you think?' The wife would have persuaded him. She had set her grey hair and put on a fur collar. You could see from her scuffed shoes that she did not usually go in for such extravagance. 'To give the children a friendly welcome and show how glad we are to have them. And I'll love them as if they were my own.'

Grace introduced herself to the elderly couple. The woman touched her curled hair and said nervously: 'We were told there might not be a train.'

'These things are very difficult to judge with any certainty.' It was one of the stock phrases she used on these occasions. 'We can only pray.' That was another.

The man pursed his lips and studied her carefully, trying to establish her credibility.

'You've negotiated with them directly, have you? You've actually spoken to them?'

'Not exactly. There are others who deal with that side of things.'

The man looked as if he wished he could speak to those others instead of Grace. 'We were told this lot isn't from Germany.'

'No. They're children from—'

'Vienna, we were told.'

Grace nodded. She could see that he was on the verge of

67

asking whether there was someone he ought to be introduced to, someone who could explain things better than she could. In a prickly attempt to assert her authority, she said: 'Of course Vienna is where it all began. I travelled there last year, when we negotiated over the very first train.'

The Nazis had set up an office for Jewish emigration in a mansion formerly owned by the Rothschild family. The tall oval mirrors, silver candlesticks and marble angels had been made for a world of sparkling delight, as if any moment the white double doors would open to display waltzing couples in morning suits and cream chiffon dresses. But when they did open, they revealed only an empty ballroom patrolled by men in black uniforms. Heavy boots creaked over the herringbone parquet. Alsatians strained against leather leashes wrapped tightly around gloved fists.

'Gosh.' The man's voice yielded a vague note of respect. 'I'm sorry, what did you say your name was? I'm organizing a lecture series, you see, and I'm sure everyone would be tremendously interested in your testimony.'

'Oh.' Grace blushed and frantically picked at a piece of dry skin on her thumb. 'There was a Dutch lady, Mrs Wijsmuller, who had some experience in humanitarian matters, and she negotiated with Mr Eichmann himself. Now if you wanted to invite *her* to your lecture series ...' the dry skin came away, '... then I'm sure that could be arranged.' And she added somewhat stubbornly: 'She did of course tell me all about it in great detail right after she came out.'

He must think her a complete fantasist now. There was an

awkward silence, and then the wife murmured that they should go and see the station assistant to enquire about the train.

It was like that time when she had told Paul and Charlie about the great bank robbery near Piccadilly; Paul had listened with awe but Charlie had needled her until she admitted that she had not *exactly* seen the robbers, nor the masks and guns she had so vividly described, but had arrived at the bank just when the police were taking witness statements.

Grace had always assumed that stories only happened to other people, that it was other people who came and went and won and lost, and that she would be forever the observer waiting outside the office, the bystander living on the experiences of others.

But then, about a month ago, her own story happened.

It began with a train. She had stood on this same platform at Liverpool Street Station, waiting for the train from Harwich. An ordinary day on a crowded platform. Quaker women kept food trolleys and tea urns at the ready. She had worn her ordinary hand-me-downs. That was how she'd looked when he first saw her: dowdy, in hand-me-downs, standing next to a tea urn. He'd hopped off the train and looked around. At first she mistook him for an older boy who had squeezed in just below the age limit, with his freckled stub nose and the open roundness of his face, still unformed, the unkempt sandy hair asking to be raked through with a comb. Then she spotted the packet of documents in his hands. She waved her list.

'You must be—'

'I'm sorry, I thought you were—'

They looked at each other and laughed. He scratched the shaven nape of his neck, and she knew at once that this was something he always did when he felt embarrassed. She almost put her hand out to run her fingers over the stubble: it would have felt familiar, she was certain of it.

They went through the list together.

'That one didn't make it,' he said, and pointed at a name.

'Neither of them?' Grace said. Her pen hovered above two surnames.

'The girl is here. The boy ... we'll try to put him on the next one.'

Grace thought: how can I know you this well, better than I know the Friends I have prayed with for years?

Then he was gone, lost in a mass of people. Grace turned to the tea urn. Frightened boys and girls descended from the train, clutching their satchels. They were served tea and sandwiches and the best smile she could muster. Grace leaned against a pillar and closed her eyes for a moment.

'Excuse me?'

Her eyelids pinged open. He stood there and scratched the nape of his neck.

He had to leave with the other Friends, he said, but ...

would she perhaps like to meet him later that afternoon? It was his first time in London and he had to go back the next day.

Of course, she said. They agreed to meet at her office that evening.

She took the children to Samhuinn House, a new school in Hampstead that had offered to take them until foster families were found. Grace's office was at the end of a long corridor of dorms on the fifth floor. That evening the exhausted children quickly fell asleep. The corridor was quiet. It was a warm late-summer night and she waited for him by the window. She thought about where they could go. She never went out at night and did not know any fashionable places. She did not know any unfashionable places, either. She only knew the tea shop on the corner, and that closed at six.

Then he came running up the stairs two at a time and she realized it did not matter.

They sat on the fire escape, their legs dangling high over the patio. He talked about his journey, the children: white as chalk on the train to Holland, green on the boat to Harwich, mud-coloured after their first day on soggy English soil. Childhood holidays spent with Friends in northern England had left him with a love of the language and a horror of English food.

'They gave us ... Scottish eggs?'

'Scotch eggs.'

'I would not have thought such a thing could exist.'

'*What God hath cleansed, that call not thou common.*'

A look of incomprehension was on his face. She bit the left side of her tongue. Proving her frumpiness by quoting the Bible: another bad habit.

'It's in The Acts. *Rise, Peter; kill and eat* – that one? When God commands Peter to eat all sorts of unclean things. Pigs, bugs, birds . . .'

'And Scotch eggs,' he said. 'But they really were *uncommon.*'

A cold English drizzle ruined the summer night. He pulled her back under the roof, protecting her head from the rain with his hand. He slid the hand down to the nape of her neck, and then he kissed her. She was dreadfully embarrassed initially, especially when he prised her lips apart with his tongue. But by the third kiss she found that they were rather good at it. The fact that as a girl she had twice practised kissing with Margaret from First-Day school helped. She would have left it at the first attempt, in which Margaret was the groom and she was the bride. But Margaret claimed her right to another round where she would be the girl; it was only fair.

He smelled of some slightly spicy soap, like scouring powder mixed with cinnamon, and she thought: this is what soap smells like in Hamburg.

It was not the first time she spent the night at Samhuinn House, but it was the first time she spent it in the company of a man. She kissed him again and dared to bite his lower lip. He bit her back a little harder. He must have brought the soap with him. She would have liked to ask him for a bar, but of course she did not. They went inside to escape the rain, sat on the floor and leaned against her desk. He talked about his group of Friends who used to cycle out to the seashore, swim and play the guitar, before their gatherings were broken up by the Hitler Youth.

She lied a little and said she loved swimming. It was forgivable, that tiny lie. Her unstoppably inventive mind pictured them on their wedding day, giggling about the fact that she had never actually gone in further than ankle-deep. 'And you told me you loved swimming!' More giggles. And she could not help but feel a little smug about this romance, about the fact that she had escaped another stifling night at home, that she had left behind her parents trapped in eternal nagging bitterness and broken free to find such giddy passion.

Dawn rose far too soon.

How could she not have asked him to stay?

'It can't be all that safe for you in Hamburg.'

He smiled. If he stayed in England, the next train might not be allowed to leave.

'I'll be back on another train.'

It had been a little awkward, taking him back to the station. He washed in the bathroom at Samhuinn House before the children woke up, and they had breakfast in the tea shop on the corner. His cheek had felt soft against her hand in the evening. When the waiter was busy serving another couple, she quickly reached out and stroked his cheek again: already it felt a little rougher. He grinned.

'I must look like a bandit.'

'It suits you.'

'Next time when we meet I'll be clean-shaven. As smooth as an egg.'

'A Scottish egg?'

The other Friends were milling around on the platform but no one smirked or, God forbid, winked. They would no sooner have suspected Grace of kissing a stranger on a fire escape than Mary Pye of performing the dance of the seven veils.

He discreetly squeezed her hand before boarding the train. She thought she should say something, make some pledge or promise, but she could not think of anything and clearly, neither could he. He stuck his round face out of the window and looked like a boy again. A freckled boy on his way to a Friends' summer camp. She waved after him as the train pulled out.

When she got back, she checked the bathroom of Samhuinn House, just in case he had left the soap there.

The platform had been warmed by the sun that day. Now it was chilly.

Brisk men in coats and bowler hats strode past, black umbrellas tucked under their arms, wary eyes on the sky. When she glanced up at the big station clock Grace saw that they had been waiting for over an hour.

She walked over to the elderly couple and told them that in all likelihood the train would not come. Yes, they had half expected that, what with the borders shut and all, but then they had hoped one more train might get through. The elderly lady smoothed her thin hair back on one side in a nervous reflex, forgetting that it had been carefully curled and set for the great welcome.

Someone tugged at Grace's coat. Little Inge had run away from her group.

'Well you really oughtn't to have done that. Now they'll all miss their train, when people will be waiting for them in Hertfordshire,' Grace said primly, and took her hand. Inge pouted and played with the cardboard tag that dangled from a string around her neck.

'What's that on your lips?' she asked. Then she let go of the card and hugged Grace with her face turned up, her chin pressing into Grace's stomach, her old-fashioned long braids swinging back.

'On my lips?' Grace ran her tongue over them. 'Oh. Lipstick.'

She took out a tissue and wiped her mouth. They walked away from the platform, two serious females.

2

Grace asked everyone. She asked the Red Cross nurses who came into her office for a cup of tea. She asked the Orthodox rabbi who brought over a whole orphanage from the Continent. She even asked Mary Pye – risking humiliation at the hands of Paul and Charlie – because you never knew, somehow Mary Pye had a way of keeping up with news from Friends everywhere. But no one had any idea of the whereabouts of a freckled, round-faced young man called Morten.

She wrote to the Hamburg address he had given her as he'd boarded the train to go back, but there was no reply. It seemed impossible that a person could simply vanish. She considered writing to the Society of Friends in Hamburg, but with all they must be worrying about, how could she bother them with such a trivial thing? She might even cause them problems for receiving letters from England.

Perhaps the government was right and the war would last three years. And after three years, a train would pull into Liverpool Street Station. A young man would hop off. Oh, the reunion! The tears and the laughter. And jokes, jokes about that innocent first meeting: 'Would you care to meet up in the afternoon?' 'I don't know ... perhaps just a quick cup of tea on the fire escape?' More laughter.

He would admire her for her steadfastness during the war.

Raw eggs, she read in the paper, raw eggs beaten with honey and a shot of brandy were the best way to strengthen one's nerves.

They stopped taking the air-raid signal seriously, and the children came back from Hertfordshire. Grace had painted the dorms blue and the hallway yellow while they were away. The widow who had helped her run the makeshift children's home at Samhuinn House chose to stay in the country, so the school sent her a German instead: a man like an evening shadow, tall and lean and very quiet, until she asked him casually if he knew any German Friends.

He pushed his horn-rimmed glasses down to the tip of his nose and stared at her as if she was mentally impaired. His eyes lay deep in their sockets, close together, and where other people would have glanced sideways, he ever so slightly turned his head. This had the most unsettling effect. His ears were like the handles on the blue jugs in the breakfast room, and Grace could not help but picture a pair of invisible hands that grabbed them and rotated the head from side to side.

'I have many German friends,' he said. 'Of course.'

'I mean Quakers. Sorry. We refer to them as Friends.'

He had never heard of Quakers. She explained that they were a religious movement inspired by—

'Ah,' he said. 'A cult.'

She sniffed. 'I'm sorry, I didn't quite catch your name.'

'Hoffnung. Max Hoffnung.'

He did not seem particularly interested in hers.

She took him into her office and explained the workings of Samhuinn House. The Nazis let a limited number of children leave Germany and Austria. The parents had to stay behind. Quakers, who were accepted as neutral, accompanied the children from the Continent to Britain. To help as many families as possible, they took only one child from each family. Regrettably, this meant—

'There is no need to explain this to me,' Mr Hoffnung said. 'I'm from Berlin.'

'Sorry.' Grace had lost her thread and shuffled some papers to buy time. It would be easiest, she decided, to simply take him through the weekly routine. Meals, school, bedtime, '... and every Sunday, the Parade.' She bit her tongue. 'I'm sorry. Every Sunday, visitors.'

'The Parade?'

'No, no, no, it's not called the Parade. It's simply the day when potential foster parents visit Samhuinn to see if they would like to give one of the children a new home.'

'Parade is a fitting name for it.'

'As I said, it's not a parade at all ...'

She was close to tears. This had been part of her script for her reunion with Morten. She had planned to tell him about all these things that went through her mind at work: *Visitor's day is the worst – I always think of it as the Parade!*

Mr Hoffnung took out a fountain pen, walked up to her weekly timetable and crossed out the entries for Sunday.

'The Parade is cancelled.'

'But—'

'From now on, foster parents can make a request for a certain age or sex if there is a good reason. But we will not let them pick the children like fruit in the grocery.'

Grace attempted a sarcastic smile. 'What a wonderfully effective strategy for finding foster parents. They will be queuing all the way from Clapham.'

Mr Hoffnung did not know where Clapham was.

'I've seen those parades you mention. Ten couples, fifty children, and in the end they always choose the blonde and blue-eyed little girls.' He leaned against the door. 'You are of course in charge. If you would like to continue the Parade, I can buy you a new timetable.'

She gave in, but told herself that it was only to humour him.

In practice, nothing much changed. The older children, the unlovely ones, were trained as maids and cooks. They spent their spare time on the Heath, skating on the frozen pond, where Grace herself tried to concentrate on her figures of eight.

*A quiet mind, a fearless heart, a tidy conscience.*

She repeated it to herself as she skated. An endless loop.

*A quiet mind, a fearless heart, a tidy conscience.*

If she knew how to swim, she could join the Red Cross and help the poor chaps in the Atlantic.

*A quiet mind …*

*Raw eggs and brandy.*

Mary Pye told her after Meeting: 'I've written to my cousin, who tells me our Friends in Hamburg are experiencing great hardship. This will come as no surprise to thee …'

Inge refused to take off the string around her neck, the cardboard tag with her name and address that she had worn since she arrived on a train from Berlin.

Grace told her it was unsightly. The cardboard was frayed, the string frayed. It made her look like a frayed, grey parcel. Would she not rather look like a pretty little girl?

'If I take it off,' Inge said earnestly, 'how will my parents find me?'

# 3

A few weeks before Christmas, Grace walked into the breakfast room where Mr Hoffnung was supervising the younger children. When one of the boys reached for the jam pot Mr Hoffnung muttered something. The little hand wandered back to the plate, leaving the pot untouched.

'What's this about?' Grace asked.

'Jam or butter,' said Mr Hoffnung. 'Jam or margarine. They have to choose.'

She laughed. 'Rationing's to start in the new year, not yet.'

'This has nothing to do with rationing.'

'Well, why shouldn't they have margarine and jam?'

'It's indulgent.'

'Indulgent! These children can hardly be accused of being spoiled.'

'No, because their parents brought them up on good principles. Like margarine *or* jam.'

Aware of children watching, Grace laughed again and pretended that she did not care. On her way out of the dining room she noticed that every single slice of toast was spread with either jam or butter, never both .

Some instinct made her avoid the breakfast room over the next few days. Mr Hoffnung, for his part, rarely came into her office. The old widow had spilled about the place like a leaking bucket, now wandering into the breakfast room, now pottering about in the office, now peeking into the dorms. With Mr Hoffnung, the division was clear. He ruled over teapots and dinner plates at one end of the corridor. She took care of lists, accounts, begging letters at the other end.

'A question. Do you know why this school is called Samhuinn?' he asked her when they passed each other in the corridor after breakfast.

'It was set up by some progressive types. They named it after a pagan spring festival in Scotland.'

Mr Hoffnung chuckled, which was a very rare sight. She mentally revised his age. His earnest leanness had made her put him at thirty or so, but when he laughed, he looked like a gawky, awkward young man of twenty.

'Why is that amusing?'

'Because the pagan spring festival is called Beltane!' He was now laughing openly. 'Samhuinn is the opposite of the spring festival. It marks the start of winter, you see. One may best describe it as the festival of the dead. They must have made a mistake, those progressive types! A big mistake! The festival of the dead!' She asked him to keep his voice down but he continued laughing until he disappeared back into the breakfast room, exclaiming between bursts of laughter: 'The-Festival-of-the-dead school!'

She concluded that Mr Hoffnung was unhinged, but it would not be very Christian to ask the school to sack him.

The following week, through the open door of her office,

she watched him walk past, awkwardly hugging a stack of paperbacks. He returned empty-handed, then walked past with another stack of paperbacks.

What *could* he be up to? Well, it was none of her business.

She looked at her watch. She had a few spare minutes before her meeting with the principal: some parents had complained about noise from the fifth floor, and the School was beginning to question whether converting the floor into a makeshift children's home had been a good idea. There was enough time to write another letter to Morten. She would write it and keep it until she saw him again, and then she could hand him a whole fat bundle of letters, proof of her unwavering affection.

'Dear Morten . . .'

She heard a loud clatter from the dining hall. Then a softer thump.

Grace changed the 'Dear' to 'Dearest'.

Max Hoffnung's paperbacks were strictly his concern. He could use them as a footstool, for all she cared.

A short silence was followed by the sound of Mr Hoffnung's voice in that lecturing, strident tone of his, then silence again. Then another loud clatter and a softer thump.

What on earth . . .!

She slid the letter under a book and tiptoed down the corridor. Very, very quietly she turned to peek through the doorway.

The children were sitting at two long tables, so deeply immersed in their task that they did not even speak. They had roast chicken legs or breasts before them, which they tried to carve with their elbows tightly by their sides, as if they had been glued into place. Their hands went up and down at such unnatural angles that they looked like rows of little puppets. At the far end of the room stood the puppet master himself, oblivious to Grace's presence.

She squinted and wished, not for the first time, that she wore glasses.

Grace peered at the boy sitting closest to her – what was that tucked under his elbow? She squinted again.

A paperback! Each child had a paperback wedged between ribcage and elbow!

She burst into the dining hall.

'Mr Hoffnung! What on *earth* is going on here?'

A few children dropped their paperbacks in surprise.

'Miss Woolman, I thought you were busy with the accounts.'

'Well, I'm glad I came over to check up on you! What *is* this?' She pointed at the paperbacks.

'Oh. This.' Mr Hoffnung smiled. 'This is a method of teaching children to eat properly.'

Grace was so aghast she let her mouth hang open. The children sat stock-still with their elbows pressed all the more tightly into their sides, shoulders hunched, forks suspended in mid-air. Thirty pairs of eyes were fixed on Grace, awaiting her judgement.

After a deep breath, she said, 'And may I ask where they use this … *method*?'

'In Germany.'

She glanced at the children.

'Mr Hoffnung.' It took effort to lower her voice, when what she wanted was to scream. 'Would you mind coming to my office for a little chat?'

As she walked down the corridor she could hear the clatter and thump of dropped forks and books start up again behind her.

He took his favourite place by the tall bookshelf in the corner. She had noticed that he always sought out tall furniture, and indeed often created a tall group arrangement, for example placing himself between a door, a hat stand, and a bookshelf. She sensed a certain mocking intent, for while Grace was of average height when compared to her sisters or the children at Samhuinn, when she stood opposite Mr Hoffnung, as she did now, and he and his bookshelf looked down at her from their great height, she felt distinctly short.

She asked him to sit down.

'I'm sorry,' she began, though she wasn't sorry at all, 'I don't intend to criticize your methods ...' She stopped. Of course she intended to criticize his methods. Come on, Grace, she told herself. Show some grit. 'The long and short of it is, we can't have this sort of thing here. First the jam, now this ... paperback business.' She lightly thumped the table in what she hoped was a display of strength.

Mr Hoffnung listened with the patience of a shadow.

'You see, this is a *progressive* school,' she said. 'We do

84

apply a lot of German methods here, you understand, but they are all *progressive* methods. Like those new classrooms in the treetops, or letting children roam about and discover their own equilibrium, or addressing teachers by their first—'

Max snorted.

Grace stood up. 'Excuse me?'

'What?'

'You snorted.'

'If you say so.'

'May I ask why you snorted?'

'I snorted because your principles are upside down.'

'Oh, they're upside down, are they? Goodness, and I didn't even notice! Perhaps you would be kind enough to rearrange them for me?'

'You talk about progressive experimentation. About classrooms in treetops. About calling the teachers by the first names. I am trying to teach the children how to eat.'

'Well—'

'Once they know how to eat, once they know to choose between butter and jam, once they know how to be human, then by all means let them be taught in a tree and call you Grace.'

Grace blushed, tripped up by the unexpected intimacy.

'Well, *Max*, there I was thinking they already knew how to eat. Because, you see, even before you arrived here, long before you illuminated this cave of ignorance with your presence, we actually taught them how to eat. In fact, you might be interested to hear that it was *me* who used to be in charge of imparting good manners.'

His lips moved slightly, but then he pressed them together and locked the reply inside.

'You'll have to concede that when you arrived here, they already knew how to eat,' she insisted.

He remained silent.

'Mr Hoffnung? When you arrived here, the children already knew how to eat, didn't they?'

After a long silence, he murmured: 'In the widest sense.'

'What is that supposed to mean? Do you or do you not concede that they knew how to eat?'

She was making herself ridiculous, but there was no stopping now. No question in the world had ever been as important to her as the question of whether Mr Hoffnung, this eccentric man with jug ears and sunken eyes that could not even glance sideways, would or would not concede that her children knew, and had long known, how to eat.

'I will concede that they knew how to eat like ...'

He fell silent again.

'Like what?'

'If I say it you will be angry.'

Grace bit her lips in fury. Any moment she would burst and send shrapnel of rage all over Samhuinn House.

'I'm not angry.'

'I'll say it if you swear you won't be angry.'

'My people have a habit of not swearing. But I can assure

you, I'm not the angry sort at all. I don't have an angry bone in my body.'

He looked sceptical, but eventually said slowly: 'I will concede that they knew how to eat like ... English people.'

She let out a noise she didn't even know she could make, a yelp mixed with a kind of battle cry. 'Like English people! And is that so very terrible?'

He opted for another silence.

'I mean, *I* eat like an English person.'

He did not respond.

'Mr Hoffnung.'

'I knew you would be angry!'

She smacked the table. 'I'm not angry! I merely stated the fact that I eat like an English person. You responded with a rather insinuating silence. And I would like to know, Mr Hoffnung – *Max* – what it is that you're insinuating. Is there something the matter with the children's table manners? Is there something the matter with the manners I taught them?'

'You don't put your hands on the table.'

'I what?'

'When you eat soup, for example, you use the spoon with the right hand and you put the left hand ... well, I don't know where you put it, but it's not on the table.'

'And that's wrong, is it?'

'It's not the way we do it. When we use one hand, the other should be placed on the table, next to the plate. Otherwise ... otherwise it could be assumed that you're doing something peculiar with that hand.'

'Like what?'

'I don't know. I've never thought that far. Scratching an itch, maybe. Or feeding the dog under the table.'

'The mind boggles, Mr Hoffnung. It boggles. And what else do I do that's so repulsive to you?'

'Well, let me just say that your parents were clearly not familiar with the paperback method.'

Another yelp escaped from her. 'They weren't, were they? Good Lord! Would you like me to correct that? Perhaps you could lend me a couple of nice heavy doorstops to practise with? *War and Peace*? The Bible? Mr Hoffnung, this is frankly the most arrogant and ... and ... insulting thing anyone has ever said to me. And I'll tell you one thing, you can go back into that dining hall right now and collect all those books and put them back where they belong, back in the library, and then you will stop pestering us with your bizarre experiments, do you hear me? I won't have it!'

She slammed her hand on the table so hard that it hurt, but resisted the temptation to wince. He sat in his chair, perfectly calm, waiting for the shrapnel to settle around him.

'Or I'll tell Mr Cartland!'

He merely crossed his arms.

'The children's table manners are perfectly fine the way they are. That's all, Mr Hoffnung. Now if you would kindly let me get on with my work ...'

She shuffled her papers with such energy that half of them slid to the floor. He remained seated.

'Really, Mr Hoffnung, I cannot think why you would want to inflict this on the children.'

He stood up, walked to the door, and with his back to her, said: 'Because their parents would want it that way.'

'Excuse me?'

He did not turn round. His hand was on the doorknob, but instead of opening the door, he appeared to lean against it for support. His shoulders began to shake. Had she not known that Mr Hoffnung was incapable of strong emotion, she would have thought he was crying. When he spoke, his German accent erupted like water from a burst pipe.

'You asked me why I inflict the children. I do it because their parents would like them to learn good table manners. One day they will come to collect the children. One day they will walk into this dining hall. And the first thing they will see is their son sticking his elbow in someone's eye. The second thing, their son slouches so badly his face dips in the soup. The third thing, their own son doesn't stand up to greet them, because no one taught him that you stand up when an adult enters the room.'

A creeping sense of unease made Grace defensive. 'That's your assumption. You don't actually *know* how the parents would feel.'

Without turning to face her, he continued: 'Of course I know. The children in that dining room are from families like my own. In my family, if you didn't finish your stew at dinner, it would be warmed up for breakfast the next morning, and then for lunch, and then for dinner, and then again for breakfast, until you finished it. If you had a shirt that was scratchy, you slept in it until you grew used to the scratchiness. You ate with your hands on the table and your elbows close to your body and you chose between butter and jam. This was our way. Now I see these children shouting and laughing with their noses in the soup bowl and their hands everywhere. I picture my mother in the room, and I ask myself, would she say these are humans or a gang of little savages? I know how these children would be brought up by their parents. You are the one, Miss Woolman – *Grace* – who does not know.'

Without another word, he left the room.

Grace rushed to shut the door behind him. She told herself that Mr Hoffnung was clearly insane, and wrong, and very, very rude. The only comfort was in the thought that she would tell Morten all about him, and they would laugh: she knew exactly how she would tell it; Morten would be in stitches.

That evening, at home, she noticed that her mother had a rather unpleasant habit of holding her spoon in her fist, like a spear. Her father had an equally unpleasant habit of puckering his lips, blowing little waves on his spoon, then sucking in the cooled soup with a tremendous slurp. Mr Hoffnung had not mentioned slurping, but it was decidedly unappealing.

The next day, the paperbacks were back on the shelf in alphabetical order. Grace told herself she had done very well to rein in the wretched man's more eccentric ideas. At lunch, she sat next to Inge and risked a discreet glance at him. He did sit very straight, it had to be said, though the pose looked stiff and uncomfortable rather than elegant. She suddenly wondered how Morten sat at table. She hadn't noticed anything particular about his table manners at the tea shop.

Then Grace almost choked on the piece of bread she was chewing.

She had not noticed anything peculiar about Morten's manners, but what if – oh, horror – *Morten* had noticed something rather peculiar about *hers*?

What if Morten had looked at her and concluded that her parents had clearly never exercised the paperback method?

She strained to remember how she had sat, how she had held her knife that morning, how she had stirred her tea, how she had sipped it. What if he had been silently repulsed by her slouching and, God forbid, *slurping*? She felt faint with embarrassment. Well, when she next saw Morten, he would have no cause to complain. No cause at all. She tried to pull her shoulders back and sit up straight.

'Inge dear,' she said impatiently, 'do sit up. And that hand, really, that hand should be on the table.'

## 4

In early December, Grace was trudging through the deep snow in her sister's old boots and her mother's muskrat coat, a sagging leather satchel slung over her shoulder. Paul had asked her to go ice-skating with him and Charlie. From the top of the hill she could see the bare black trees brittle with frost, the snow-covered bathing hut and the white pond. A person was skating on the pond in wobbly circles, with two others watching from the bank. She squinted but could not make out more than the three dark shapes. The skater glided towards the bank and all three huddled together for a moment or so. Then one of them slowly, awkwardly, stepped on the ice, fell, got up again with the help of the others. Slowly he or she gathered confidence and ventured out alone into the middle of the pond, fell, got up, fell, got up, fell again.

And then, with the jolting stumble of a child stepping into a rabbit hole, the person crashed through the ice.

Grace dropped her satchel and ran down the hill. When she reached the pond, Paul was dragging a girl in soggy black clothes over the ice towards the bank. Charlie was waving his arms and shouting instructions – 'Careful! That way!' – but for once Paul ignored him. He had hooked his arms under the girl's shoulders and half walked, half slid backwards over the treacherous crust. By the time he gently set her down on the bank, her wet hair had frozen and her blue lips quivered in speechless shock. Charlie pulled a flask from his bag but Grace waved him away. She hurried them, the boys half carrying the girl between them, back over the Heath to her office at Samhuinn.

Someone had stoked the fire in the stove. Perhaps the

school's caretaker was feeling the season's spirit of good-will and charity: these days, Grace's office was always warm when she arrived in the mornings. She fetched blankets and an eiderdown, helped her off with her coat, and soon Miriam's thawing hair was dripping all over the letters and lists. Her cheeks filled with blood and her eyes grew bright with a strange, hungry vitality. She was precisely the type of girl that Grace had always envied. The type with vibrant eyes and a mouth always ready to smile; the type who crashed through the ice one minute and laughed about it the next. Grace lent her a green jumper. She noticed that on Miriam the drab garment looked original and interesting, as if she had thrown it on in a moment of happy carelessness.

She had been doing her rounds as one of the neighbourhood's air-raid wardens, Paul explained, and the boys had talked her into taking a break and borrowing a pair of—

Charlie interrupted him with an anecdote from the previous winter, when Mary Pye had attempted to skate on the ice. It was a Charlie sort of anecdote, full of embellishment and exaggeration, and they all laughed rather dutifully, but Grace noticed that Miriam was not looking at Charlie at all. She was looking at Paul. For a moment the happy carelessness gave way to an expression that was earnest and still, the expression of someone contemplating a familiar figure in a new light. Then Max walked past carrying a pile of fir branches, his jug ears hidden under a red hat with white bobbles, and the moment was broken. It turned out that he and Miriam knew each other; her parents were his landlords. There was much chatting and exclaiming. Miriam touched her hair, which had dried into a frizz, and said it was high time she went home.

Grace watched them run down the steps, Miriam skipping ahead, Paul carrying the wet coat, and thought how odd it had been to hear about Max's life outside Samhuinn, to hear that he had friends and liked to play the piano until the neighbours thumped on the wall.

On her way back to the office, she walked past him when he dropped a basket of pine cones, destined, like the branches, to decorate the breakfast room, which scattered and rolled into the furthest corners of the hallway. It was the final insult that she should be crouching in a cold hallway on her knees, picking up gilded pine cones, while others were gallivanting about outside.

She found a silver ornament in the shape of a Christmas tree among the pine cones and held it up.

'May I ask you a question?'

'Yes?'

'I was under the impression that you were Jewish.'

He paused. 'And?'

'Jews don't celebrate Christmas!'

Mr Hoffnung smiled. It was not a dry or sarcastic smile, but a warm and rather amused one. 'Well Miss Woolman, I'm afraid this is something that would take far too long to explain.' The smile gave way to an uncertain frown. 'Unless, of course, you are saying that I *have* to explain . . .'

'Oh, no, of course not. I'm sorry. It was simple curiosity, nothing more.'

'Dearest Morten,' she wrote in her fifteenth unsent letter.

The yule-tide spirit is working its wonders! Despite the strain of this strangely quiet war, we are all letting ourselves be softened a little by the mood of celebration and good cheer. Even our eccentric Mr Hoffnung appears to have yielded to the ~~yule-tide~~ festive spirit. The children persuaded him to act as Sugarplum Fairy in the Christmas pantomime!! I am to be a shepherd.

Mr Hoffnung has been surprisingly enthusiastic about it. Perhaps this means we have finally buried the hatchet?? ~~We have even taken to calling each other Max and Grace.~~

When the war is over – oh Morten, I pray that it will soon be over! Those poor people in Finland and Norway! I feel particularly sorry for them since it must be so awfully cold there.

Grace read through the letter. It was embarrassingly bad. She scrunched it up and used it to light the stove in her office.

Later, Max dropped in with a bag of chestnuts to roast in the stove. Neither thought of making incisions in the shells. The explosions rattled and banged in the heat like a trapped farmer with a shotgun. They ran for cover, crouched behind her desk with their hands over their ears, and Grace thought, if only Morten was here: he would know what to do.

# 5

When the pond thawed, the sons and daughters of the Baltic stripped off their pullovers and splashed into the cold fresh water. Max said he was an excellent swimmer, had swum half the length of the Rhine once, but would wait until the weather was warmer before sampling the ponds.

'There is no need to be ashamed,' Grace said, and splashed water at him with her foot. 'I can't swim, either.'

He wagged his finger in mock outrage. 'I once swam from Munich to Berlin!'

'Berlin is not on the Rhine.'

'You're right. Neither is Munich.'

Then he wrapped himself in a woollen blanket, sat on the grass with his back against a tree trunk, pushed his horn-rimmed glasses down to the tip of his nose and began to read a newspaper.

Grace dipped her toes back in the water and shuddered.

Little Inge said swimming was good for the constitution.

'I'm surprised you even needed a boat to come to England,' Grace said. 'You swim like a duck. Much more elegantly, of course.' She lowered her voice so Max could not hear and added: 'I'm going to take swimming lessons, you know.'

'Swimming lessons? With a teacher who draws waves on a blackboard?'

'That's where the fishes learn how to swim,' Max called over. 'At swimming school.'

Inge loved that. 'Will you be taught by a trout or a goose?'

'Geese don't swim, actually,' Grace said, though she was not too sure.

'You mustn't be very annoyed with Mr Hoffnung,' Inge whispered suddenly. 'At home, we always had butter *or* jam. It's true. He didn't invent it.'

'Inge! Were you eavesdropping on us?'

'Only by accident.'

'Well, that was weeks ago. We are all good friends now.'

'The only time my brother and I were allowed butter *and* jam was on the morning when Mama took me to the train station.'

And then Inge, true daughter of the Baltic, ran to the end of the wooden pier and jumped straight into the pond.

Grace preferred to take her lessons at the ladies' pond, where Max Hoffnung could not see her. The swimming instructor, a ruddy and cantankerous retired seamstress, made Grace wedge an inflated rubber ball between her knees, which seemed the surest way to tilt her, duck-like, head down, legs up, into the water. She pushed weeds and feathers out of the way with her arms as two ducks glided past, ignoring the giant invader. When she dipped her head underwater without closing her eyes, she could see their frantically paddling feet.

In her mind she was teaching Morten to make pebbles skim across the pond. The trick was to give them a hard flat spin with your fingertips just before you let go. She managed three hops and Morten was duly impressed.

# Swords and Ploughshares

## 1

Mary Pye had taken to putting her hat in the icebox and the butter dish on the book shelf between the Bible and the dictionary.

'Which *was* the right place from an alphabetical point of view,' said Charlie.

She put her confusion down to war nerves and announced at dinner that it would be best if she moved back to her old cottage in Ulverston. The idea sounded reasonable. Everyone felt frayed and jittery because of the pesky false alarms, and she was not bound to London by work.

'And Charlie will be going up there, too,' his father said.

Charlie dropped his fork on his plate, a trick he had recently adopted to register wordless protest. He had easily passed his tribunal, moving the lay judges with his pure and eloquent Christian steadfastness and dedication to the Quaker faith. He had rejected arguing for exemption on political grounds as too risky: most of his comrades had failed their tribunals. The judges exempted him from military service on the condition that he make himself useful on a farm or in a hospital.

'He might as well do his land work in Ulverston,' their father continued, looking at Mary Pye. 'There are some conchies at Swarthmoor Hall.'

'Land work?' Charlie's knife hit his plate right next to the fork.

'Or you could be a stretcher-bearer, like I was. But I wouldn't recommend it.' Their father kneaded his lean fingers. 'Prison would be another option. I wouldn't recommend that, either. They make you work in there. You might not enjoy that.'

'I work!'

'Do you?' His father raised both eyebrows in a great show of astonishment. 'When?'

'Every day.'

'But that's wonderful!' He turned to their mother. 'Margaret, did you hear? Our firstborn has grown bored of being idle!'

Their mother ignored him. She took Charlie's hands in her own.

'Land work is not the worst, dear. Three boys from Hampstead Meeting have signed up for human experiments at the hospital. Now they're all down with yellow fever.'

Mary Pye muttered something about the hardest service being the most rewarding. 'Think of our Saviour on the cross.'

'That's just the sort of life I have in mind. Crucified at thirty-three.'

'Charlie!'

'Mother!'

'He's quite right, Maggie, he's quite right, it *is* a wonderful life to emulate,' said Mary Pye.

Paul wished his family would talk about his own tribunal for a change.

'Land work is supposed to be all right, you know,' he told Charlie later that evening. He took the *Book of Christian Discipline* from his shelf and leafed through it in the hope of finding a useful line for his tribunal. They were still sharing a bedroom. Paul had dropped out of Bentham College after his failed statistics exam and was working as a sculptor's assistant in Hampstead; neither his nor Charlie's more obscurely sourced income stretched to their own digs.

'It's not the land work I mind. It's Ulverston.'

'At least you won't have to help out in the soap shop.'

At this, Charlie leaped up from the bed, seized the *Book of Christian Discipline* and threw it across the room. 'Not another word about the soap shop.'

Paul went to pick up the book, smoothed the pages and wiped down the cover with his sleeve.

'It's not the fault of the *Book of Discipline* that you don't like soap.'

'I hate soap. And I hate the *Book of Discipline*.'

'There's no reason to hate it.' Paul held on to it tightly in case there was another outburst, but Charlie merely sighed.

'Don't worry about tomorrow,' he said, and boxed Paul's arm. 'Come out tonight, have a few drinks, get a good night's sleep and you'll be fine.'

## 2

Charlie's friends were waiting by the pier. Flasks of cider and gin circulated, and Paul took a few sips for courage. A group of girls arrived with torches and impatiently switched them on and off in the twilight. The local air-raid warden would no doubt have put a stop to the whole thing, had she not been busy fighting through the undergrowth with a scrawled map in her hand. She stepped into the circle of torchlight, and Paul looked at her face and realized that nothing else mattered, neither his tribunal nor Charlie's land work nor the worrying news from the Continent, because he was at a twilight bathing party, and there was Miriam, ready to change into a swimming costume and glide into the pond.

A line from a poem or a song came to him: 'She wants to eat of the fruit of all the trees in the garden of the world'. Yes, that was exactly how she looked.

She reached the bank on the other side of the pond first and climbed up into the tangle of foxgloves, ferns and marsh marigolds. Paul burned his leg on some nettles when he joined her. Someone jumped in from the pier and there was much shrieking and whooping, but in the darkness of the night they couldn't see who it was.

'This is my favourite moment,' Paul said, 'when the daylight's gone and you see all the windows in the distance light up one by one.'

'Sorry to spoil it, but you're sitting next to an air-raid warden. I'm personally responsible for all that darkness.' She leaned back and propped herself up on her arms. 'That vicarage next to St Matthew's? I had to fine them three times. After the third time I went down there with some black tape and sealed the window myself.'

'I'm surprised they didn't stop you.'

'They were out. I climbed in through the bathroom window, which was the one they refused to seal. Then I sealed it. Then I realized I'd sealed my way out. Luckily they hadn't locked the front door.' She lowered herself all the way to the ground and folded her hands over her stomach. 'The thing I ask myself is, is this really the best I can do? Is this what I *should* be doing, going round Hampstead with a roll of sticky tape?'

He did not answer because he was too dazzled by the spectacle of light and dark that unfolded itself above them. 'Look! I told you the lights would come on.'

Someone had picked up a bucketful of stars and poured them over the night sky. They no longer competed with streetlamps and chandeliers, and their light flooded the darkness, so brilliant and dense that Paul could not even make out any constellations.

He thought: Now. I'm going to tell her all about my tribunal right now, and she's going to tell me it'll be fine, and that's all I need to hear.

Just then, Miriam sat up and pulled her knees to her chest.

'There's the Plough!'

'Where?'

'There. See, the handle, the blade ...'

'I can't find it.'

'Just follow the line of my arm.'

Their cheeks almost touched. He could feel her shiver with cold.

'Can you see it now?'

'Yes.' He let his cheek touch hers, and she did not move away.

'I don't want to be like that,' Miriam said with sudden, intense fierceness. 'Millions of them, and you can't tell one from the other. We have to make up patterns to even remember which is which. Don't you sometimes think that at the end of one's life, one must lie there and think: I hope I counted? Do you know what I mean? I so desperately want to *count*. That's why I wanted to study art, because – don't laugh – because I thought it would be so wonderful to sign my name on the canvas, and then it would be there for all eternity. It's why I had to join every single student society at Bentham, and then volunteer as an air-raid warden as soon as I could. I thought that surely being part of some greater idea, some movement, surely that was a way of ... of mattering. Of being seen. But now I'm thinking that it isn't, really. It's more like being that star on the bottom right of the Plough. Everyone knows the Plough and no one knows the star.'

She rested her chin on one knee and the warm connection between their cheeks was broken.

'I want that, too,' Paul said quietly. 'I want to count.'

'I know you do.' He could almost hear the concentrated frown and he knew what her face must look like now in the dark, that almost scowling look she had when she was thinking hard. 'And I envy you, because you're going to make a choice that matters. What's there to do for a woman in a war, really? Knit socks for the boys, tape up the vicarage. Stir the stew for when the boys come home. And give birth, of course, give birth to lots of boys who will go out and defend us.'

'Well, being an artist is also a way of counting.'

She let out a quiet laugh.

'Is it? It makes me think of that cartoon of a man in a beret standing behind an easel, and the caption, "Hampstead at War". Because I'm not sure it is, you see. King David played the harp *and* smote the Philistines, didn't he? I'm not sure I'd think of him quite so highly if he'd *only* played the harp.'

'You might if he'd played the right song. Or written the right song. There's a famous woman columnist at *Peace News* who often writes about—'

'*Peace News*?' She pronounced it exactly as she had that first time they met, somewhere between incredulity and contempt. 'Sorry, I don't mean to be rude, but when I listened to

Charlie and his friends rant against the war machine just now, well, they don't know anything, do they?'

'But I'm not Charlie. This isn't my set, either.'

'Then what *is* your set?'

'Why do I need to belong to a set? Why can't I just have my own beliefs?'

'Fine, but what are they? You can't still believe what you said in that debate – that everything will be fine as long as we're nice to the Germans.'

'Of course not.'

'I mean, I just assumed ...' Her voice grew a little uncertain. 'I suppose I assumed you'd changed your mind since the war started. I don't know why I assumed that.'

Because you wanted it to be true, Paul thought. And at that moment, it was what he wanted, too. He wanted to sit here with Miriam and feel that they were one, that they had the same beliefs and the same fears and the same notion of right and wrong, and he wanted them both to mean the same when they said, 'I so desperately want to count.'

'If you want to know what I believe in ...' he took her hand, '... I believe in this. I believe in the two of us sitting by a pond at night. I believe that everyone has a right to sit by a pond at night without being shot at, without being attacked or robbed. There is a scene in *All Quiet on the Western Front* where the German protagonist spots an English officer sitting at an easel in a crater from a blast, painting with watercolours, and he retreats, rips the ring off his hand grenade and throws it into the crater. If you talk about the choice I'm facing, well, it's that. Do I want to be the Englishman at the easel, or do I want to be the soldier with the grenade? Do I want to be the victim or the perpetrator? I tell you what, I don't think for a moment that the German soldier drew the better lot. From the moment the grenade explodes, he's as dead as the Englishman. It's just a different sort of death.'

There was a rustle in the undergrowth behind them. Miriam sat very still, then suddenly clapped her hands, and with another quick rustle whatever had been hiding there scurried away.

'The way I see it,' she said calmly, 'is that we're in the crater, we can see the German with the grenade peering down at us, and you've got a rifle. And you're about to throw it away.'

'But I'm not.' Two forces were tearing at Paul, two entirely contradictory thoughts. The first one was, *I renounce war*. The second one was, *What sort of man would refuse to protect his own?* There was no conceivable way of reconciling those thoughts. No, there was only one way to avoid being torn apart, and that was to separate them. The first thought belonged to the world of First-Day meeting, and a pledge signed in a crowded hall, and – oh, he almost laughed at the absurdity of it – his tribunal in the morning. The second thought was all that mattered right now, here, with Miriam by his side.

He told himself that he wasn't about to lie to Miriam, he wasn't about to represent views that were not his own. He was merely letting one side of his character breathe a little. He was only giving a little more room to the side of his character that wanted the English officer to turn round, shoot the invader, and finish his watercolour.

'I'm against war,' he said carefully, 'and I would never *volunteer* to pick up a rifle. But if there was no other choice – if someone put a rifle in my hand and asked me to help defend our country – then of course I wouldn't throw it away.'

It astonished him how easy it was. The words slid so effortlessly off his tongue. There was something about the image of him defending their crater that felt natural and instinctively right. And it was such a relief not to have to be complicated, contrarian Paul any more. It was such a relief not to have to sit here and tell Miriam that it was certainly bad luck for her relatives on the Continent, but bombing Germany wouldn't make their luck any better. It was such a relief to believe, at least for this night-time moment by the pond, that his choice really did matter, and that he would go off and fight and be heroic, and come back to find Miriam waiting for him with loving admiration in her eyes.

'Of course you wouldn't.' She leaned into him, and he put his arm around her. 'I'm sorry. It was a horrible thing of me to say.'

The clouds parted and they looked up at the stars. He could see the Plough very clearly now. He took her hand and lifted it towards the sky.

'Merak,' he said. 'The star on the bottom right is called Merak.'

# 3

NATIONAL SERVICE (ARMED FORCES ACT)

—

APPLICATION TO LOCAL TRIBUNAL BY A
PERSON PROVISIONALLY REGISTERED IN THE
REGISTER OF CONSCIENTIOUS OBJECTORS

—

Name in full ... Paul Jeremiah Ezekiel Lamb

Any statement you wish to submit in support of
your application should be made below:

'I object as a Quaker to war and have dedicated my
life to abolishing the horror and futility of violence.
I cannot, when my soul cries out against war, take
up a rifle and fight bloodshed with bloodshed. God
has taught us not to kill but to love all men, even
the Germans. On battlefields do not grow vines! As
an artist trained in print-making, I have expressed
this sentiment in a sketch of a crippled vine that
was published by the Peace Pledge Union, which I
joined in 1937. Enclosed is a copy of the sketch and
some other samples of my work as a pacifist artist,
guided by the conviction that 'the pen is mightier
than the sword'. My most recent design, which
aims to depict the true nature of war in the guise of

an all-consuming sea-monster, was published in *Peace News*, a publication I also support. I plan to devote my life to art in the service of peace, but given the limited scope for using draughtsmanship to save lives in this war, I would be willing to serve in a Friends' Ambulance Unit, binding the wounds of war.'

I conscientiously object:-
(Strike out any of the items which does not apply)
a) to being registered in the Military Service Register
b) to performing military service
c) to performing combatant duties
and apply to the Local Tribunal to be registered accordingly.
I declare that the foregoing information furnished by me is true.

Not bad. Not bad at all. Reading through his copy of the application, he was rather proud of the little flourishes here and there – 'the pen is mightier ...' and so on. The tonic of romance still warmed him, and he easily dispelled any feelings of guilt. He had not exactly lied to Miriam. If everything went well, he would be allowed to serve in the Friends' Ambulance Unit, and that was as good an outfit as any of the ones she had in mind. There was no need to tell her about the details, about his objection and the tribunal; he would simply wait until he had his place with the Ambulance Unit, and she would probably think it was the same as being a stretcher-bearer with the army anyway.

'There's only one thing to remember.' His father coughed into his fist, took a deep, rattling breath and coughed again. 'Excuse me. There's only one thing to remember: if you speak freely from your heart, you have nothing to fear.'

His mother cut another slice of cake and poured a mug of thin tea. 'And do remember not to mumble, dear.'

'For goodness' sake, he's a Quaker!' Paul's father coughed again. 'The judges won't care if he mumbles, stammers or talks backward.'

Paul's mother suggested he wrap himself in a blanket, but her husband waved her away while still coughing into his fist. Even indoors he wore a maroon scarf and a thick brown cardigan that his wife had knitted from unravelled old jumpers.

'I'll make some more tea,' she mouthed, mindful of his father's mood, and went into the kitchen.

When she was gone, his father pulled a plain brown envelope from the inside of his jacket and placed it on the table.

'This is for you.'

Paul slid his finger inside the envelope. It was empty. He turned it upside down. A white feather slid out and slowly drifted to the floor. Paul picked it up and held it in his palm.

'Someone gave this to me in the Great War,' his father said. 'It was intended as an insult, of course, a symbol of cowardice and all that, but in the end I grew rather fond of it. It occurred to me one day that it could well be the feather of a dove, and from then on I decided to keep it as a symbol of peace.'

'Was that one of your epiphanies in Meeting?'

'It was an epiphany on the 24 bus to Tottenham Court Road. I have most of my epiphanies on the 24.'

'Fancy that. With me it's usually the 168.'

'To Euston? That one tends to be too crowded.'

'I like crowds.' Paul took a deep breath. 'I find noisy, boisterous crowds more inspiring than the silence of Meeting, to be frank.' He braced himself for his father's reaction and wished Charlie could see him now. There it was, his bolder, louder new self, striding out into the world.

But his father seemed unruffled, as if he knew his younger son was only sampling the taste of rebellion. He shrugged and said: 'You'll learn to appreciate the silence of Meeting. There'll be times when you'll feel like the entire world is shouting at you, and then you'll be grateful for silence.'

'Or perhaps I'll shout back. That would be another option, wouldn't it? What did *you* say to the chap who gave you the feather?'

'It was a girl.' His father shook his head. 'I came out of prison, went to Flanders with the Friends' Ambulance and saw more blood and gore in a single day than that girl had seen in her entire life. But she was a sheltered little creature, people told her things and she believed them. I was back on home leave, and one day I was sitting under an apple tree with John Balding, a friend from school, who'd joined up as

112

quickly as he could, gone to Flanders and got his arm blown off. Anyway, the two of us are sitting there, munching apples in the sun, and there comes the girl. She's planned this, of course; I haven't seen her since I left and I'm so happy I drop my apple and jump to my feet. And what does she do? She opens her purse, takes out two white feathers and gives each of us a feather. Some horrible old shrew had put her up to that. She wasn't a mean girl; she thought she was doing something clever, or she'd seen it at the pictures or something. Anyway, she gives us our feathers and walks off, all pouting and dignified, and Balding gets up and runs after her, waving his empty sleeve. He grabs her with his good arm – not really the way to treat a lady, if you ask me, but he was, as it were, a bit touched after Flanders – so he grabs her and yanks her round and flaps his empty sleeve in her face, jabbering away about his arm. "Have you seen my arm? Have you seen my arm, miss? God knows, I must have left it in Flanders!"'

They sat in silence for a while. Paul put the envelope in his bag. 'Well, let's hope it brings me luck. You know, just in case ... There are, of course, chaps who fail their tribunal, and then they go and join the Royal Army Medical Corps, which I suppose is just as good.'

'Yes. And then their unit is ambushed and before they know it, they've pulled out a gun and killed three Germans who were forced to enlist just as they were forced to enlist.'

'Perhaps I wouldn't pull a gun. That's just your assumption.'

'Assumption, no. It's my experience. You think *this* is war, don't you?' His rattling lungs struggled to support his voice. 'Stacking up a few sandbags. You think *this* is where your faith is tested, going to a courtroom and telling a bored judge about your conscience? Well, imagine death swapping his scythe for a machine gun. *That's* war. *That's* a test. The officer walking up and down the line with his cocked revolver, ready to shoot anyone who isn't going over. Thousands of men emerging from the trenches and walking into the fire and going down, and then the next thousand, and then the next. And you think in the midst of all that – when you're cowering in a trench next to some trembling little soldier holding on to his rifle for dear life – you think in that situation, when that soldier asks you to grab a rifle and help him defend the trench, you'll say: "Sorry old man, unfortunately I can't touch a rifle, but how about a cup of tea?"'

Paul put up his hand to block the assault. The effect of the night's tonic was beginning to fade. It irritated him that his father would burden his mind with unnecessary detail and complexity when he would have rather entered the courtroom fresh, clear and confident.

'Your mother and I,' his father continued, 'spent an entire afternoon in Flanders trimming off the military insignia on the uniforms the army had asked us to wear even though we were with the Friends' service. We cut them off with a pair of nail scissors. Then we dyed our uniforms grey, and after that we painted our ambulance grey, too. Do you think that was ridiculous? Do you think it was ridiculous to

114

be so obsessed over details? Well, it wasn't. Because that's how we defend our faith, Paul. We don't do it by ranting and shouting. We do it by etching our principles into our lives like a groove in a steel plate, and we follow that groove, and if it means sitting in a muddy field and fiddling with nail scissors, then that's what we do. Because once you leave that groove, Paul ...' his father rapped his knuckles on the windowpane, '... once you leave it, you'll be skidding and sliding over the steel plate with no moral direction at all. If it's not important whether there's an army badge on your shirt, then perhaps it's not important if there's a gun in your ambulance, and if that's not important, then perhaps it's not important if you're taught to shoot as part of your training. And when you finally stand up and say, I draw the line here, well, then everyone else will stare at you and reply, but you accepted the badge, didn't you? And you accepted the training and the camaraderie, didn't you? You're one of us now.'

Paul looked away.

'That doesn't help me, though. What if I fail the tribunal? What if they tell me to go and join the army, or the Army Medical Corps?'

'They won't. And if they do, then you'll do what generations of Friends have done, you'll let them send you to gaol, and we will come and visit you and see to it that you're treated reasonably well, and you'll come out a stronger man, a man who knows that the world has tried and failed to break him. That, Paul, is a feeling of strength that will stay with you and nourish you all your life.'

His father was talking about himself, of course, and patted his chest to reinforce his point. But the gesture had the opposite effect. As soon as he touched his chest, he let out a cough, and another cough, and Paul remembered him saying that his lungs had never been the same after the cold dampness of the prison cell. That was what had stayed with his father all his life: weak lungs and a fragile constitution. Some nourishment.

'Better not tell your mother about the feather,' his father said when Paul took his coat off the hook in the hallway. 'I never saw that girl again. I went back to Flanders and that was that, but you know what your mother's like, she'd think it queer of me to keep a feather, wouldn't she?'

He took off his scarf and wrapped it around Paul's neck, as he had sometimes done when Paul was small.

# 4

In the waiting room of the court house in Bloomsbury, Paul sat down next to a dark-skinned man who studied him with open curiosity.

'Conchie?' the man asked.

Paul nodded and took off his father's scarf.

'Christian or Socialist?'

'Quaker,' Paul said.

'Christian, then.'

Paul considered this. 'Well, we do base our testimony on

the teachings of Christ, of course, though you see, it's quite different from Catholicism, for example, in the sense that it would be possible to be a Quaker and something else.' He gave a nod. 'It would be perfectly possible to be a Quaker and a devoted follower of Mr Gandhi.'

'You think I'm a Gandhian?'

'Oh, it was just an assumption, since you look like a Hindu.'

The man burst into full-chested laughter. Paul felt embarrassed but could not have said why.

'It's fascinating to follow the parade of your thoughts there,' the man chuckled. 'You see my brown skin, you think Hindu, you think Mr Gandhi, who also has brown skin. Oh, please don't blush, comrade. I am absolutely delighted by your reply. You see, I am planning to study this subject in depth. "Thought and deliberation in the pre-revolutionary bourgeois mind" ... now I've said it, it's going to be the title of my thesis.'

'So you're not a Gandhian?' Paul asked cautiously. How smoothly and eloquently the words had flowed last night by the pond, and yet here he was again, mumbling and struggling to keep up with another's arguments.

'It's fair to say that I have much admiration for Mr Gandhi, but I'm not convinced by the idea of non-violence, no. I believe in armed revolution. From a theoretical perspective, of course. I'm too short-sighted for marksmanship.' He stretched out his hand. 'A. S. Chatterjee, truly pleased to meet you.'

'Paul Lamb,' said Paul, utterly confused now. 'To be

honest, I'm not sure I support the idea of an armed revolution. You see, I'm a pacifist. Well, it goes with being a Quaker, really. I hope you don't mind.'

A. S. Chatterjee smiled and locked his fingers behind his head. 'Do I mind? Why, I'm delighted! I hope we'll have a lifetime to discuss our views, Mr Lamb. You strike me as an interesting fellow, and frankly, an interesting case study.'

Paul exhaled with relief. 'If I may ask ... what are you doing here if you're not a pacifist?'

'Oh, I'm fully intent on refusing to serve the Empire. As you would say, it goes with being an anti-imperialist, really.'

A gruff-looking chap in a twill suit sat down next to them.

'Conchie?' Chatterjee asked.

'Arsonist,' said the chap.

'Oh,' Chatterjee said. 'I beg your pardon. Different courtroom.'

Paul tried to give the arsonist a friendly, forgiving smile, but the man turned his back to him.

'Is that what you're going to tell the tribunal then, that you're against the Empire?' Paul asked his new friend, more sure-footed now that he found himself on the familiar terrain of forms and tribunals. 'I hear objection on political grounds is awfully hard to pull off.'

Chatterjee dismissed the comment with a wave of his hand. 'My dear comrade, do you think anyone in there gives a hoot about the nature of your objection? If you took a more analytical view of the mind, you'd find the decisive factor at a much deeper level.'

'Really?' Paul's throat tightened. The feeling that had kept him floating two inches above the ground all the way from the pond to his house had entirely vanished; the entire bathing party might as well have been a dream that left no trace in daytime. 'What level?'

'Class, obviously.' Chatterjee replied, and locked his hands behind his head again. 'It all comes down to class. Picture some clean-collared Etonians, their voices ringing through the room, loud and clear, and the old hams on the tribunal are practically sighing with pleasure because it makes them remember those sun-dappled days of their youth, those wine-splattered evenings with the debating society: "Fine young fellow, don't quite agree with his views but I can see there's a heart and a conscience ... Conditional exemption. A few weeks in a wheat field will do him good." In comes some example of the unwashed, a lumpen pig farmer perhaps – no, those are central to the war effort – well, you know what I mean. A carpenter's apprentice, say. Picture him standing there, pigeon-toed, looking down at his scuffed brown shoes, and he mumbles something, and our honourable tribunal member cups a hand around his ear and bellows, "WHAT?" And the fellow mumbles again. He's only ever spoken to the men working alongside him, see, or to his family, to his sweetheart maybe, but certainly never to a whole roomful of strangers. He blushes, and he tries to speak up, but now he is nervous and ashamed, and in the end the tribunal will conclude that his argument was, on the whole, not convincing: "Couldn't even hear what the young blighter was saying, dash it!"'

'Are you telling me,' Paul said, swallowing hard, 'that it is dangerous to mumble?'

'My friend …' Chatterjee placed his right hand on his heart. 'It is fatal to mumble.'

# 5

The judges sat behind a barrier of polished carved oak. They did not wear wigs or gowns but simple suits. There were three of them: a wiry little man with round spectacles and a stiff, strangling collar on the far left; a taller man with tired, bloodshot eyes on the far right, and an enormous, slouching beast of a judge in the middle. The middle seat was slightly raised so that the senior judge towered a head above the others even as he slouched. He blinked and snuffled slowly like a large predator digesting a rabbit.

Paul was so mesmerized by the trio that it took him a moment to notice the painting behind them. It was a portrait of the late King in red and ermine, as tall as the room. One royal hand discreetly pointed at three rows of medals, the other was gripping a sword.

The sense of gravity was lost on the handful of journalists who sat to Paul's left and scratched their scalps with their pencils.

The wiry little man cleared his throat.

'Mr Lamb,' he began, leaning over the barrier like an eager mouse, an impression that was reinforced by his squeaky voice, 'would you be good enough to tell us a little more about your objection? You say you are against the taking of life.'

'Yes.'

'Does that include animal life?'

'I've lived as a vegetarian for the past year.'

'Though you brush your teeth and would not hesitate to fumigate a flea-infested mattress, one should hope.'

'Naturally.'

'So you do appear to support the notion of taking a life in order to ensure your own comfort. Very good, Mr Lamb. Enough of fleas, then. I would enjoy hearing your views on a different matter. Given that you think it is wrong to fight the Nazi hordes, even though they pose a somewhat greater threat than a few insects, could you tell us what we ought to do instead?'

'I believe there's still room for a negotiated solution,' Paul said somewhat mechanically. 'Even in the midst of war, it's always possible to negotiate peace.'

'And hand Europe to Hitler and his henchmen?'

The little man leaned back and looked up at his senior for approval. He was perhaps less experienced than his peers, who sat through the proceedings with weary indifference.

'War will only lead to more war,' Paul mumbled, glancing down at his freshly buffed shoes. 'If you remember, the last war was meant to end all wars, and yet—'

'And so on and so forth,' said the tired judge on the far right, rubbing his eyes as if he had been up all night. 'You do realize, of course, that if all of us took your attitude, Buckingham Palace would now be decorated with black eagles and flying the swastika flag.'

'One could always engage in peaceful resistance, I suppose.'

The journalists emitted a few snorts.

'I for one would refuse to learn German,' he added uncertainly. He had read this in an essay by Russell. It had somehow sounded more convincing then.

'Well, that would show them, wouldn't it?' the tired judge said. He propped up his head with his fists and his knuckles dug deep into his jowls. Paul wondered whether he had a son in the army: there was something personal in his contempt.

'Mr Lamb, you describe yourself as a pacifist,' squeaked the first judge. 'What, then, would you do if a German soldier were to break into your house and attack your mother?'

It was not the best moment for Paul to discover that when under extreme mental strain, his face twisted into a grimace that could best be described as a grin.

'I don't see why this question should be so terribly amusing, young man.' The judge squinted through his round spectacles with the injured air of someone used to being mocked.

'Oh, it isn't, it isn't,' Paul said, grinning. 'Not at all.'

'Well then, once again, what would you do?'

Paul was about to say, *I hope I would have the faith and strength of mind to peacefully resist and dissuade him.* It was the answer he had rehearsed dozens of times in his head, but it suddenly struck him as naïve to the point of idiocy. He willed himself to say it, simply say it, but instead his mind was invaded by the powerful image of a soldier grabbing his mother by her hair. It was such a strange and repulsive image, and he managed to push it away almost immediately, but when his mind returned to normal, he found that he did not know what to say.

'I'm afraid I cannot answer that question,' he said weakly. 'I cannot answer it because I truly don't know what I would do.'

He told himself that it was, all in all, not a bad reply; some people had advised him not to fall into the trap of answering hypothetical questions, so he might have done well to forget his prepared answer. And yet, he felt dishonest. The man had asked him a hypothetical question, but nevertheless a reasonable one, and Paul had failed to give a clear and courageous response. He felt hot and constricted in his father's suit and wished he could at least loosen his tie. A distinct smell of essence of lavender rose from the warm tweed.

The tired judge pressed the sagging blue pouches under his eyes for a while.

'Mr Lamb, it strikes me that when you talk about your objection to the taking of life, the life you are most concerned about is your own.' His nostrils widened with a stifled yawn. 'Rest assured, this is quite a natural feeling in a chap, but I am

123

not sure one can call it conscience.' He tapped his pen on the wooden barrier. 'A more appropriate term might be *cowardice*.'

And still, Paul thought, this is for the taking. I can still bend it round. They don't expect any great speeches here, whatever A. S. Chatterjee says. If I just put my mind to it and remember not to mumble, I can still bend it round.

It was only then that the friendly glutton in the middle, who had remained silent with his hands folded over his stomach, shifted in his raised seat. The other two looked up at him in reverence and expectation. He gazed at Paul in a lazy, kindly way, and when he spoke, his voice sounded as creaky, deep and inviting as a much-loved old armchair.

'Tell me, Mr Lamb,' he said, 'what would you say if I asked you to give me one good, solid, simple statement that summed up your views? You see, we've been batting back and forth the same questions and the same answers with a dozen young men like you.' He bounced an invisible ball between his big hands. 'One gets a little tired of it all; one comes to see it almost like a tedious and rather repetitive game. And no doubt you, too, have heard all about it from your like-minded friends. So what I like to do, and I believe this to be to the benefit of all involved, is to give you chaps a chance to speak up for yourselves. Why not? Mr Lamb, please give us a good, solid summary of what it is that moved you to come here.'

Paul stared at him and grinned.

'Take your time, dear fellow,' the judge said. 'Collect your thoughts, take your time.'

'Well ...' Paul began. He looked up. There was the King with his sword. All he had to do was explain that he was loyal to the King but would not, and could not, be loyal to his sword. And that was, after all, what his people had done through the ages; there was no reason why he should fail. He squared his shoulders and said with sudden confidence: 'It's really all in the scriptures, isn't it, but of course in worship we have this principle of "what dost thou say" – it's a principle of our faith, if you like – and so I suppose I should, as you say, express it all in my own words.' The man gave a phlegmatic nod. 'Now, having said that, I always did feel they made rather a good point in Isaiah – Isaiah two verse four to be precise – where they talk about there being no more war. There is a good line in there about mankind rejoicing in the creation, about growing and nurturing things rather than, as it were, destroying them: *They shall beat their swords into ploughshares and their spears into pruning-hooks*. You see, if you were to ask me to give you one line that summed up all my views, then that would be it, really: *beat swords into ploughshares*. Not exactly my own words, of course, but I couldn't really put it any better myself.'

Phew. He was through. He was through. Paul felt elated, dizzy, giddy with the satisfaction of a man who had stood his ground and made his point.

He turned back to the judge, who had slumped even deeper into his seat, one hand dangling by his side, the other resting comfortably on the barrier. He was playing with his fountain pen and looked at Paul calmly, almost without interest. For a moment Paul thought he had not even listened.

'Thank you, Mr Lamb, for giving us this little exposition. Interesting that you should mention those poor wretched ploughshares. We all know, of course, that Isaiah is not the only one who talks about them. As it happens, they are mentioned at least twice in the dear old Book of Books. Could you do an old man a favour and quote the other passage for me, Mr Lamb? Or would you like me to give you a hint? I quite understand that one's memory does tend to fail in these rooms.'

Paul felt the blood rush to his face. He shook his head, so utterly thrown that he was no longer even grinning. The court reporters, bored no more, sniggered. Their pens were poised to take down this unexpectedly interesting tribunal, which would merit more than the usual four-line write-up in the paper.

The judge sighed with tired disappointment. 'No? Nothing there? Here's my hint then, Mr Lamb. The other passage has almost the same wording as the one you quoted. One might almost call it a mirroring passage. And if you were to ask my opinion, which is only by the by, since I am not the one whose conscience we are all grappling to understand here, I'd say the two passages should never be torn apart and quoted as casually as you did just now. They should always be quoted as a pair.'

He stretched two fingers over the wooden barrier and

126

opened and closed them like a pair of pincers. Paul, close to tears now, could only shake his head once more.

'Well then, I am, of course, referring to the passage that begins, *Prepare for war, wake up the mighty men,*' the judge said in a bored drawl. '*Turn your ploughshares into swords and your pruning-hooks into spears: let the weak say, I am strong.*' He paused. 'Joel three verse ten.'

And then he repeated: '*Let the weak say, I am strong.* Do you disagree with that, Mr Lamb? Mr Lamb, would you rather let the weak stay weak?'

# PART TWO

# Under the Noise

# Café Brilyantn

'The purpose of this paper is to develop a mathematical formula for the perfect cut, allowing even a
cutter of modest means and average ability to achieve
maximum brilliancy.'
*A Theory of Diamond-Cutting*

# 1

When Mrs Morningstar went to see the Wizard at the Institute, she did something rather peculiar. She stepped off the
bus at Hatton Garden and walked the length of the street
from Clerkenwell Road down to Holborn Circus. Along the
way she discreetly touched certain walls and windows with
her gloved fingertips. Had someone stopped and asked her
what she was doing, she could not have explained herself. It
was a primitive impulse, a superstitious ritual of the sort she
usually despised.

When she had married, left her parents' home and moved
to Hampstead, she had walked the length of the road and

touched certain buildings while a stern voice in her head commanded: *And you, and you, and you, do not dare to follow me.* Now she retraced her steps and touched those same places as if to make amends.

She touched the mud-smeared windows of the corner café. It was a grim place, which Nathan had mockingly called Café Brilyantn. Inside, a dozen men with thick grey, black and reddish beards bent over rickety tables. They shook diamonds out of small white envelopes onto the dark wooden surface and sorted them with quick merchants' fingers. During the last war, all of Antwerp had been compressed into this café: the fur-swaddled merchants from the Antwerp Diamond Bourse, the brokers in frock coats with silken lapels, the apprentices in mended cotton shirts. Esther had expected it to be crammed with wartime émigrés once more, but many of the chairs were empty. The waitress in her black dress moved about easily with her tray of coffee in glasses. Where shoulders in black coats had once pressed against the windowpane, there was now a cautious gap. The men gathered at the back of the room, instinctively avoiding the glass.

Esther let her fingertip trail along the windowpane. When she had left Hatton Garden for good, she had stopped here and drawn a line through the gesticulating men. She had deleted them with her finger. *Farewell, diamond café.* Now she retraced that line. She turned up her palm and stared at her black fingertip with sudden guilt: she should not have been so glad to leave Café Brilyantn behind. Once it had contained the hopes and ambitions of her entire family. Her father, mother, her three brothers, her four sisters. Each of them had looked at the mud-smeared windows as an enchanted mirror holding a wonderful future: a rich husband with a Belgian accent; a merchant with a beautiful daughter; a formula for the perfect cut.

'*That* would be a way to make a packet,' Nathan had said.

Inside the café, one of the men sat his little son on his lap. He drove a needle through a sheet of cardboard and angled a diamond so that the light struck the stone and was thrown back onto the cardboard in an explosion of brilliant dots. The galaxy of miniature rainbows danced and changed size as the father slowly moved the stone. The boy tried to catch them with his fingers.

The man's lips moved and Esther knew what he was saying: *Look, this is what we call the fire of the diamond.* Her own father had shown them the same trick one afternoon by the kitchen window. And as soon as Nathan had seen it, any thoughts of forged emeralds had been replaced by an unceasing ambition to perfect that fire. It had become her ambition, too. Her father cut stones the way his father and grandfather had cut them. The wonder girl smiled condescendingly at their traditions, their superstitions. As soon as she learned about dispersion and diffraction, she drew lines, angles and arrows on a piece of paper and showed them to Nathan. He smiled and tugged her frizzy braid: '*That* would be a way to make a packet.'

The man with the boy on his lap looked up and she quickly walked on.

Some of her family's dreams had come true. Others, like the calculation of the perfect cut, had vanished. It was wrong to draw a line through a window that had at least partly kept its promise.

There was a scratched black door two blocks down from the café and she gave it a light affectionate tap. Red Leybesh had lived up there, her studious brother Solly's friend, who had dashed off to Russia.

Tap, tap, tap. There was the pawnbroker's. A woman with a shawl drawn deep over her face slipped inside.

Then Rubin & Sons, owned by Leybesh's father. The optimism of that 'Sons': Leybesh's older brother worked in the shop. Perhaps Leybesh would tire of hammers and sickles and come back to the scaife, too. *Do not be heartbroken, Mr Rubin. One son is better than no son. Adler & Sons have not been that fortunate.*

A cluster of men in long black coats blocked the door to the staircase that led up to the attic. Esther's hand touched the brick wall and stayed there for a breath or two. When she had left Hatton Garden for good, she had bundled up her scraps of Yiddish and Flemish and sent them up to the workshop. There was to be no talk of shlemiels and scaifes in Hampstead.

A few of the men nodded at her in recognition. She nodded back and quickly walked away from them. And again she was pricked by guilt for having deleted those men in the café with her finger all those years ago. How clever she had felt that day! She remembered it so clearly. She had bidden farewell to the attic and the shops. She had banished the whole of Hatton Garden from her life, had taken the bus

134

up to Hampstead, had walked into her big empty house carrying one man's child and another man's wedding ring.

Tufts of white hair wafted around the Wizard's massive bald head. The prominent widow's peak had disappeared, making his face appear rounder and larger. His stomach blocked the door.

He must have a house in town by now and another in the country, Esther thought. It surprised her that he would still cram his mahogany cabinets and grandfather clocks into this flat above the lab. Then again, there might be certain advantages. Presumably the wife was now conveniently tucked away in one of the houses.

'Miss Adler.' He slapped his forehead. 'Mrs Morningstar. I apologize.'

'I'm the one who ought to apologize. I've been meaning to respond to your letter for, gosh, for months now, I suppose.'

'Ah. I did wonder why I didn't hear from you. Whether there was a case of, as it were, divided loyalties.' He chuckled and wagged his finger.

She was once again the earnest student forever failing to catch the joke.

'I'm afraid I don't understand.'

'Forgive an old man for a bit of mischief. It was a sly dig at your German roots.'

'My roots are Belgian and Russian.'

'Quite, Miss ... Mrs Morningstar. Quite.' And he made a flourish with his hand as if to say, it's all the same anyway, isn't it? 'In any case, I'm very pleased to see you. Loyalties aside, I was a little worried that you were holed up in some evacuated physics department in Shropshire, gathering cobwebs and brooding over old grudges.' He chuckled again.

'I don't hold any grudges.' She smiled. 'No one's ever given me any reason to hold a grudge. But I suppose the bit about the cobwebs is true. I haven't exactly fought at the forefront of science over the past couple of decades, which is why I've been struggling to imagine how I could be of any use.'

'I don't remember you being this bashful in the old days. They've ground you down in Shropshire, eh? Or ...' he scratched his stomach, '... or is it Mr Morningstar?'

He did not ask her in, and she wondered whether there was someone sitting in the green armchair. It had been madness to walk up these stairs, to knock on this door. But the lines she had prepared so carefully could no longer be held back.

'I have been thinking about your offer every day for the past months.' She cleared her throat. 'If it still stands, well, it would be an honour and a privilege to work at the Institute again.'

Her daughter had once unsuccessfully tried to teach her a piece on the piano. It was a simple piece, no more than half a page, that began in an 'allegro moderato', held its breath for three long notes in the middle, then continued in the same 'allegro moderato'. But as much as Mrs Morningstar tried, she could not find the stillness in the middle. 'Just imagine time being suspended for three bars, and then it picks up again,' Miriam had said. But she could not do it; she needed to rush on because she feared nothing more than those moments that were suspended in time.

The Wizard stood in the door and she waited for his reply. One bar passed, two bars, three bars.

'Very good,' he said. 'I shall see you next Monday at eight o'clock then. I suppose you still remember how to find your way to the east wing.'

She hardly heard what he was saying. All she heard was that he did not reject her, that the letter had not been a mistake. An unbearable sensation of tension and discomfort fought with her grateful joy at having been chosen, at having been plucked out of Statistics for Freshers. She wanted to break out of this suspended moment that they had shared in the past and shared again now, and yet wanted nothing more than to work in his lab again. It was impossible that he should have chosen her: but he *had*, he *had*, and nothing else mattered.

# 2

Bentham College had no option but to let Esther go for this project of national importance. She delighted in her colleagues' envy. Every morning she ran to the lab as she had not run for twenty years and arrived with the flushed cheeks of a young girl. No one was more solicitous to the Wizard than she, no one more modest and industrious. It had been magnanimous of him to invite her back; it showed he was able to put personal feelings aside for the war effort. And so was she.

Every day she walked past the empty glass cabinet at the centre of the lab and cast a guilty look at the top shelf, which held a wooden stand with a semi-circular hollow. There was one thing she must do, and yes, she would see to it; but for two, three weeks she and the Wizard had behaved with impeccable politeness, and she feared upsetting the delicate balance. If she asked him for permission and he said no, she would have to do it anyway. Better perhaps not to ask him, and hope that the righteous nature of her plan would leave him no room for objection.

It took her two, three weeks to summon up the courage to do what she knew she must. She ran to the lab, as every morning. She unpacked her books, her folders and pens and lab coat. Then she reached deep into her bag and pulled out the heavy Nobel medal. She held it aloft for everyone in the lab to see.

'Who in here remembers Mr von der Weide?'

A few men of her own age raised their hands. The younger ones stared at them with admiration. She turned to a pale weedy chap and held out the medal for him to look at. He touched the golden rim with his fingertips.

'Hold it. All of you, take a good look at it. Mr von der Weide used to stand where you are standing now, yes, right here. I assume you've heard about his recent difficulties. He's given me his Nobel prize medal for safekeeping, and

I don't know what you think, but I can imagine no better place for it than right here, in the laboratory that was so dear to him.'

The man closest to her began to clap. The others joined in the applause. Drunk on their approval, she climbed on a stepladder and opened the glass cabinet in the centre of the room.

'I suppose some of you may have wondered why there is an empty wooden stand in this cabinet.' The stand, with its moon-shaped brace, sat on a high glass shelf where it could be seen from all sides. The medal fitted perfectly into the semi-circular space. Still standing on the ladder, Esther turned to face the room. 'You see, when I was here as a young researcher, we were told that the stand had been designed to hold the laboratory's first Nobel medal. Well, as you know, other laboratories in the institute have collected carat after carat of gold since then, but somehow our corner of the building must have been a little cursed. I'm pleased that our dear Mr von der Weide's prize will grace this cabinet until he is in a position to take it back.'

There were shouts of 'Hurrah!' Esther half expected them to carry her across the room on their shoulders. She was the darling of the lab again, the spoiled wonder girl, the pet. She hopped on the floor, stumbled a little, was quickly steadied by gallant hands.

*And to think I once sold shoes in Passau*, she heard Gottfried say. He said it every time he succeeded at something in the lab, though she could not remember whether he had in fact ever sold shoes or whether it was some German saying. When she had sent him her congratulations on the Nobel Prize, he had added a mischievous handwritten addition to the pat thank you note: 'And to think I once sold shoes in Passau.'

Esther was about to tell the others about this famous man's little quirk when the door at the other end of the lab opened. She could just glimpse the expression on the Wizard's face as he stared at the Nobel medal on the shelf. The door closed and she was left with the excited faces around her, fizzing with eagerness to get to work and do their absent peer justice.

# 3

Everything sparkled at the lab. Everything reflected the light. And she herself sparkled, too; and was in the light once more.

Belgium was invaded and at home the mood was one of dull, dark mourning, as if all the mirrors and all the silver had been covered. Sometimes when she turned the key in the lock she was so tired and the house was so quietly sad that she could not tell whether she was stepping into the house in Hampstead in 1940 or the house in Hatton Garden in 1918. Her husband acted as if the Germans were already in Kent and even persuaded her to procure four vials of morphine from a medic at the institute for the worst case. She felt repelled by his defeatism now, yet could not deny that his general yielding softness had been very useful to her once. At night the carousel of dread and regret turned and turned in her head, but when the sun rose she dressed without washing and went to the bright world of the laboratory without even waking Mr Morningstar.

Let other women be wives, mothers, sisters. Esther had no time for domesticity. Let other people be defeatists. Esther was neither numbed nor subdued by the fall of Belgium. Even the worry over her relatives in Antwerp did not paralyse her. Let others sit in gloom and fear, like medieval peasants awaiting the marauders. She was alive and ready for battle. There was nothing supernatural about the speed and force of the German assault. It was a function of the quantity and quality of their tanks, bombs, planes and ships. If they met an opposing force greater than their own, they would be pushed back. Her one task was to help increase that opposing force.

The clarity and precision of her purpose filled her with an optimistic vigour she had known only twice before: when she first joined the Wizard's lab, and before that, when she had promised Nathan to help him make a packet.

## 4

Esther arrived at the lab and did not immediately spot what was wrong. The muted atmosphere, the nervous glances were not unusual these days. She walked past the men with spectrometers; her current work was mostly theoretical. When she passed the glass cabinet she glanced at the stand in quiet triumph as she did every morning and only then did she see that the medal was gone.

'Where is it?'

A few men glanced at each other. No one spoke.

'Where is the Nobel prize medal?'

Not long ago she had been the darling of the laboratory once again. Now she relived another role she knew too well. Here she caught a smirk, there a shifty look. They were all in league. Her voice reached that high pitch she loathed, and which they must think of as typically female, uncontrolled, with a touch of hysteria.

'Did any of you take it? It was entrusted to me. It was entrusted to me by Mr von der Weide, our friend and colleague Mr von der Weide, prisoner in a Nazi gaol. I hope you all understand that this is not some trinket you can use for your pranks.'

The schoolmarm's tone earned her a roomful of resentment.

'The Wizard has it,' one of the men said without looking up.

'Does he indeed? It's not *his* Nobel prize,' she snapped, and there it was: the summary, the reason why the Wizard hated von der Weide and hated the medal, and now hated her for having accepted his offer and then put the medal in its rightful place.

'The Wizard didn't win the prize. The Wizard has, as you

142

may have noticed, never won a Nobel Prize. This medal belongs to Gottfried von der Weide, who took great risks to—'

Turning her head, she saw the open door, the tufts of white hair, the Wizard's expressionless face.

'Miss Adler, if you wouldn't mind seeing me in my study...'

She did not correct him.

'Thank you for reminding us all that I have never found favour with the Nobel committee,' he said with an awful smile. 'It's interesting to see that this is all you measure someone's work by. How would you evaluate your own achievements by that standard? I hear you taught a very successful statistics course for accountants at Bentham College. Perhaps it was selfish of me to disrupt such a promising career?'

She sat in the green armchair. He slouched on a swivel chair by his desk. The woven brown wallpaper had not changed, nor had the olive-green curtains with the pattern of rhomboids. She half expected to hear a muffled cough from the next room.

He looks like a glutton, she thought, like a glutton who swallows all he sees and desires. He had fed on his students, on their adoration and their need to please, and had grown monstrously fat on them over the years. And she ... she had shrivelled up like a hard, bitter plum, all the juice of her youthful hopes and ambitions gone. His scorn did not touch her; there was nothing for it to touch.

'So, Mrs Morningstar, you suspect me of having pocketed the medal for my own profit?'

'I never—'

'You did not for one moment consider that I had good reasons?'

She told herself not to apologize. He would sack her, he would force Bentham College to sack her too, but it did not matter, she would not apologize.

'Let me put it this way, Mrs Morningstar. What do you think the Germans will do if they invade Britain and find a Nobel medal in my lab that bears the name of a political prisoner back in Berlin?' He moved the curtain aside with the back of his hand and gazed over the domes and spires of Westminster. 'Not to mention what it would mean for poor Gottfried. I don't think having smuggling added to his many charges is quite what he had in mind when he sent you the medal for safekeeping.'

She tried to hold her ground. 'The Germans haven't invaded Britain yet. We shouldn't act as if they have.'

'Some might say it's important to take precautions. I am sure, my dear, that you have taken yours.' And his eyes flickered over to her for a moment before returning to the view.

The comment silenced her. She felt cowardly, ashamed; the medic must have told him about the vials of morphine.

'Where are you going to hide it?' she asked quietly. 'Mr von der Weide will want it back one day, and I would like at least to be able to lead him to where you've buried it.'

The Wizard withdrew his hand and let the curtain swing back. He pulled an encyclopaedia from the shelf behind the armchair, opened it and let the medal hidden in its hollowed-out pages drop heavily into her lap.

'Bury it?' His stomach was at her eye height but she refused to flinch. 'Bury it where? In my wife's kitchen garden? In the institute's courtyard? Have you heard of the Gestapo and the SS, Mrs Morningstar? Have you heard what they do when they raid a house?'

'Yes,' she said with slow emphasis, 'I have indeed.'

For a moment, that shut him up. Then he sighed and said: 'You see, I was going to melt it down in the lab and donate the gold to the war effort. But you're quite right, he sent it to *you*, and I shall let you take care of it. My advice would of course be to melt it down, but it's your choice. You may hide it in your house if you wish, though if that's what you choose to do, I would ask you cut your ties with this institute. I have two dozen researchers under me, men with families and decent lives that I must protect. You may leave us and do as you please, or stay with us and destroy the thing. I would call that a fair deal, and frankly, not one to agonize over. It's a slice of metal, for Christ's sake, not a person.'

Back in the lab, the men avoided her. She remembered that it had been like that during her very first week, so many years ago. On her first day they had assumed her to be the tea girl, someone's wife, a seamstress in the wrong building. Even after she put on her white lab coat, they continued to ask her for cups of tea. There were crude jokes, hostile mutterings about homely spinsters who would be better off knitting socks for the boys in Flanders. Only Gottfried had been nice to her. She remembered an evening in the empty lab. A trembling hand set down a mug of tea next to her spectrometer.

*They always ask you to make tea, so tonight I thought, maybe I will make a tea for her for a change.*

He had reminded her of her brother Simon. Something about the shy pudginess, the tremor. Yet when he fixed a crystal on a metal thorn his hand was as steady as a surgeon's.

Her notes lay before her, columns of data to be gutted. She smoothed the paper with her hand, and it trembled more than Gottfried's. 'Applications of mathematical statistics to the assessment of the efficacy of bombing' by E. Morningstar.

Only the day before, the Wizard had told her that her research was much appreciated, had been read in the highest circles and found to be very useful indeed. Statistics for Freshers had not been such a waste of time after all.

If she did not destroy the medal, she would have to leave the lab just when her life finally had some meaning and purpose again, when things were finally fitting together again. She told herself that she must stop trying to connect all the best and worst moments of her life, must stop trying to fit it all into a pattern, but already the carousel in her head was turning again, already she was letting the present yield once more towards the past, and her white-coated lab colleagues hunched over their spectrometers became tall gaunt cutters bent over their spinning scaifes.

# 5

Mrs Morningstar decided to consult Max before mentioning the medal to her husband and daughter. After all, he had personally witnessed more than one Nazi raid. Max rarely spoke about Berlin, but once, when she had helped him write a letter to a potential British sponsor for his mother, he had described to her in his slow, precise way how her shop had been looted. The upturned drawers, the smashed wood panelling, the bruises on her face in the morning. If he thought hiding it at home was too dangerous, she would melt it down right away, and the rest of the family need never know about it.

She pulled Max aside one evening when the others were out. He listened to her clipped explanations while turning the medal in his long thin hands. Something seemed to upset him.

'You must have heard of Gottfried von der Weide,' she said.

'Physics is such a mystery to me,' he said with a strange stiff smile, and handed her the medal. 'I suppose the name rings a bell. Yes, I suppose I saw it in the paper once.'

*But it must do more than ring a bell,* she wanted to say. *You're the son of a German physicist.* And she could see that he knew this was what she wanted to say, and knew, too, that she would not say it, because Max's father was a subject that could not be mentioned.

Instead, she told him about the Wizard's concerns. Max nodded, and said in an impartial tone that this was quite true; if the medal was found at their house after a German invasion, they would all be taken away and interrogated.

'Enough,' she said decisively. 'I'm sorry I came to you with this hare-brained idea. Professor Littlewood is of course right – it's a medal, not a person. I'll melt it down myself in the lab.'

His rigidly composed expression cracked, and he grabbed her wrist hard and cried: 'Please don't melt it down.'

'Max! It's too dangerous to keep it here, you've said so yourself.'

'I know. And if you ask me what the sensible thing would be, well, you should melt it down. But if you ask me to speak from my soul, I would ask you not to. I can't explain the reason, it's how I feel. It would seem like another punishment to Mr von der Weide.'

'Well, I feel that way, too, otherwise I wouldn't have kept it safe in the first place. But we can't put ourselves into danger for some Swedish gold. I don't think that's what Gottfried would want.'

'Then why did he give it to you? He gave it to you, not to one of his friends in Göttingen or Heidelberg or Passau, because he knows you will keep it safe for him. And please do that, please keep it safe for him.' He held out his hands. 'Or I will keep it safe myself.'

'That's out of the question.' She put it in her pocket. 'I'll try to think of something. I promise you I'll do my best to find a place for it. And then let's pretend I never showed you the medal.'

A few days later she mentioned to the Wizard in passing that she had followed his advice.

'I think our friend from Heidelberg will understand,' she said in a tone that was meant to make it sound like a light and insignificant act.

It was only then that she realized what had been so odd about Max's reaction. 'He did not give his medal to one of his friends in Göttingen or Heidelberg,' he had said, 'or Passau.' The first two towns were well known and he might have used them as figures of speech, as a way of saying, 'friends at famous universities'. But Passau? How could Max possibly know Gottfried's little joke about selling shoes in Passau?

# The Teapot

## 1

Grace and Max cut the children's hair. The girls were given sporty bobs; the boys, shaved necks and floppy fringes. Grace herself experimented with a fashionable fringe. It made her look a little more playful, and she had a feeling that Morten might like it. He would run his fingers through it, perhaps, or gently blow it from her forehead.

There were not many children left at Samhuinn. Most had found homes, or at least farmhouses in need of labour. When Inge's turn came, Grace had to restrain herself from letting the pair of scissors slip a little, just enough to snip away that awful, ratty string. The cardboard name tag was long gone, dissolved by rain and soapy water. The string clung on.

The scissors clipped neatly around Inge's thin neck, through her mousy hair, as thin and dully brown as Grace's. She saw herself in Inge's reserved earnestness, in the stern silence that was so unusual in a child. Inge looked at herself in the mirror and frowned. Grace pouted.

'Are you saying you don't like my work?'

'It's not your work that I don't like,' Inge said. 'It's my face.'

'You have a lovely face.'

'My brother looks much nicer. That's why Mama kept him with her.'

She hooked her finger around the grey string and pulled at it so it cut into the soft skin on her neck.

It was hard to believe that the blue dorms had once seen happy children, wild chases down the yellow corridor so loud they brought up sour teachers from the floor below. Now the mood was anxious, cowering. Like little mice in little mouse-holes, Grace thought.

Inge had taken to placing small pieces of cheese before the mouse-holes in the kitchen. The other children copied her. No amount of scolding from Grace and Max could deter them. When the cook put out traps, the children sabotaged them with sticks. Once they left out a pan of grease overnight. It was crisscrossed by tiny paw prints in the morning.

'These are not currants, I think,' Max said after staring into his bowl of nature-cure oat flakes for five minutes. He shoved the bowl aside and told the cook to put out more traps.

They had discussed whether the children ought to be

exposed to news from the Continent. Max said there was no point in trying to protect them: it was better for them to know.

Grace missed the music-hall performances in her door-frame. No more glimpses of Max carrying pine cones, paperbacks, fir branches that scattered needles all the way down the corridor. He barricaded himself into a storage room behind the kitchen and dived into some frantic correspondence that she dared not ask about. His face grew gaunt and his ears protruded even more prominently. He looked more than anything like a tragic clown, a broken rag doll.

She tried not to disturb him. They rarely spoke, and the shy camaraderie that had emerged around Christmas faded and was replaced by awkwardness. She longed to ask him what the matter was, whether he had received bad news from Berlin, but the question was too daft at a time when there was nothing but bad news from Berlin; what other news could there be?

Only once did she venture into the storage room. It was after the hairdressing session. She remained in the doorway, half in, half out.

'I was wondering if I could ask your advice on something.'

'Anytime.'

'It's about Inge.'

He nodded.

'It's the fact that she insists on wearing that string around her neck. I can see why she does it. She has some idea that

152

her parents will find her. It's become some sort of symbol of loyalty. But I'm not sure it's healthy. In fact, I worry that it's downright *unhealthy*. And I was wondering ... well, I was wondering if I ought to, you know, accidentally snip it off next time I cut her hair.'

There was a look of such utter horror in his eyes that she stopped.

'It was only an idea. Another idea would be for someone to tell her to take it off. You see, if *I* told her, she might simply resist, since she sees me as a friend rather than a figure of authority. But if someone else were to tell her ... perhaps ... if *you* ...' She was openly pleading now. 'You could tell her it's an order from the headmaster. Max, she has to get rid of that thing.'

Max shrugged. 'In my opinion, she can wear it as long as she wants to.'

'But it's for her own good! It's not a necklace, it's a horrible, hideous, morbid noose. Can't you see that? The only purpose it serves, the only function it has, is to remind her and everyone around her of all she left behind, every single minute of the day. It chains her to that very moment when her mother knotted it around her neck in their kitchen in Berlin, with her little brother watching. And we need to cut her free from that, we need to cut her free from that morning in the kitchen with her mother and her brother and a plateful of rolls with jam *and* butter.'

Max shrugged again, and Grace hated him as she had hated him during his first week.

'Have you even looked at her?' she cried. 'It makes her look *odd*. It makes her look like ... like a suitcase that someone left on an abandoned platform in the pouring rain.'

'She is odd. All of us are odd. Let her wear her piece of string.' He folded his hands under his gaunt face. 'Sometimes I wish I had one to wear myself.'

Grace realized then how much she had relied on her work to sustain and nourish her. From the time when she had accompanied the Dutch official to Vienna to negotiate exit permits for Jewish children, she had prided herself, congratulated herself on being one of the few people who did good in this dim and evil world. Yet it occurred to her now that the chief beneficiary of all those hours in train stations, in offices, at Quaker fund-raising lunches, had really been herself. She had created a world where she could paint the walls yellow and laugh at Max's wonky Christmas ornaments; where people spoke to each other in kind, calm tones and worked for a common purpose. Now the very air at Samhuinn was jittery and fearful, there was no place left where she could replenish her spirits. When she prayed, she found her mind puzzling over Max's sullen hostility. When she closed her eyes in Silent Meeting, she saw nothing but a piece of grey string around a slender neck.

The worst aspect of this new situation, however, was that it made a certain time of the day even more unbearable than before: the time when she would lock her office, and walk home alone.

# 2

A week later, in May 1940, Holland fell.

Grace decided it was time to move the remaining children to the countryside again.

Max responded to the idea with a shrug. An awful fatalism wafted through the yellow corridors. Grace refused to be polluted by it. One could not be fatalistic with children in one's charge. The headmaster, Mr Cartland, told her he would evacuate Samhuinn to a farm in Somerset; there was enough space for the children from the fifth floor. However, in order to save costs and space, he thought it best if his wife and the school's nurse took care of all the children on the farm. They would cook, clean, supervise meals and so on. He and a handful of teachers would deal with academic matters. Since all the children at the farm would be full boarders, there was no need to have separate sleeping arrangements for the fifth-floor lot.

Grace nodded. It was a fair arrangement. There were enough other people in London, or indeed Europe, who needed her help; she would find another job to do. She went back to her office, where she was storing a batch of yellow paint bought to freshen up the hallway. It upset her to sit and look at the paint that would never be used. She went into the breakfast room. Max was there, stacking plates.

'Max,' she said quietly, 'it looks like we won't see your lovely Christmas ornaments this year.' She told him about the plan.

He said it sounded sensible. The clattering plates in his hands reminded her of that day with the paperbacks. Clatter, clatter, soft thump.

'Is that all you have to say?'

'It sounds sensible, responsible and efficient.'

'I thought . . . I thought you might be a little sad to see the children leave.'

'I would be sadder to see them bombed.'

She refused to let it go. 'Some of the children *are* very sad.'

'They will enjoy the farm.'

She could not understand this new hardness, this surface that made every comment of hers bounce like a rubber ball on stone.

The children were downstairs, in class. She picked up a plate, held it with both hands and shook it.

'Max,' she said with urgent despair, 'I had hoped you would be a little . . . a little kinder. It *is* sad. Can you not admit that? I know it's the sensible thing, but I thought . . . I thought we had begun to set up something rather pleasant here. Something rather successful. The children were happy here. Inge said something yesterday – it was one of those things she says, but still – she said that if she had to leave this place, she would no longer want to live.'

'She said that?' He lifted the stack of plates. The way he stretched backwards to balance the load reminded her of more cheerful times, of books and pine cones. 'If that's what she thinks, she ought to have stayed in Germany.'

'Max!' Grace dropped the plate.

'That's a shame about a good plate.' His German accent had thickened.

'You can't mean that.'

'I do. It's a shame.' He began to sweep up the shards. She kicked at the broom, and it flew out of his hands.

'How can you? She's eleven!'

'I am only stating a fact. If she does not want to live, if she has no will to live, if she is unwilling to use this life that has been given to her, then she should have stayed in Germany. She could have given her place on the train to her little brother.' He calmly picked up the broom and continued to sweep. 'Or my mother.'

That afternoon, she let Inge help her punch holes into official letters and receipts, then file the papers into different folders. It was Inge's favourite activity and seemed to calm her, though Grace usually tried to discourage it and make her play with the other girls instead.

They were sitting on the floor with two big hole-punchers when they heard a great commotion in the staircase.

Grace went out to check. A flustered girl came running up the stairs and pushed open every door. It was Doreen, an acquaintance of Grace's from Jewish Relief.

When she saw Grace, she cried between deep, panting, exhilarated breaths: 'There you are! Grace, the train's here! The train's here!'

Grace's first rush of ecstasy was wiped out by one look at Inge's face. The little girl was lit up by bright and shining joy.

Grace frantically tried to shut the door, tried to buy just one minute to warn Inge, tell her that this was not the right train, that she must not expect her parents and her brother to be on this train.

But Inge, burning with fiery joy, pushed her out of the way, pushed the Jewish Relief girl out of the way, raced down the stairs two at a time and shouted at the top of her voice: 'Mama! Mama!'

She could of course have held Inge back. She could have forced her to stay in the office with her. Indeed, she *should* have held her back, should have protected her from staring longingly at every single person who stepped off that train until the train was empty.

She could have, and yet she couldn't. She should have been responsible and sensible, but the force that gripped her was too powerful. Half-way down the stairs she almost trampled over Max Hoffnung. She did not care. She pushed him out of the way, took the last steps two at a time and all she could think was Morten! Morten! Morten!

Doreen had borrowed a car from someone and they hurled through the streets with giddy recklessness, straight to the Friends' House on Euston Road, where volunteers were already feeding tea and sandwiches to the tired travellers. Grace jumped out with the motor still running. That they should meet again at Friends' House!

Men, women, children were flooding in and out of the

front door, a thick flow of refugees, helpers, Jews, Quakers, girls with clipboards, a man with a dozen loaves of bread stacked high on a trolley.

Friends were pouring out tea and listening to stories about the ordeal. When the boat left Holland it came under fire from the Germans. There were tilted heads, rounded mouths, sympathetic interjections: 'Gosh!' and 'How awful.'

Someone passed Grace a teapot. She poured tea into chipped mugs and looked at faces, faces, faces, so many faces but none that fitted. Her eyes were a question and she was looking for the one face that would be the answer.

Voices around her told the story in fragments. Holland under fire. A train to Holland, then the boat to Harwich. The boat under fire. Yes, but where was the face?

A tired, ash-blonde girl of about twenty tapped her on the shoulder and held out an empty mug. 'Would you mind?' She was American. An American relief worker, probably.

Grace could bear the tension no longer. She filled the mug and when she had finished, asked straight out if Morten was on the train.

'Sure.'

*Sure*. She pressed her palms against the hot sides of the pewter teapot.

'Morten is here?'

'Uh-huh.' The girl could hardly speak for tiredness. She moved towards an armchair in the corner.

'He's *here*?' Grace wanted to throw her arms around the American and kiss her dear sweet blonde head. She would remember that voice for the rest of her life, that kind, limp voice uttering that word. *Sure.* Morten, here! He might be walking in any moment! It couldn't be possible. She was dreaming. She did what she thought people never did in real life: lifted a bit of skin on her arm with her thumb and knuckle and gave it a hard squeeze. It hurt. He really was here. He was here!

She grabbed the girl's hand: 'That's wonderful ... you cannot imagine ... well, first of all, welcome to England. We're so glad you made it. What's your name?'

'Tipper.' The young woman closed her eyes when she spoke and rubbed her hand over her face. 'It's been a long journey. Morten should be here any minute with the rest.'

Grace followed Tipper to the armchair. The red lipstick was in the pocket of her dress and she must find an excuse to run upstairs and tidy her hair and rouge her lips before he arrived. She did not give a hoot about what the others thought if they saw her emerging from the bathroom with red lips. Let them think what they wanted, her lover was here! And she would kiss him with bright red lips!

Then she saw the crowd shuffling and shifting to let someone through. She jumped up but it was only Inge. The child wriggled through the crowd and looked up at every face with earnest grey eyes. Grace felt a sharp pang of guilt and pain and then annoyance, because this was *her* moment, her moment when she must run upstairs and put on lipstick.

Tipper carried a bundle of papers under her arm.

'Is that the passenger list? May I see?'

They went through the names together. Inge's parents were not there, as Grace had expected. Neither was Inge's brother. She would tell her later. She would have a quiet word with her. Oh, why did Inge even have to be here!

'Is there going to be another train?'

'Are you kidding? Amsterdam's burning. We came under fire when we left the port. I was sure we'd never make it.'

Grace's thoughts were on her lipstick but it would be callous to leave this girl now. She offered another cup of tea.

'Thanks.' Tipper eased into her seat. 'Cake! Swell.'

She told Grace a little about her work for the American Friends. She and one other American had stayed in Berlin when Britain declared war and all the others left. What a winter.

The tea revived her and Grace could see that underneath her exhaustion lay one of those practical optimists. She began describing her journey in great detail and it was all terribly brave and interesting, but Grace was beginning to wonder why Morten was delayed and whether he had gone straight to some hostel.

As soon as there was a suitable break in Tipper's stream of words she said: 'You cannot imagine how glad I am that you're all here. Do you think I should go out and see if Morten is all right? I hope they're not held up at the station.'

'No, he's fine. He'll just be lingering, as usual. You know Morten. Never on time.' Tipper laughed with an easy familiarity. A tired sunny laugh. Grace felt mildly envious that she knew details that were new to her. Morten, never on time! Well, it was a tiny weakness, hardly worth remembering.

She stood up. The minutes passed by so slowly and she thought: he must be stuck somewhere or he would come rushing, running to me. And she held tight that image of her standing there and pining for him, stretching towards him, as he stood in Liverpool Street Station with his suitcase in hand, pining and stretching towards her.

'Have they arranged for your lodgings?' she asked Tipper. It was rude to stand there and think of love when there were dozens of travellers aching for sleep.

'Yeah. We'll be staying with an American friend, but you know, we're not planning to hang around for long. Just a few days and then we're off to Philadelphia.'

Grace stared at her. 'The whole group? Morten's going too?'

*But he's German. He can't go. He has to stay here, with me.*

Tipper shook her head. 'Not the whole group. Just me and him.' She held out her mug. 'That tea was good. Any chance I could have some more?'

Grace filled up her mug and did not even tremble.

'Sounds like quite an adventure.'

'We talked about staying in London but we've only got transit visas. And my parents really want us to live with them. They're in Philadelphia.'

'I see.'

'It'll be a honeymoon. Of sorts.' She took a sip and flinched. 'Ouch. Hot.'

When she flinched, she pursed her lips and the effect was very pretty.

'Congratulations. I didn't even know. Wartime correspondence ... sporadic ... erm ... wartime, you know ...' Grace had run out of words.

Tipper had not. 'Yeah, exactly, wartime. We barely had time to say our vows. I wore yellow.' She shook her head. 'Some wedding party.' But then she smiled again and Grace could see that in peacetime she would be ever-sunny. 'The bride wore yellow. That's what we'll tell our grandchildren. It's what I always say, y'know? It's all really hard now but one day it'll be a great story for the grandchildren.'

A good sport, a loving wife, a beautiful mother.

'Right.' Grace shook her teapot. 'If you wait here, I'll go and fetch more tea. One can never have too much tea, don't you think? That's what I always say. Tea, tea, tea.'

She crossed the room and walked out of the back door, round the house and all the way to the bus stop where she waited for five minutes until the bus came that took her home. Only when she sat down did she realize that she was holding her satchel in one hand and, in the other, the empty pewter teapot.

# Swarthmoor Hall

# 1

It had been raining for a solid week when Charlie's train pulled into Ulverston Station. Wrapped in a stiff coat, with his collar yanked awkwardly over his head against the rain, he splashed through the puddles on the platform towards a dry patch under the station roof. He shook the droplets out of his hair and looked around for a motor car, a horse-drawn cart or at the very least a friendly person with an umbrella. But the station was deserted. He waited for a while, shrank into his scratchy coat and hopped from foot to foot. The wind grew stronger and blew the rain under the roof, soaking his dry patch.

'Sod it,' he muttered, turned up his collar and plodded out into the rain, shoulders raised, chin tucked in like a reluctant ox. His city shoes became heavy with the rainwater. He squelched across the field and kept roughly to the right. There was no path, only a bumpy meadow blurred by rain and fog. Fields and fog to the left, forest and fog to the right. Straight ahead, uphill, a glimmer of light. He speeded up, his cold fingers clamped around his suitcase, which grew more cumbersome with every step. When he had almost reached the top of the hill, he could make out the gloomy, towering outline of Swarthmoor Hall.

If his father had sent him here in the hope of bringing him closer to his ancestral faith, he could not have failed more spectacularly. The sight of the bleak bastion reminded Charlie of everything he loathed about Quakerism. Those stark, unadorned stone walls, the narrow latticed windows, the plain, sensible wooden doors: it was a house that drew its walls around itself and hunkered down before the wind and rain. And that's what we do, Charlie thought, we hunker down; for all that talk of striding out into the world and gladly carrying our inner light hither and thither, we're really happiest when we're holed up in a cottage with latticed windows where no one comes and bothers us.

His father would, of course, have countered that Quakers had travelled far and wide, the early Quakers especially, that they had gathered strength from the first meetings at Swarthmoor Hall and then fanned out across the whole world, founded an entire state on the other side of the Atlantic, fought the slave trade, reformed prisons. Yes, Charlie thought, but where are we *now*? If Quakerism is such a topping religion, then why are we the only Quakers on our street – and by the way, people *still* think we're spies? That's where you got us with your hunkering down and your meekness, our own neighbours think we're spies!

The last stretch led him through a splintered wooden gate, an unkempt garden and, finally, to a back door that he attacked with his fists. There was a stench of manure and shuffling and rustling sounds, like animals moving through dry straw. The dull windows gave nothing away. He cupped his hands around his face and brought his eyes close to the glass. A large heavy shape shifted about in there. Cow or horse. He picked up his suitcase, walked round the side of the Hall and tried the front door. It was open and he entered a clammy stone hallway.

'Hello?'

The door to his left opened, just a foot wide. A plump blonde with rosy cheeks and small suspicious eyes peered through the crack with her hand shielding a candle.

'I just saw someone stomp around the garden, shouting at himself,' she said cautiously. 'Was that you?'

'I wasn't shouting. I was thinking aloud.' He wiped his nose on his sleeve.

'I suppose you're the new conchie.'

'You're not wrong.'

'And what a little ray of sunshine you are. Come on in. The kitchen's over there, if you want to get changed.'

'Thank you.'

'No need. And do feel free to go on shouting at yourself if you feel the urge. The walls are thick and we're very tolerant here.'

In the chilly kitchen Charlie ripped off his wet clothes and tossed them on the black iron range. The flagstones were cold and he hopped from foot to foot.

'Lovely summer,' he shouted. 'Picnic weather.'

The door opened and the girl came in, stared at his full frontal nakedness, clapped her hands over her eyes. She showed no inclination to move but simply stood there with her eyes covered and asked: 'What did you say?'

'I didn't mean to make you come in!'

'Then why did you call me?'

'I didn't!'

'Were you thinking aloud again?'

'Can you please leave the kitchen so I can put on some dry clothes?'

'No need to be shy.' She giggled. 'It's not as if there's much to see.'

'Out!'

And he slammed the door shut behind her.

He took his time, dried himself slowly with a tea towel, put on the winter clothes he'd brought in wise foresight. The door opened again.

'I'm not looking! I'm only going to make tea.'

She made a great show of keeping her back to him while she filled the rusty kettle with water, and chatted easily over his sullen silence. Her name was Georgina; a land girl, not generally fond of conchies but the ones at Swarthmoor were all right, she was glad of the company. The farmer had put her up in an abandoned cottage next to the Hall but it was cold there, and she preferred to sleep in the room above the cow.

She revived the dying fire in the kitchen with a couple of logs and brought him a blanket. He felt a bit bad about having been rude to her; it was not her fault that this place made the Highgate troglodytes look futuristic.

Her voice rippled on pleasantly. Like a gurgling stream. Charlie abandoned himself to the warmth of the fire and drifted into the toasty comfort of sleep.

He was woken by shouting. The door swung open. Three men stumbled in and left a trail of puddles on the flagstones. One of them pulled off his jacket, sweater and undershirt in one single violent tug, grabbed a towel from a chair and began vigorously to rub his thick neck and torso. He bowed his head to towel his hair and the swell of his broad back.

'Lamb, I suppose,' he said without looking up. 'Good to have you here. One more hand at the udder.'

His name was Jack and he was a political objector, not a God-botherer. Just to be clear.

'Same here,' Charlie said, and crossed his arms. Who was going to check his papers here, anyway?

'Good.'

Jack grabbed five bottles of stout from a roughly built shelf, carried them effortlessly between the fingers of his massive hands and set them down on the kitchen table. He drank straight from the bottle and Charlie copied him.

Georgina began to ladle out bowls of soup. It was only

now that Charlie took a good look at the other two men. Short, wiry, and fizzing with nervous energy, they were twins, and had previously worked as printers in London. Camden Plumbers & Roofers brochures by day, Workers' Revolt by night: they too were political conchies. In London they had been known as Marx and Engels, nicknames that made it over to Swarthmoor.

'So there aren't actually any Quakers here?' Charlie had been prepared for a group of meek half-wits he could impress with impersonations of the Elder of Snotsborough.

'Feeling lonely?' Jack licked his beer-moistened lips. The twins snorted with derision. Charlie noticed a lino print on the wall, probably the work of one of the twins. It showed a grinning man in a cloak and hood, and underneath the caption: 'Guy Fawkes – the only man to enter parliament with honest intentions.'

Charlie pointed at the poster with his beer bottle. 'Not bad.'

'Thanks. I made it,' said Marx, or perhaps it was Engels.

'My brother's a printer,' Charlie said. 'Well, an artist, but he occasionally makes prints.'

'Fascinating.' Jack pulled a chunk of wood and a knife from his pocket and began to whittle away at the wood. The shavings fell in his empty bowl, on the table, on the freshly washed flagstones. Georgina groaned.

'I couldn't ask you to do that over some newspaper, could I?'

'You could.'

'Here. Newspaper. Take it.'

'I'm not in the habit of taking orders from anyone.'

Georgina turned to Charlie and widened her small blue eyes.

'You see what they're like?'

'I only said I wasn't taking orders from anyone.' Jack stood up, grabbed a broom and swept the wood shavings towards the middle of the kitchen, where he brushed them neatly into a metal dustpan. 'And I'm not.'

'Unless they're from Moscow.'

Jack kicked the dustpan, scattering the shavings he had so carefully swept up.

'He's in a mood,' Georgina stage-whispered. 'Moscow hasn't called in a while.'

'Bit rich coming from someone who thinks Moscow is a type of coffee,' Jack replied.

She blushed and said to Charlie: 'It was only because the twins printed a poster that said "Moscow" in Cyrillic, and in Cyrillic it looks like "mocha", which reminded me of the little blue mocha cups we had at home. So I thought the poster might be a Russian advertisement for coffee.'

'And when we tried to explain that it was Cyrillic . . .' Jack grinned at the twins.

'. . . she said . . .' Marx nodded at Engels, who shrieked in a high-pitched whine: '. . . "Cyrillic? But I thought they all spoke Russian!"'

'Hilarious.' Georgina stood up and lifted a big enamel pot off the counter. 'I hear that in Russia conscientious objectors are imprisoned as enemies of the people and sent to shovel snow in Siberia.'

'And who told you that? Father Duffy after choir practice? Yes, he's a particularly reliable source.' Jack's grim mood had evaporated, and he even picked up the broom again and whistled as he swept the flagstones.

Marx, on the other hand, twitched with anger. He kneaded his sinewy hands as if to stop himself lashing out. Eventually, he said: 'One ought to be very careful about spreading those sorts of lies. It might seem like jolly good fun now, but . . . just think about what you said. Conchies in the Soviet Union. Well, we all know there are no conchies in the Soviet Union. And here's why. Let me spell it out for you, Georgina, dear. What does "Soviet" mean?'

'Coffee.' Georgina appeared to be thoroughly enjoying herself, and even winked at Charlie as if to say, isn't this tremendously entertaining? The strings of her apron had been pulled tight to emphasize her waist, and her hips were wide enough to support the pot, which she steadied with her strong arms.

'No, Georgina dear,' said Marx, and his tight little mouth twisted itself into an awful smile. 'Soviet does *not* mean coffee. It means council. As in workers' council. Now who do you think would oppose the army of a workers' council?'

'A group of girly chaps who enjoy milking cows?'

His hands squeezed and pulled each other ever more furiously.

'Father Duffy,' Georgina added, with the recklessness of a

child testing how far she could go, 'has asked us *especially* to pray for the poor frozen Soviet conchies, but you'll be pleased to hear he also suggested we pray for the generals in the Red Army, because their souls are not only stained by atheism but *also* by the horrific treatment of—'

'Father Duffy can go to hell!' The hands flew apart, knocking bowls and bottles to the floor. 'Here I am, a proud urban proletarian, having to listen to the verbal farts of a peasant priest! If you *must* go to Mass, if you *must* have your virgin birth celebrations with Father Duffy, then at least spare us the details, and in fact spare us the overview, too. Poor Soviet conchies, you say? I say Tsarist lackeys! Imperialist retrogrades! Bourgeois vampires feeding on the cracked bone marrow of the people!' Marx climbed onto his chair. 'I say cannibals! Cannibals bent on sucking every last drop of blood from the revolution until the red flag pales to white! Pedlars of perversity who've made it their sorry lives' mission to drive a dagger through the heart of the Red Army, to feast on the smouldering ashes of the workers' state and pick through its charred ruins for gold.' With his last words he jumped on the table and shook his fist. 'Saboteurs are like rot. Now don't you ever describe this rampant fungus, this blood-sucking plague, this . . . this . . . necrotizing fasciitis on the body of humanity, as a sentient being with an *objection*, let alone a conscientious one.'

Georgina balanced the pot on the counter and applauded the raging, stomping creature on the table with genuine delight.

'You did it again, Marxy! Hooray, you did it again! One

day you'll break that table, by God you will. Pedlars of perversity and necrotizing something, well, I've certainly learned new words today.' She smiled at Charlie. 'I've told you this bunch is priceless. I'm having *much* more fun than I ever did at home. And now I'm going to take the soup over to little Mrs Pye.'

Charlie, dizzied by the mad exchange, clung to the familiar name like a nauseous boy stepping off a carousel. 'Mrs Pye?'

'A cranky Quaker lady we've got to feed along with the cow. She lives just across—'

A deafening cacophony exploded in the kitchen. Marx was still ranting on the kitchen table. Jack decided to use the dustpan as a hammer, the table as an anvil, and with much banging and noise accused Marx of having an urban superiority complex: let it not be forgotten that the Russian revolution started in the countryside. Engels tried to make a point quietly, but no one listened.

Charlie fled the din, and did not mind one bit that it was still raining outside.

'Until the red flag pales to white!' Georgina sang under the rain, and swung the pot from side to side with such vigour that he feared she might drop it.

## 2

The cottage consisted of a sunken thatched roof and concave walls yielding to the wind. Weeds devoured the front porch and crept over cracked dull windows. The door opened straight onto a squalid parlour.

Mary Pye sat by the fire, wrapped in a ratty grey plaid, her head bowed as it had always been in Silent Meeting. In the few months since he had last seen her, her hair had thinned and there was a bare patch of skin on her crown.

'Well, hello!'

'Charles!' She raised her thin arms. 'Darling boy!'

He was uncomfortably aware of Georgina watching him, and greeted Mary Pye with a little more distance than he would have liked. Only when Georgina left did he give her his best smile. 'The chaps at Swarthmoor Hall are a rather frightening bunch, aren't they? There was one who jumped on the table – I thought he was going to grab a knife and murder us all. Another attacked him with a dustpan, and the girl, well, she looked as if she was going to pour boiling soup over us. It rather made me look forward to a bit of quiet Bible study with you.'

She waved him away with her hand. 'Serve me some soup, will you?'

There was something rather odd about her, but he could not decide what it was.

'I suppose they're all right once you get used to them,' he mumbled uncertainly.

'Who?'

'The chaps at Swarthmoor.'

'Oh, them. They mended my roof the other day.'

'Well, when I said they were frightening, of course I didn't mean *frightening*. I only meant . . .' But he wasn't sure what he had meant.

She said her usual prayers before beginning to eat, and that comforted him a little. Then she asked him to serve another bowl.

'Thank you, I've already eaten.'

She insisted. He filled another bowl and sat down in a musty armchair next to her. But as soon as he began to eat, she rapped the wooden arm of her chair and said: 'Then serve one more, will you, and put it on the table. Just leave it there on the table.'

He did as he was told, looked up and cried: 'That's what it is! You've dropped your plain speech!'

'Well, I haven't really, but the girl finds it so very queer . . . and also, you know, Charles, in London it felt somehow right to preserve the old ways, but when I came back here I looked at all the people in Silent Meeting thee-ing and thou-ing, and going on about our Friend Mary Pye, and everything was first-day and seventh-month, and it rather got on my nerves.'

She pointed at the bowl. 'Just put it there, dear, by the fire.'

They slurped their soup.

'Are you expecting someone?'

She didn't reply and he decided to ignore the third bowl.

'And how is Paul?' She speared some bread on a toasting fork.

'Not too well, unfortunately. You remember he failed his tribunal.'

She let go of the fork and upset her bowl. Soup spilled into her lap.

'Oh, oh dear – oh dear.' He brought her a dishrag and she dabbed at herself with mounting distress and confusion. 'He's going to join the army, is he?'

'No, he—'

'It's evil of them to force him. But that's how it is, the maws of war must be fed.' She wrung the soup-stained dishrag and her breath quickened. 'There was nothing he could do, was there? They wanted my Seth, and they got him.'

It surprised him that she muddled the names. Her mind was sharp one moment, fuzzy the next. He picked up the toasting fork and pushed the now-burning bread away from the fire.

The blanket had slipped from her shoulders, freeing an unpleasant smell of decay. She rocked back and forth.

'I did copy out the peace testimony for him,' she mumbled. 'I said, here it is, our testimony that has held true since 1660, a testimony against all strife and wars! We are a people that follow after those things that make for peace, love and unity.'

She stopped rocking and stared at Charlie. 'Seth, dear, we are commanded to bear our testimony. Out there in the slaughter, thee shall remember thy mother's words.'

Charlie glanced at the third bowl of soup.

'I'm not going to join up,' he said in a soothing voice, hoping he could bring her back to the present. 'And neither will Paul. They told him to go and join the army, but he refused, so they arrested him and sent him to gaol, and that's where he's going to be for a few months.'

'Gaol!'

'Oh, it's not as bad as it sounds. There is a special wing for Friends, and ...' He thought of something else he could invent to cheer her up. '... There are Silent Meetings every morning. And very good cells with stoves.'

'Oh, that *is* good.' She frowned with nervous confusion. 'Still, it is never pleasant to be in hospital.' Then she took his hands and held them in her own. The smell of decay became overpowering.

The third bowl sat there, all the more prominent for being untouched. The chunks of chicken and potato had sunk to the bottom and clear broth remained at the top. There was a thin line of liquid and herbs smeared around the inside of the bowl just above the soup, like a water line after the tide has gone out. Like the mark left in a soup bowl after someone has drunk from it. Charlie told himself not to be daft. The third bowl had been placed close to the fire; some of the liquid had merely evaporated.

Mary Pye appeared to have dozed off. Charlie was about pick up the tray and to tiptoe to the door when she grabbed his arm.

'It is good for us to be here,' she whispered. 'I am as comfortable, and well in my spirit, as ever I was.'

She pulled the blanket around her and turned towards the fire.

The next morning, Charlie went to see her again. The fire was cold and she was in the same armchair, huddled in the same blanket, asleep. He felt bad then for not having helped her into her bedroom despite her obvious frailty. He boiled some water for tea in the kitchen, trying not to wake her. The cottage was very quiet. Now and then he turned to see if she moved, or shivered, or stirred. The third time he turned round, he looked at her, looked at the stiff fingers, the parchment skin, the closed eyes, the still face, and realized that she was dead.

## 3

The Quakers' founding mother, Margaret Fell, was buried at Sunbrick burial ground, not far from Swarthmoor Hall, in 1702. Mary Pye, who had always believed herself to be Fell's direct descendant, was laid to rest there on a July morning in 1940.

The funeral was as plain as her life: half an hour of silence; a handful of Friends from Ulverston. On the insistence of a Pye cousin, a local vicar, an additional Anglican service was held in the parish church. It was a sunny day and Charlie lingered in the cemetery for a few moments. There he found Mary Pye's late husband and her son.

Charlie would not have made the connection had the vicar's wife not sidled up to him and pointed out an inconspicuous grey slab: 'That's him.'

'But Mary Pye never married.'

'Did she not! You never saw such a loving wife. Only her husband wasn't a Quaker. They almost threw her out of the Society for that, you know; they used to be rather strict around here. If you ask me, she would have liked to be buried next to him, even if it is an Anglican graveyard.'

'That's a shame.'

'Not just for the husband, but for him as well.' The woman gestured towards a memorial by the church entrance.

There was Seth Pye, inscribed between the names of sixty other men who had died in the Great War. Charlie wondered who would fill the spare bowl of soup now that Mary Pye was gone.

To his surprise, Jack, Marx and Engels turned up for the Anglican service. They stood at the back, cloth caps in hand. Georgina sat in the first row, wearing a stiff black dress that emphasized her ample bosom.

Charlie had never been to a church service and was surprised by the way it went on and on. Hymns, prayers, the sermon: '... and Jesus Christ our Saviour ... our dear sister ... in heaven as on earth ... How sweet the sound that saved a wretch like me!'

Once he glanced towards the back and caught Jack singing along. Georgina looked rather sweet with her round rosy cheeks and her lips pursed in earnest piety. Her blond hair was tucked under some sort of black bonnet, which gave her the air of a young widow.

Finally the hymns and preaching ceased.

'Let us stand in silence and remember the life of Mary Pye, our dear cousin, aunt, and friend,' the vicar said.

Charlie stood up, rather relieved to have reached a familiar part in the proceedings. He closed his eyes and settled into the silence. He thought of Seth and the other men from the memorial. He thought of Mr and Mrs Pye – *you never saw such a loving wife* – raising their son in this little town where people could be rather strict. He thought of the Mary Pye who had lost her son, sitting in Silent Meeting in London, and he wished what one always wished on these occasions, that he had spent more time with her instead of always trying to ...

'And now let us sing hymn number twenty seven,' the vicar said. '"Abide with Me".'

The congregation burst into song. '... *fast falls the eventide.*' Charlie stood half perplexed, half amused. '*The darkness deepens ...*' Was this what a service in the steeple-house was like then? '*Lord, with me abide.*' One minute to remember eighty years lived on this earth?

For the first time in his life he felt a deep yearning for silence.

# 4

They set off early.

'Last week I killed three hundred and fifty-seven rats,'

Georgina told Charlie, who was putting on his boots. She adjusted her land girl cap. 'In one week alone. Three hundred rats can eat three tons of wheat a year, did you know?'

'Fancy that,' said Charlie, down on one knee, his fingers stiffly fumbling with the laces. Her breeches were rather tight around her buttocks.

'Fancy it,' she said, and nudged him out the door.

He carried her bag for her, an unwieldy knapsack filled with instruments he would rather not think about. They strode towards a glum brown cottage. Georgina whistled a tune, Charlie whistled along. The farmer's wife was waiting for them in the kitchen with steaming bowls of porridge.

There were two ways to kill rats, Georgina said between hasty spoonsful of porridge, her head dipped close to the bowl. One was neat and one was messy. The neat one was to find all their escape holes, plug them securely except for one, then pump in gas through the one remaining hole into their burrows. That way they died underground and one didn't have to fuss over the corpses. In a bumpy field like this one, however, finding the holes would take all day, and it was better to use the other method.

'Which is more fun anyway,' she said, pushing aside her empty bowl and licking her lips. 'Stuffing all the holes one by one is *such* a bore. As long as there are enough people to help out, I far prefer the messy way.'

They went outside, and Georgina efficiently instructed the assembled farm hands, even turning the scrawny, sullen farmer himself into an attentively listening schoolboy. She handed each of them a shovel. Charlie made no move to take one, and she frowned and said: 'Have you just come to watch, then?'

'Of course not.' He picked one of the smaller shovels. Out of the corner of his eye he saw Jack arrive, carrying a spade over his shoulder.

Following Georgina's orders, they swarmed out over the freshly mown hay field and took their positions. Georgina had lugged a canister and a long black tube across the ground. She wedged the canister between her knees, squatted down a little with her shoulders leaning forward and her bottom sticking out, and began pumping gas into a hole. Charlie averted his eyes, forcing himself to focus on the horizon and the oak trees in the distance. He shifted his weight from foot to foot and breathed on his reddened hands to warm himself.

The first terrified squeak made him jump.

There was another, louder squeak, and then another.

The rats were fleeing their burrows, sleek grey torpedoes darting across the field in terror. The farm hands hopped about, lifted their feet in their heavy boots and stomped and whacked the rats to death.

Georgina let go of the pump and leaped across the field like a dervish, lifted her shovel high and cracked it down on a rat, and another one, and another one, until the scurrying stopped and limp fat bodies with half-open snouts and broken backbones dotted the mown earth.

Charlie feebly whacked a few clumps of earth and weeds and hoped no one noticed.

'What's that you're doing, a spot of gardening?' Jack stood behind him. He lifted his spade and brought it down on a lone rat that was racing towards his boots. The rat let out a squeak, and Jack struck it again, and again, until it was a squashed lump. 'That's how *I* like my gardening.'

When they cleared away the dead rats, Georgina exclaimed: 'Three tons of wheat, think how many loaves that makes!'

'Plenty,' Charlie said, and thought he might throw up.

Georgina playfully picked up a rat by its hind legs and tossed it at him. He dodged it but was too slow. It hit his thigh and left a dark smear on his breeches.

'What a girl you are,' she said, and giggled.

'Astonishing,' was all Charlie could muster.

They washed their hands in the cold kitchen, where the farmer's wife had laid out bread, cheese and pickles. Charlie told himself he ought not to have any appetite after the massacre, but in truth he felt as ravenous as a starved rat. He cut off a big chunk of cheese, slapped it on a slice of bread with some pickle, devoured it, and when he had filled his stomach, he wiped his sticky hands on his thighs, leaving a pickle smudge next to the rat blood.

# Press Barons

## 1

Paul gave his clean clothes to a guard at Wormwood Scrubs and was given a set of dirty prison clothes in return, like a laundry in reverse. He was allowed to take his Bible with him. When he entered his cell he could not help but think that his father had in fact wanted this for him, that this was somehow the most Quakerly of experiences. They believed in plainness and his new life could not be plainer. Here he possessed nothing but a spoon, a bowl, a towel and a brush, all of which he expected to lose to a stronger, more violent inmate at any moment. The one window was so high up he could not look outside. The straw palliasse on the metal frame had been thinned by many restless bodies.

However, Paul lacked the one resource that would have made all this bearable. His conscience had none of the clarity and strength that had fortified the early Quakers. He had lied to Miriam, he had betrayed both the pledge and the peace testimony to win her affection, and when his time had come to defend his stance before the tribunal, he had lazily parroted a Bible quote. His punishment was all the worse for being fully deserved. 'I joyfully entered prisons as palaces,' Margaret Fell had written in her journal, 'telling mine enemies to hold me there as long as they could, and in the prison-house I sung praises to my God.' Well, he did not feel like singing praises. He certainly did not feel joyful. He felt like a fool.

His anger was like a trapped animal that threw itself against the bars of its cage: now it threw itself against Miriam for having lured him into lying, now against the judges for having tricked him, now against his father and Charlie for having failed to advise him well. But the real target of the anger lay beyond those bars and was Paul himself.

That night he read the three chapters of Joel and constructed a response that would have left his judge roundly defeated. 'Let the weak say, I am strong,' Joel wrote: and in another passage, 'My great army ... will restore to you the years that the locust hath eaten'. In his imaginary response, Paul argued convincingly that there were peaceful, Gandhian ways of strengthening the weak; and that the great army was a metaphor for the restorative effect of faith.

'I see you have spent a great amount of thought on this, Mr Lamb,' the judge said in this satisfying script. 'It is rare to find such depth, faith and courage in a man of your age.'

But he had not said that. It was nothing but a script. It had not happened.

The bars of the cage gave way, and anger and shame burst out in hard, furious sobs. He had wanted it *so much*. He had wanted to say the right thing to Miriam, and the right thing to the judges, and the right thing to his father. He had wanted to be admired and respected by them all and despised by none. He had wanted to oppose the war, yet do his bit. He had wanted to be a good Quaker *and* a war hero.

King David had started out as a shepherd who played the harp and carried ten cheeses to a camp of soldiers. He felled Goliath and smote the Philistines, just like Miriam had said, but then he had done something else, Paul remembered it now: there was an incident in King David's old age that he really ought to have brought up at his tribunal. Yet nowhere in the pages of the Books of Kings could he find the incident he was looking for, and he wondered whether Mary Pye had perhaps made it up.

He fell asleep with the Bible on his chest and dreamed of a great locust eating up his years.

The next day they moved Paul into a cell with a bunk bed. The upper bunk stayed empty. It surprised him, since the gaol was clearly overcrowded. Still, it was a relief. The cell was dark and cramped, a concrete box with a window so high up he could not see outside, but at least there was no one to harass him. He had heard that one of the most basic rules in gaol was never to ask any of the inmates about their crimes. Yet all the men who shouldered past him in the corridor, who took the full bowl of porridge from his hands as if it had been offered to them, seemed to know why he was there. Some of them were tense, quick and scrawny, the type who would be good with a knife. Others clearly needed nothing more than their rake-sized hands to smash a face or wring a neck. Had Paul met them on a dark street in Highgate, he would have crossed to the other side or sought safety in the next pub. Here, there was no avoiding them.

He started out with a towel, a bowl, a brush and a spoon. Soon he had only a bowl, a brush and a spoon. Then, only a bowl and a spoon.

His father sent him buttons and lavender soap and advised him to use these as currency. He also told him to find other conchies in his wing – other Quakers, ideally – and gather every night for Quiet Meeting.

'Thank you,' Paul wrote, 'but there are no other conchies here. Yes, I'm surprised, too.'

The buttons and lavender soap bought him some protection. He took the fact that they left him his bowl and spoon as a kindness, until he discovered the real reason: without a bowl, he would not be served porridge, and if he wasn't served porridge, he couldn't give half of it to whoever was standing behind him in the queue.

The screws locked all the cells, then hurried into their shelters. Paul lay there, locked up, listening out for enemy planes. In the next cell, a man began to scream with the rise and fall of an air-raid siren: 'Let me owwww-t! Let me owwww-t!'

There followed a terrible rhythmic series of thuds. Paul could not make out what they were. Someone banging his fist against the wall, probably.

'Let me owwww-t! Let me owwww-t!'

Thud, thud, thud.

Then he heard the raiders. There was something so personal about a raid. He knew, of course, that there were hundreds of German bombers and hundreds of targets, and how they matched up was a matter of gravity, wind and luck. And yet, when he heard the raiders overhead, the roar of their engines growled, *Where are you? Where are you? We will find you! We will find you!*

He pressed his face into the crook of his arm as if that would make him invisible.

If only that awful thudding noise would stop.

## 2

'We found a pal for you.' The guard grinned and shoved a carefully groomed, dark-skinned man into the cell. Paul recognized the Hindu he had talked to before his tribunal.

'Chatterjee!'

'Have we met?'

'The court house in Bloomsbury. We were waiting for our tribunals.' It was beyond Paul how anyone could fail to have every single detail of that infernal day carved into his mind. 'You were advising me on my defence.'

'Why, of course! The Quaker.' Chatterjee raked his thick black hair with his fingers as if to stimulate his brain. Neither the cell nor their dirty uniforms seemed to make the slightest impression on him: he moved with the lazy confidence of a gentleman at his club. Paul half expected him to turn round and ask a waiter to fetch his coat. 'You must forgive me, but I've forgotten your name. I think it's this diet of cocoa; what a thing to give to anyone over five. We are all steadily regressing towards infancy in here; another month and I shall be rocking to and fro on my back. Was my advice of any use?'

'Oh, yes, thank you,' Paul said politely. 'Though I failed my tribunal, as you can see. Paul Lamb.'

'The sacrificial Lamb! Now I remember everything.'

There was something about Chatterjee that reminded Paul of Charlie. Perhaps it was the way he wore his grey prison uniform, with the dishevelled charm of a pair of daytime pyjamas. He settled down on the lower bunk with his back slouched against the wall, one leg casually draped over the other.

'How about your own tribunal?' Paul asked. 'I assume . . .' He glanced up at the barred window.

'You assume it didn't go all that well? In a way, you assume correctly. It didn't go all that well *for the judges*.' Chatterjee lifted a forefinger to emphasize his point. 'Can you see what I'm doing here? It's a theory I'm in the process of developing. For now I'm calling it "systemic reversal". If you think of *yourself* as a failure, my dear

Lamb, you will be a failure. But if you think of the *system* as a failure – with the judges failing to recognize and appreciate your argument – then ...' He paused importantly, raising his elegantly arched black eyebrows. 'I leave you to draw your own conclusions.'

'I see,' Paul said.

Chatterjee grinned. 'I apologize, I did not intend to confuse you.'

'Oh, not at all, it's just ... I'm impressed you can even think about theories. All I can think of is – I don't know – how nice it would be to have a toothbrush.'

'Ha! Let's see ... they gave me a brush with a wooden back.' Chatterjee inspected the pillowcase that held his belongings, took out a brush and turned it in his hand. 'The question is, hair or boots?'

'I'd say boots,' Paul ventured.

'I'd say hair, but I can see that if in doubt, one might want to opt for boots. Which means I'll have to wheedle a comb off someone who is about to be discharged. I've already noticed quite a few who scratch their scalps; those certainly won't do. Not to worry, we'll find a toothbrush. I also need some buttons.'

'My father sends me buttons, but the men always steal them.'

'And you let them?'

'There doesn't seem to be any alternative.'

'Thank goodness we won't have to rely on Quakers for the revolution. I've been to this place before, you see. Let me introduce you to the house rules. Here's what you do. The next time someone as much as touches one of your buttons, you take your spoon like this' – he closed his long fingers around the concave end – 'and then, my friend, you drive the handle right into his eye.'

After a week, Chatterjee had organized toothbrushes for both of them. It was a mystery to Paul how he had succeeded in drawing a boundary around himself in the space of only a few days. There were men who were stronger than Chatterjee and men who were more overtly aggressive, but Chatterjee kept them at bay with a mere glimpse of something unstable and menacing under his affable veneer. He and Paul sat alone at the far end of the long table in the canteen and ate their porridge together.

'You see, I was utterly truthful at my tribunal,' Chatterjee said. 'I told them they could do me no greater favour than throwing me into gaol. What a tremendous chance to build up an army of criminals for the revolution! What revolution? they asked. Any, I replied. Communist, anarchist, nihilist, the label is of no importance, it's the energy unleashed by the great chaos of transition that matters. The idea terrified them, of course, and what did they do in their terror? They threw me into gaol! Panic wrestled logic and pushed it to the ground. I find it very entertaining, the things men do when they panic. It always reminds me of the time I watched a horse in a burning stable. It ran round and round in circles even though the door was open.' He laughed, and ate some porridge, and laughed again at the recollection.

When they returned to their cell, Paul asked: 'But it got out in the end, didn't it?'

'What did?'

'The horse. The one that was trapped in the stable.'

'No.' Chatterjee carefully wiped his hands on a flannel. 'I'm afraid it didn't. Daft creature.' He sighed and tossed the flannel into a corner. 'But what can I say, the door *was* open.'

In the afternoons, Chatterjee liked to lie on the top bunk and read a book, all the while letting out an incessant stream of patter.

'Have you been to the library? You need to bribe the guard. I like to think of it as a subscription fee. Most of the books are of the opium variety – you may, of course, be perfectly satisfied with that. What's that you're reading? I see. Opium!'

'Opium?'

'It's just that I try to avoid religion of any sort. It stupefies a man more than any narcotic, but the library doesn't offer much else. I've been forced to entertain myself with this.'

He held up the cover of his book. It said *Black Beauty* and showed a galloping horse, its mane blowing in the wind.

'Any good?'

'It's a rather sentimental story of a carriage horse who falls on hard times. I suspect it was left behind by someone's child after a weekly visit. However, after the first chapter I decided to read it as a parable on the chained proletariat, and, *voila*, it became perfectly enjoyable. Do you see what I did there? It is all a matter of perception. The human mind is but a malleable lump of clay.'

'Fascinating.'

Chatterjee jumped off the top bunk and landed lightly on his feet with the elasticity of a cat.

'Anon, anon, we must make our way to the canteen. I bribed the cook: we'll be served a double ration while four new boys will get half. Sometimes, my friend, sometimes I fear that Socialism will never work because of people like me.'

# 3

The toilet paper at Wormwood Scrubs came in waxy rolls marked 'Government Property' and there was always a shortage. Paul soon discovered why. Chatterjee had organized a ring of men who smuggled roll after roll into his cell. He drew explicitly posed nudes on the lengths of paper, tore them off and sold them for buttons, which he then used to pay off the men and buy a spoon whose sides had been carefully filed into razor edges. He liked to shave himself with the spoon while the others could see him.

'A little bird told me I'll be transferred to another wing soon.' Chatterjee rinsed the spoon in a mug of water. 'Ten buttons and the magic razor spoon is yours.'

'Thank you. I'll pass.'

'Ah. Is it because you think our friends down the corridor have grown fond of you? I'm sorry to say, my dear Lamb, that they'll shear you as soon as I'm gone.'

Paul shrugged.

'Shrug away, Atlas, shrug away.' Chatterjee began to clip his toenails with the spoon. 'Shrug as much as you like, but the damned thing will still be on your shoulders when you stop shrugging. See, you have two choices if you want to get on in here. You can be violent, or you can be useful. The man who filed this spoon, for example, is useful. But I can't see what particular skill you have that would keep them off.'

Paul pointed at the waxy rolls. 'I could do those.'

'And I could have sworn you'd never seen a naked girl.'

Paul picked up the sooty toothpick. He drew a sitting nude, a reclining nude, a nude getting out of a bathtub. He drew a standing nude with her arms crossed over her head, a walking nude casting a coquettish glance over her back, a nude on a plinth with her head twisted towards the viewer. When he was done, he let the whole length of paper travel through his fingers. A dozen nudes, and they all looked a little like Miriam.

Chatterjee let out a low whistle.

'You might have told me earlier. One thing – with all due respect, if you want these to sell, you need to make them less polite.' Chatterjee sat down, spread his legs wide and drew two arcs over his chest with his hands. 'That sort of thing.'

He paused and listened for the hum in the distance that grew into a roar. In the next cell, the methodic thudding sound began.

'And pubic hair,' he said. 'Men pay up to three buttons more for convincingly drawn pubic hair.'

After Chatterjee was transferred, Paul drew for his survival. He churned out nude after nude with the anxious creativity of Scheherazade spinning tales for her executioner. The men began to make specific requests for poses, body types, hairstyles. But whether he drew light-haired girls or dark-haired ones, skinny dancers with bobbed hair or voluptious whores, there was always some expression in their big, vivacious eyes that reminded him of Miriam. There was nothing he could do about it. He tried to evoke other nudes he had seen at Bentham, other women he had seen on the street or in pubs, but his hand always defied his intention and drew only that one face in a hundred different guises.

He sent out pictures of Miriam into cells full of leering men and it felt as if he was selling his most treasured memories, as if he was selling the loveliest images in his head; yet there was nothing he could do to stop it. He asked the guards if he could have a cellmate, hoping another Chatterjee would bolster his status, but it took them a while to find someone who was willing to share a room with him.

The new man was stocky and neckless, with a bald head covered in scabs and scars. He had been moved after his previous cellmate had refused to put up with him any longer, and Paul soon found out why. He also discovered the source of the mysterious thudding noise.

At night, when the air-raid sirens howled, the bald man screamed: 'Let me owwww-t! Let me owwww-t!'

And then he whacked his head against the wall. Thud, thud, thud.

'Are you the barber?' he asked Paul in the morning. The blood had dried in brown patches on the side of his head. The man was like Chatterjee turned inside out: all of Chatterjee's hidden, internal madness was on full physical display here, and Paul was not sure whether this was any better or far worse.

'No.'

'Are you sure you're not the barber?'

'I'm sure.'

'But the barber would say that, wouldn't he?' He had spotted the mouse trap in the corner that Chatterjee had bequeathed Paul as a parting gift, picked it up and tenderly examined the cheese on the spike.

'Maybe . . .' Paul tried to remember what his mother had taught him about speaking to people who were soft in the head. With loving kindness. 'Are you looking for a barber?'

The man ate the cheese, pocketed the mouse trap and put his scabby mouth very close to Paul's ear. 'I need him to shave the inside of my head.'

# 4

When Miriam was at the factory all she thought about was her drill and the steel mould before her. Never in her life had she felt such purposeful concentration. She was one of a hundred links in a perfectly forged chain, one of a thousand minds that formed the collective spirit. The great surge up the stairs in the morning, clocking in, a turban among a hundred other turbans, shirtsleeves rolled up, a smile on her face, humming along to the rhythm of *Music While You Work*. She learned not to compete with the noise of the machines, not to shout over it and lose her voice, but to speak *under* the noise, as one of her supervisors told her. She did not understand that at first; how could one speak under the noise? And then, one hot summer day in 1940, she found that she simply did it, she was conversing with the other women at quite a normal level, moving her lips carefully, speaking under the great noise.

At the Bentham College Women's Union and the Debating Society, and even in the air-raid precautions team, her initial fire and energy had fizzled out when she sensed that her efforts were not truly needed; that the Women's Union already had plenty of spirited speakers, that the short-trousered grocer in Highgate would have noticed the chink in his blackout board even if she had not sternly pointed it out to him. Here, the demand for patient labour was immense and ceaseless, and all she had to do was dedicate herself to it. She did not need to question her job because the chain's perfection was clear to all. Her task was to drill out an impeccably smooth steel mould. Other women would use the mould to cast bullets; soldiers would use the bullets to win the war. Here was the purity and simplicity that all her other causes had lacked.

When there wasn't any music on the wireless, the women sang. And that, too, contributed to the wonderful satisfaction of belonging to a useful whole. This new life had a rhythm and a tune where her old life had been aimless and disordered, a constant lurching from unfinished job to unfinished job.

They worked and sang, and every now and then, Mr Baxter, the director, descended from his office to the factory floor and said something wise and profound that they would all laugh about afterwards.

'I've been in this business longer than you've been in this world, and one thing I've observed is that northern girls are better with their hands. Why do you think that is?'

Miriam shook her head. Mr Baxter wiggled his fingers.

'Northern girls have longer fingers. And do you know why?'

Miriam tried not to look at the red-haired girl next to her, who was biting her lips while her cheeks inflated with pent-up laughter.

'It's the mills. Just like we developed an upright gait to be able to throw spears at mammoths, northern girls developed long fingers to work the textiles at the cotton mills.'

'Is that so, Mr Baxter?'

'Just take a look for yourself. It's never too late to learn something new.'

'I'll make sure I do, Mr Baxter.'

He walked back up to the factory floor and shut the door behind him. The girl next to her released her lips and released a howl of hilarity. It was so infectious that Miriam laughed until her laughter turned into pig-like snorts. When Miriam finally calmed down, the girl wiggled her fingers and both were helplessly convulsed once more. It was only when one of the older women muttered that she wished she could afford a good giggle, but unlike some she needed the piece work to feed her children, that Miriam and her new friend returned to their drills.

They were walking away from the factory after their night shift when they heard the explosion. People came running towards them. Her friend disappeared in the crowd and Miriam's instinct was to retreat too, but then she reasoned that there might be injured victims. She held on tightly to her bag and ran the other way, into the noise.

The blast had hurled a double-decker bus against a house. It stuck in the wall like a giant loaf. A photographer overtook her and began to snap away. The banner on the side of the bus advertised Hovis sliced bread. Miriam began to laugh hysterically. It was not the worst hit she had witnessed and the bloodied bodies being pulled out of the bus by ambulance workers were not the worst she had seen. Yet her hand was shaking so hard she could hardly hold on to her bag.

The photographer left. The ambulances left. Miriam was still standing there shaking. The warm blanket of the factory had been pulled away and she felt so alone, so utterly alone. A dog emerged from behind the bus, sniffed at something on the ground and began to lick it.

Miriam tossed a stone at the dog. Then she picked up a leg in its thin black stocking, which had been sliced off neatly by a flying piece of metal. She put it high up on a window ledge.

She began to walk south until she reached Marylebone. Her feet hurt and the streets were bright now in the morning sun. She turned west. Gradually the deserted pavement filled with typists and civil servants. The crowds thickened and she walked on with a rigid smile; bumped into briefcases and sharp elbows; apologized.

When she reached the high gloomy prison walls she thought she would linger a little and then turn back home, but there were dozens of women waiting at the gate and one of them gave her a friendly nod. Her curly red hair reminded Miriam of her friend at the factory. She felt the warmth of the herd and stood there very comfortably, as securely as she stood every evening at the factory gates.

The woman nodded at her again, unscrewed a little jar and rubbed some red colour on her cheeks. She offered the jar to Miriam. Miriam copied her.

'They won't let us in for another hour,' the woman said. 'It's a disgrace.'

'That's fine. I can wait.' She marvelled at the calmness of her own voice. 'I forgot to make an appointment. Do you think they'll let me in anyway?'

'I should think so.' The woman screwed the jar shut.

Miriam felt the hysterical laughter rise within her again.

## 5

She looked as fresh and apple-cheeked as if the big gates had opened and let in an entire summer. He had assumed the walls of the visitors' room were white but when she sat down opposite him in her white wool jumper and blue rayon scarf, he realized the walls were grey. The room filled with her warm scent. His own smell must compare to hers as the walls compared to her dress.

'That's a nice jumper.' He did not know what else to say. It was as if he had forgotten how ordinary people spoke to each other. If she had grunted at him, he could have grunted back. If she had started banging her head against the wall, he would have known how to make the right soothing noises and pull her away. But she did nothing of that sort. Instead, she made some comment about the weather, and he said: 'Yes, it's very cold.'

His eyes met hers and she flinched.

'I probably look quite rough.'

'Of course not.' She placed her hands flat on the table. 'I

must be looking rather wild myself. I've walked all the way from the factory. Though after all your tall tales about joining the army, I'm not sure why I did that.'

'I've been meaning to explain ...' he said uncertainly, expecting her to interrupt him. But she nodded in encouragement and he realized he had no explanation. 'I suppose I told you what I thought you wanted to hear.'

She waited for him to say more.

'That's all,' he said.

'That can't be all.' She tucked a loose strand of hair behind her ear. Had there ever been a lovelier movement? He wanted to ask her to do it again.

'Well, it is. I implied I was going to sign up because that's what you wanted to hear.'

'But I don't understand it!' The strand came loose again. She swept it back with both hands and smudged the rouge on her cheeks in the process. 'I don't understand any of it. Are you trying to be a martyr? But martyrs don't lie about their beliefs one day and go to gaol for them the next, do they? See, if you'd lied and then gone and sat out the war on a farm – that I would have understood. But this, this just doesn't make sense.'

'I shouldn't have told you I was going to sign up. I'm sorry.'

'You know what I think? I think you told me the truth that night. I don't think you ever meant to go through with this. It just sort of happened, didn't it? You wanted to please your family, and now you're here and you're probably not even sure why.'

She was right, in a way, and yet it irked him that she should think of him as someone who didn't have views of his own. He *had* views of his own. He was not very good at expressing them; he was not even capable of fully articulating them for himself, but he did have them.

'I do know why I'm here,' he said firmly. 'And it's not as senseless as you think. When they let me out, I can apply to be registered as a conchie again and this—' he gestured at the bleak thick walls – 'this will support my case.'

She looked exhausted and confused, and he thought, it can't be easy for her. The patches of land where their families had pitched their tents were just too different. When he listened to her talk about the war and what it meant to her and why everyone should go and fight, it made perfect sense. When he was alone in his cell and explained to the judge in his head why the swords should be turned into ploughshares, it also made sense. Isaiah was right, and Joel was also right. They were even bound together by the same book. But if you put them right next to each other, if you read 'they shall turn their ploughshares into swords' and then read as the next sentence, 'turn your swords into ploughshares', well, that was a mess. There was no way of reconciling those two. They could exist in their different patches – just like the old Quakers had said 'thank thee' and 'third-month' while their neighbours said 'thank you' and 'March', but they could not live together.

He was about to try to tell her this when she reached out

and, instead of saying anything, very gently touched the left side of his face.

'This isn't as bad as it looks,' he said quickly. 'I ... I fell down the stairs.'

'It's horrible to see you in here.'

'It all looks much worse than it is.'

'Is there anything I can send you to make it better?' She took her hand away. 'Books?'

He shook his head. 'In the early days, I had a Bible.'

'And then?'

'Someone took it off me.' He cracked his knuckles. 'Look ... there was a bit of a paper shortage. It was my own fault. Hell, I'll say it as it is. Some men needed toilet paper and they took my Bible. And that's why I don't want you to send me any books. It wasn't a personal thing. They were ordinary men who needed paper, that's how I've decided to see it. I was partly to blame for the shortage, and I happened to have a book with a lot of pages. What I don't want is for you to send me books because ... well, I'd only get angry if they tried to take those, too.'

'And you'd get into a fight.' She glanced at his ear. 'That's what this is, isn't it? They took your Bible and you got into a fight.'

'It was only because ...' His excuse was lost in a mortified stammer. He tried again, and again the stammer defeated him. 'It wasn't because it was the Bible as such,' he said eventually. 'It was because I had nothing else. It was the only thing I had left, so I was sort of attached to it.'

They fell silent. Paul wanted to get up and pace up and down as he did in his cell. Instead, he drew his finger up and down along the edge of the table between them. 'You're going to say this just shows that it's important to defend yourself. But it wasn't like that. I was angry, and I got into a fight. If anything, it convinced me that fighting is a bad idea.'

'That's not at all what I was going to say.' Her eyes followed his finger. There seemed to be something on her mind, and several times she began to say something. But then the guard told them visiting time was up.

'I'll come and visit you again,' she said quickly. 'There's only one thing. I might as well tell you, I've signed on at a munitions factory. If that's a problem—'

'It isn't,' he said quickly. 'Of course not.' He held out his hand. 'How about a deal? Whenever you're here, we'll just pretend there's no war. We can't go on arguing about it every time we meet. And I do want us to meet. I want us to talk about paintings, and books, and ... life. There are so many things we can talk about other than war, aren't there?'

'Of course there are,' Miriam said. She took off her thin light scarf, crumpled it into a ball and pressed it into his hand.

In his cell he unfolded the scarf on his pillow and rested his head on it.

# Pack My Unwanted Love into Bombs

## 1

Grace would spend another week or two at Samhuinn. All they were waiting for was the signal from Somerset, the message that the farmhouse was ready.

Max suggested that they give the yellow paint to his landlord, Mr Morningstar, an architect who would use it to brighten up an air-raid shelter or two. Grace agreed. For all she cared, they could use her unwanted yellow paint in air-raid shelters, turn her unwanted love letters into fighter plane fuel, pack her unwanted love into incendiary bombs. She was spent, empty, as numb as a tied-off limb.

Once she thought: my heart is broken. But the phrase was not hers; it was a phrase from a world of actors and poets that had no place for her. Her phrase was: *Grace, dear, now what on earth made you think you were so very special to him?*

206

Max carried away the yellow paint. As he passed her he briefly touched her shoulder and said: 'I am sorry.'

What did that mean? He did not know about Morten, so it meant nothing at all. His sympathy meant nothing to her.

Yet when he came back, a weak current shivered under the numbness and made her put her hand on his arm. 'And I'm sorry, too. I'm sorry I never asked … I suppose I didn't want to intrude.'

'There's nothing you could have done.'

'Have you heard from her?'

He shook his head. 'I don't even know where she is. She's stopped writing. It's as if … as if my mother has just completely disappeared.'

Max emptied his storage room office. Not that there was much to empty. He packed up the pots and crockery in the kitchen, donations mostly. Grace still remembered how she had collected them from Friends' House. She would continue to use her office for a while; work in the empty building as long as she could. She told herself this had nothing to do with memories of a night on the fire escape.

A parcel appeared on her desk. A rather big parcel. When she opened it she found a wonky Christmas straw star, a folded card and a gilded pine cone. Two books: *War and Peace* and the Bible. The writing on the card was tall and lean. 'Two books – in case you still want to practise (though it is not necessary). (It never was.) Max'.

She ran out but the children were in their classroom and Max was out.

'Oh, Mr Hoffnung, you crazy man!' she shouted into the empty corridor, and laughed, and laughed some more, and then noticed that it was the first time since the teapot day that she had laughed.

## 2

Inge's belongings she packed last.

'Promise me you'll read this book. And then you'll write to me about it.'

A chewed old teddy bear.

'Hello, Herr Bear. Listen, you will look after this young lady. And please remind her to write.'

Inge watched with her knuckles in her mouth. But when Grace shook the bear and grunted a reply, she smiled. Grace shook it again.

'Vell vell, Frau Inge, ve are going to a farm, yah?'

She was pulled up short by a sudden concern that Inge might feel mocked, might feel she was imitating her, or her family, or Max. But Inge was still smiling.

'*O Tannenbaum, O Tannenbaum,*' Grace made the bear sing. And because she did not know the rest, she continued: '*O Tannenbaum, O Tannenbaum.*'

'*Wie grün sind deine Blätter,*' sung a voice behind her.

With the bear pressed to her chest, Grace whipped round.

Max stood in the doorway, singing. Inge laughed until she began to hiccup, and ran out to fetch a glass of water.

Max put his hand on the hat stand, which was one of those things he liked to do.

'It means, how green are your leaves. Well, needles.' He cleared his throat. 'You once asked me why I celebrate Christmas.'

'I didn't mean to pry.' She stood up.

'When I was a boy I didn't even know my mother was Jewish. She went to church with my father and she always decorated our Christmas tree. It was only when the Nazis came to power that she and I were categorized, so to speak.'

'I'm sorry. I shouldn't have asked.'

'No, it was normal to ask. But if you knew my mother, your question wouldn't be why I celebrate Christmas but why I don't celebrate it even *more*. Every year she began decorating earlier. First the flat, then the flat and her shop. First in early December, then in late November, then in early November.' He let go of the hat stand and coughed into his fist. 'You see, the last time we decorated a tree together was the night when Gestapo smashed the windows of all the Jewish shops and set the synagogues on fire. We were in the shop in the evening, long after closing time, and we enjoyed decorating the tree so much that we forgot about the time.'

He stopped, then looked into the hallway to ensure Inge was not eavesdropping.

Grace wanted to tell him how sorry she was, how much she wished she had helped him more, how much she wished she had used her Quaker channels to open an exit route for his mother, to find a sponsor for her in England or perhaps in America, instead of thinking only of tracking down Morten. She wanted to tell him how much she wished she had asked him more about his life in Germany, about his family and friends, and about his life in London, too. But there was simply no way now of making up for all those lost moments. She had wasted too many hours, too many weeks daydreaming about her fantasy romance, writing unsent letters to a lover of her invention. It was impossible now to turn round and suddenly show great interest in matters she had never once bothered to ask about. It was impossible to suddenly declare to Max that he and his life were in fact terribly important to her, that they must be great friends. It would sound ridiculous; as if she was once again inventing a deep emotional connection where there was really only a casual friendship.

'If there is anything I can do to help ...' she said, and remembered that she had said this before. He shook his head. Then he reached out and took her hand. There was a sadness about his dark eyes but also, she thought, a certain warmth that made her feel strangely reassured, as if her stumbling words and awkward apologies were not all he judged her by, as if he could see beyond that; as if, in fact, he could see her where others failed to see her. And she thought what an unsettling and yet wonderful feeling that was, to be seen.

'Mr Hoffnung?' said a deep voice.

For a moment Grace thought it was Inge play-acting.

She dropped Max's hand and turned round. A policeman stood in the door. Behind him was Mr Cartland, the headmaster.

'Mr Hoffnung,' the bobby said, 'I must ask you to come with me.'

Max did not show the slightest surprise. 'One moment, please. My bag is in the other room.' He calmly moved towards the door but Grace grabbed his arm.

'Excuse me – what's this all about?'

'Good evening, ma'am.' The policemen tipped his helmet. 'This gentlemen here's been reported as an enemy alien.'

'But he isn't!' She refused to let go of Max's arm. 'Mr Cartland, surely you can clear this up. He's ... if anything, he's a friendly alien.'

Mr Cartland looked away.

'And what do you mean, reported? Reported by whom?' Grace stared at the headmaster. 'Are there spies in this building? While we were doing all we could to give the children here a home, were people spying on us? Mr Cartland, will you look at me and—'

The policeman interrupted her. 'Ma'am, I'd ask you not to be obstructive. The order is to round up all enemy aliens. Are you contesting the fact that your friend is a German citizen?'

'But he's—'

'Please.' Max shook his arm. 'Let me go. It's all right.'

'But where are they taking you?'

Max turned his head slightly towards the policeman, who

seemed to interpret this as a menace and bellowed a rough: 'Right then, are you coming or is this going to be difficult?'

And Grace suddenly thought, he doesn't know that this is Max's way of glancing sideways: and where they are taking him, no one will know, and no one will be there to explain it. She tightened her grip around Max's arm, but the policemen stepped forward and grabbed his other arm.

Just then Grace saw Inge's pale little face appear behind Mr Cartland. She was holding a glass of water in both hands. One breath, and then she was gone. Grace let go of Max.

'Where are you taking him?' she shouted after them, but they ignored her.

Inge was not in her dorm. She was not under Grace's desk. She was not in the empty kitchen. She was not in the breakfast room.

There were still three long tables in the dining hall. The tall double windows stood open and a warm breeze blew in and swelled the curtains.

She was not behind the curtains.

But there on the wooden floor, right by the open window, was a glass of water.

Grace closed her eyes, folded her hands, clenched her fingers together.

Then she slowly leaned out the window as far as she could. A car disappeared around the corner. She squinted at the street, the pavement. Nothing. Oh dear God, she thought, oh dear, dear God, please. I will do anything you want.

She was about to pull back into the dining hall when she heard the hiccup.

It was to her left. Outside the window, to her left.

She held her breath and then said very slowly: 'It is all right. Everything is all right.'

Then she looked to her left.

There was Inge, standing on the narrow ledge outside the window with her face to the wall, gripping the old stone ornaments with all her might.

She hiccuped again.

'It's all right, my darling. Don't move.' Grace tried to see which limb carried the most weight, which hand was gripping the stone tightly, which hand could be stretched out and seized.

'He is gone?'

'Yes. Everything's safe. You're safe.'

'I know him.'

'It's only Mr Cartland. It's nothing to worry about.'

'No. The policeman. I know him.'

Five floors below, the street and the pavement.

'Don't worry, my love, he's a nice policeman. Now hold that gargoyle tightly with your right hand. That's right. You're doing really well. And now give me that other hand. Your left hand.'

'I know him. He arrested my father.'

'You can tell me all about it when you're back inside. Now you must give me your hand. Don't look down. Look at me.'

'You don't believe me! He arrested my father, I swear!' Inge shrieked. Her left foot slipped off the ledge.

'I believe you. But he's gone now. Please, Inge, your hand.'

Grace held on to the windowframe so hard that her hand hurt, then leaned out until her other hand touched Inge's left arm. 'Your hand. That's it. That's it.'

The small hand was in her own. She gripped it. Nothing could happen as long as she gripped it.

'Now come back to the window. It's only two steps.'

'I can't.'

'You can.'

'He's hiding in the staircase.'

'Inge, it's a different policeman. He might look similar, but it's not the same policeman. It's an English policeman.' An urge overcame her to simply yank Inge towards the window. 'Don't look down. Look at me.'

'Then why did he arrest Mr Hoffnung?'

'He didn't arrest him. It's a long story. I'll tell you when you're inside.'

'But I saw him.'

'It was a misunderstanding. Mr Hoffnung is going to be fine.'

'You're lying.'

'I'm not.'

'Promise that you're not lying.'

'I promise,' Grace whispered. 'Now come.'

Inge took two steps along the ledge. Grace pulled her in through the window and clasped her arms around her. The hiccup was gone.

'You lied,' Inge said simply. She pressed her wet cold nose into Grace's neck.

'I didn't. It wasn't a real arrest. They are only taking Mr Hoffnung with them to ask him some questions.'

'That's what they did with my father. He never came back.'

'Mr Hoffnung will come back.'

Though suddenly she was not so sure. Suddenly she was not sure of anything. This little girl, she thought, this little girl knew so much more than she did.

She let go of Inge, who walked to the other side of the room.

'First they take Mr Hoffnung, then they take you, then they take me and all the other children from the train,' Inge said. She reached into one of the cardboard boxes. Before Grace could stop her, she pulled out a pair of large metal scissors and took them to her neck.

With a snip, the string came apart.

The scissors clattered to the ground; the grey piece of string floated down slowly.

'That way they won't know I'm from the train,' Inge said.

# Trapped Light

> 'It follows then that the back of the brilliant must be cut in such a way that when light enters the stone, it does not pass through it but is wholly reflected by its back. It is the diamond cutter's task to temporarily trap this light inside the stone.'
> *A Theory of Diamond-Cutting*

## 1

Esther's willingness to destroy the medal had mollified the Wizard. She could not fault his courtesy, his appreciation for her research. It was only her own mind – her own elastic mind that insisted on stretching back to the past – that prevented her from feeling comfortable in his presence. When he stood behind her, her movements became jittery and unfocused, and once or twice she botched a very simple calculation on the blackboard and had to rub it out.

She asked the medic who had provided the morphine vials to give her a weaker mixture for her sleep.

'It's not helping, Essie,' her husband said one evening. 'You're still doing it.'

'Then let me! There must be hundreds of people who fidget in their sleep. I can't see why my particular form of somnambulism is so very upsetting to you.'

He sighed and went on polishing an old horse harness he had found heaven knew where. In the morning, he would probably hang it up on the kitchen wall, next to the butter churn, the copper pans and the old Welsh love spoons. There were brilliantly modern architects all over Hampstead, men who built clean lines in steel and concrete, but her husband was not one of them.

'It's this house,' she said, and pulled at her nightgown as if it were a straitjacket. 'I would sleep wonderfully well in a clean, warm, modern house. We ought to pull it down and build a new one.'

'If we wait until the end of the war, the bombs might do the work for you.'

'I wouldn't mind.' She defiantly swallowed her nightly mixture. 'As long as we're all out when it happens, I wouldn't mind one bit to come back and find it all rubble.'

Her husband winced. She was unkind, perhaps, but what other woman would tolerate a husband who polished horse harnesses in bed? Admittedly, it was rather endearing, the way he sat on the edge of the bed in his flannel pyjamas and hummed as he rubbed the cloth over the leather.

'You were going to say something about Miriam,' she said and yawned.

'Yes.' He paused and scratched his head. 'I suppose you've noticed it too.'

She nodded, but could not imagine what he meant. Was there a problem with Miriam? She had assumed her daughter was busy working at the munitions factory. It had always been this way; it had always been her husband who noticed the red measly spots on the forehead, the best friend who no longer visited, all those tiny signals in a child's life that other mothers seemed naturally to receive and respond to. It was not that she did not love her daughter. But Miriam's arrival had so utterly erased Esther's achievements up to that point, had marked such an abrupt transition from a life that was satisfying and purposeful to one that was dreary and dull, that it was difficult to see the arrival as a blessing and the child herself as endlessly fascinating.

Before she could quite complete the thought, she fell asleep.

She used numbers to control and calm herself. When the Wizard trapped her in a corner with some research question, she found that mentally reciting prime numbers or the decimal digits of pi allowed her to keep a perfectly placid face. Then she recited the numbers even when the Wizard was not present. The strain of the long working hours, her restless sleep jolted by air raids, demanded she subject her mind and body to a rigorous discipline. She forced them to march to the rhythm of her mantra.

At some point, ancient words of prayer replaced the numbers. How did she even remember them? They were part of a faith that meant nothing to her. And yet, when she sat in the reinforced basement at night, she recited them in her head:

> Who shall live and who shall die,
> Who shall reach the natural end and who shall not,
> Who shall perish by water and who by fire.

And then she made up more lines:

> Who shall perish by fire and who by suffocation
> Who by rubble and who by blast
> Who by gangrene in a trench
> Who by thirst and hard labour
> Who in the hull of a torpedoed ship
> Who by morphine in a Hampstead kitchen ...

Before the end of the year, Mrs Morningstar completed a theoretical assessment of systematic bombing that was seen as particularly timely and useful. It formed part of a body of research used to shape Britain's response to German attacks on Coventry, Birmingham and Bristol. The Prime Minister gave instructions for plans to be prepared for retaliation in kind, and a list of suitable German towns and cities was drawn up. Britain would not be able to send over more than two hundred aircraft on one night, and the view was that destroying the greater part of a relatively small town would have a more devastating impact on morale than destroying a small part of a large city. In a war cabinet meeting in

December, the Chief of the Air Staff specifically cited Mrs Morningstar's paper to reinforce his argument that they should largely rely on fire, and choose a closely built-up town where bomb craters in the streets would hinder the fire fighters.

On the night of 16 December, Mannheim was bombed. The operation was thought to have yielded excellent results. About 100 tons of high-explosive bombs were dropped and 14,000 incendiary bombs, the Chief of Staff reported. Extensive fires were caused, some of which were still burning when the air force struck again on the night of 17 December.

Mrs Morningstar felt neither pride nor pity when she saw blurred footage of the attack at the pictures. Her first thought was that the flashes of light on the dark screen did not look like explosions or raging fires at all, but like the white dots on a Laue photograph.

## 2

Mrs Morningstar watched the screen turn into a Laue photograph; young Esther Adler picked up a pair of tweezers and pulled the photograph out of a tub filled with developer.

The country was in the middle of the Great War but there had never been, she was certain of it, a more exciting time to be a scientist. They numbered twelve at the lab, guided by the Wizard. Twelve pence to a shilling, twelve researchers to a lab: it was such a pleasing number, one that could be cleaved like a crystal to produce threes or fours or sixes, or indeed twos.

She pegged the photograph to a washing line and hurried into the Wizard's living room with the others. They sat down on the floor, balanced hot mugs of tea on their knees and waited for the circus to begin. Gottfried laid out a hypothesis in his slow, long-winded way and was soon interrupted by the Wizard: 'You are aware, of course, that your Laue photographs will continue to be blurred until you learn to control that trembling hand of yours?'

The others laughed. Perhaps Esther laughed, too. The Wizard, sitting in a dark green velvet armchair, lit his pipe. He was a horse trainer leaning against a fence, smoking his pipe, watching the colts and thinking to himself: this one needs more guidance, but that one, with a bit of encouragement, could win the National.

When her turn came, Esther explained her latest ideas for examining the structure of graphite. She had built her own cylindrical camera out of brass tubing, bits of lead and sealing wax. Her brother's alarm clock and a nail served to turn the crystal.

'It works beautifully,' she said, 'though I'd still be without a spectrometer if Gottfried hadn't taught me how to weld.'

The gratitude on his face was an expression she would remember years later, when an emigrant in a long coat turned up at her door with that secret smuggled parcel in his hands.

*

That night, she packed away her tools and looked around to find all the others had left. She locked up the room and fetched her coat. The Wizard's private flat was above the lab, and she decided on a whim to show him the dried Laue photograph.

'Miss Adler.' He opened the door himself, as if he had been expecting her. His fingers curled snugly around a glass of wine. The hair was clipped close around his widow's peak and she wondered whether it was true what they said, that he sympathized with the Bolsheviks.

Flustered, she began to talk about the lab, increasingly nervous as she noticed his eyes flitting in distraction from her face to the books she held to her chest. She tucked a stray strand of hair behind her ear. He told her to wait in the doorway and came back carrying a small pouch.

'Open your hand,' he commanded. 'Palm up.'

She did as she was told. He let six, seven small stones tumble into her open palm.

'Rough diamonds,' he said softly.

She knew what they were. She was the daughter of a diamond cutter. It was infuriating that the Wizard thought these glassy pebbles would dazzle and impress her: she was a scientist, not a chorus girl. To her, diamonds were interesting the way rock salt was interesting, and graphite, and benzene. Most infuriating, of course, was his apparent idea that *this* was why she had knocked on his door, to flirt like an infatuated schoolgirl; and there was no way in which she could now right this misconception.

'Oh,' she said. 'How very lovely.'

He smiled, picked the diamonds from her palm one by one and dropped them back into the bag. His fingertips tickled her nerve ends, but she held still.

The following week, she taught one of the young men in the lab how to weld. He was an Irish mathematician, charming and brilliant, but he had two left hands when it came to building and handling instruments. The interrupters for his Shearer gas tube would fill up with gas and pop off with a loud bang. Esther tried to help him handle the gas tube, causing much laughing and jumping and shrieking, and their coats were smeared with grease and dust. When she looked up, the Wizard was standing there in his pristine white coat.

'You've come out to save us, have you?' the Irish fellow cried, lifting his hands in helplessness. Esther hoped the Wizard would wave his hand over the Shearer tube and silence it with a single command; such an unscientific thought.

He joined them and scrutinized the bad-tempered instrument; tapped it with the stem of his old brown pipe.

'There's a straightforward solution to your predicament, but I would like to see if you can find it yourselves.'

Esther held his gaze.

'I know what we're going to do,' she said. 'Let's put it on the roof. Then it can bang away as much as it likes.'

His thin mouth widened into an amused grin and he rubbed his hands with boyish delight. 'Splendid.'

'Was that the solution you were thinking of?'

'No, but yours is far more original.'

They carried the instrument up to the roof and spent the rest of the afternoon building a protective shed around it. It continued to pop off twice a day, and the muffled bang became the lab's very own gong for luncheon and tea. The Wizard loved nothing more than to startle visitors with the mysterious noise. And since it had been Esther's idea, he invited her out for dinner in Soho as a treat.

They talked about graphite. He confided in her that he found Gottfried's work a little slipshod, it did not have quite the rigorous quality he expected from his men. What were her views on the lab? He did not mind about the Shearer tube; that kind of bang-smash-boom could be invigorating, but only when underpinned by rigorous work. Did she agree? What did she think?

He pulled his pipe from his mouth and tapped the back of her right hand with it. The end was still a little moist and warm on her cold skin.

When they finished their baked salmon he took her hand, turned it upside down and gently stroked the life lines on her palm.

'You'll think me a fool for saying this, but I have never met anyone quite like you, young lady.' He leaned forward now and whispered urgently: 'Esther . . .'

And she felt strangely powerful in that moment, more powerful than any of the men at the lab. The mighty Wizard had turned into a glassy pebble she could roll around in the palm of her hand. When he told her he had a room nearby where they could talk more privately, she thought of the horror this question would cause in everyone she knew in Hatton Garden, and then she said yes, that would be very nice.

They walked down the road, up a fusty staircase, into a grubby room. He slammed the door shut and lunged at her with what she presumed to be an expression of unfettered desire. She was a little taken aback but let him squash her against the wall with his large soft body. He kissed her on the mouth. It would hardly do to voice a sudden change of mind now. His hand crept towards her left breast and squeezed it somewhat desperately but he did not try to remove her dress. She kept her eyes wide open and stiffly bore the squeezing and rubbing, and he was mercifully unbothered by her lack of enthusiasm. He continued to chafe against her through their clothes in an angry act of physical exertion that left him huffing and red-faced. Up close, his flushed skin was porously lined and his breath smelled of tea and curdled milk. She turned her face away.

So this was the passion people wrote about in poems. She had never much liked poetry.

On the bus home, she made herself invisible in the corner of her seat. A whispered conversation with an old school friend came to her: 'I'm always worried about going too far, because I don't really know what "too far" means.'

How utterly ignorant they were. And she a scientist!

Later she told herself that she must have enjoyed it in some way. It was a logical conclusion. No one had forced her to meet the Wizard in Soho, and no one forced her to return to his flat two days later with a paper she wanted him to see. She had done it out of her own free will, and therefore must have found some pleasure in it.

The paper was not related to any of her research in the lab. She had started working on it long before the era of the Wizard. 'A Theory of Diamond-Cutting' was its modest title; she had never shown the final version to anyone.

Esther knocked on his door.

An hour later, she buttoned up her blouse and hoped she could scrub the ink off her skin before her mother or any of her sisters saw. What a lot of nonsense he had written on her breasts with his tickling fountain pen. And then she thought that she was perhaps wrong to call it nonsense, and that other girls would find it romantic. She was a cold fish, lacking in the warm-blooded vitality that men found so attractive.

Her shyness was charming, he said.

She gathered 'A Theory of Diamond-Cutting' from the floor, wondering if she could ask him now to read it. There was a muffled cough. She glanced up, but the Wizard was still talking. Another cough. It came from the next room.

She clasped her paper to her chest and ran out and down the stairs.

The next day, a handful of men marched up to the roof to dismantle the Shearer tube and bring it back into the lab.

'The Wizard's orders – we're to rebuild it until we get it right.'

They came back down laughing, hooting, carrying the components of their trophy high over their heads: 'Put it down, gently does it! Here he is ... Sir, sir, where would you like us to put it?'

The Wizard smiled and directed the spirited traffic into a far corner of the lab. He grabbed his belt and hitched up his trousers over his protruding stomach. It was a tic she had not noticed before, and she found it unpleasant.

She accompanied him to a lecture a week later, a luncheon talk for a circle of gentlemen with a leisurely interest in wine and science. They were financial supporters of the institute, and as such had to be entertained by the Wizard with popular, greatly simplified presentations of his research, a task he referred to as 'throwing pearls'.

He had brought two raw diamonds, which the gentlemen weighed in their palms as if they handled such stones every day. The Wizard, once again enjoying his role as circus magician, held one of them up between his thumb and index finger.

'Gentlemen, how many of you believe that the diamond is the hardest substance known?'

Dozens of white hands with signet rings went up.

'And quite right you are, too. I assume the same number of you would be happy to wager that the diamond is indestructible?' He placed the diamond on the polished table before him. Esther handed him a hammer, which he wielded over the stone.

227

Heads nodded.

The Wizard passed the hammer back to Esther, faithful assistant to the great conjuror.

'I am sorry to say, gentlemen, that you would have lost the bet as well as a perfectly good stone. Diamonds cleave along certain planes and can be split by a light blow on the right spot, as many a rash gambler and many a diamond-cutting apprentice will have learned to their cost.'

'Which is why they add a culet,' Esther, stiffly occupying a chair in the corner, murmured absent-mindedly.

'Miss Adler?'

'Oh, nothing. I was only pointing out that diamond cutters tend to flatten the sharp tip of their stones for precisely that reason, to prevent them from splitting. They call it a culet,' she said. 'Which is French for posterior.'

The gentlemen sniggered.

'My assistant has a passion for jewellery.' The Wizard spoke with a slight distaste that evoked images of dirty, crowded, loud Hatton Garden, the cutters and merchants scurrying along the narrow dark streets. 'Our problem with women scientists,' he continued, winking at his audience. 'They do become distracted by pretty stones and sparkle.' This was met by another round of laughter. Esther tugged at her collar for air. She caught some of the men glancing at her with interest, and was certain that they all pictured her and the Wizard in a damp Soho room. The image was unbearable to her.

When they left the club, the Wizard did not speak to her.

She felt dreadfully awkward but did not know how to apologize for interrupting his lecture. His disdain was quite justified; she had acted like a goose.

The next day, the nice Irish mathematician approached her with some hesitation. He cleared his throat, rubbed his nose, bit his lip.

'We are ordering a hamper for the Wizard's wife, the poor thing.' He gave her an embarrassed glance. 'Would you care to contribute at all?'

They all knew, then, or thought they knew.

Not long after that day, she became Mrs Morningstar and left the lab. When she took up a teaching position at Bentham College, her students were greatly impressed by the fact that she had once assisted the famous Wizard.

Yes, she said, his lab was a wonderland; they had all had a marvellous time.

# You, You, You

## 1

Paul left Wormwood Scrubs to find the streets thronging with khaki. Soldiers and their sweethearts were everywhere. Front pages and posters blared at him to do his bit. Girls wore yellow and red scarves printed with fire-bomb fighters and patriotic slogans: 'London! Alert!', 'Dig for Victory!'. The main change, however, was the proliferation of injured young men in the streets. Paul had entered prison when the main thrust of the war had still to be outward, an outward flow of men and guns that he refused to join. Now some of the flotsam and jetsam of that initial flow had been washed back. Paul saw men of his age who had already learned to butter a piece of toast with one hand, who kept their face slightly turned when they spoke to girls to hide the missing eye. He received a letter from the Ministry of Labour and National Service exempting him from military service on the condition that he do medical work. Instead of relief, he felt a vague sense of shame, as if he had cheated his way out of an unpleasant duty. He hoped this feeling would pass once he joined an ambulance unit, once he was part of a group of Quakers who bound wounds under fire. But then he found out that hundreds of young pacifists thought exactly like him: everyone wanted to serve in an ambulance and no one wanted to mop a floor in a hospital under the judging glances of strangers.

Paul added his name to the long waiting list for the Friends' Ambulance Unit and in the meantime found a job mopping floors. Sometimes he went for a Sunday walk on the Heath with Miriam, but after a few of those walks he had to admit to himself that their friendship had been easier when he was still in prison. On the Heath, they saw limping men in khaki, and tired nurses sitting on benches with their eyes closed, and more than once Miriam quickly steered him down a wooded path to avoid a family friend coming the other way. They might as well have tried to take a Sunday stroll around the fields of Flanders and pretended they were picking poppies for a bouquet. Both knew this could not continue, that they were trying to keep up a friendship that had no anchor in the real world. But then there were those moments when they entered a dense stretch of woodland with no one else around, when Paul helped Miriam up a slippery rock and she held on to his shoulder to steady herself, and she smiled that lovely smile at him, and the outside world and the war ceased to exist.

When the air raids started again he slept in the shelter at the hospital. He loathed the shelter: the smell of so many ill and exhausted people reminded him of prison. To escape it he volunteered to help with the casualties and was thanked for his indefatigable bravery. Again he felt that he was cheating, that he was pulling a mask of bravery over an act of cowardice: to him, rushing around amid the sirens was far less frightening than being trapped underground behind a closed door.

It was during one of those nights, when he was taking a quick nap in an office, that someone hammered on the door and he opened it to find Miriam stumbling in. There was a peculiar expression on her face, a look of confusion and a certain helplessness, as if she had lost her bearings, as if that natural confidence that carried her through life had vanished from under her feet. He thought of the time he had dragged her over the frozen, cracking pond towards safer ground and was gripped by that same urge to help her.

Her words came out in quick garbled bursts but he gathered that the munitions factory where she worked had been hit and one wing destroyed.

'You'd better go back there. I can come with you if you like. They'll be counting the ...' He almost said 'dead', but the look on her face made him change it to '... girls.'

When he moved towards the door, she held him back with rising panic in her eyes.

'I can't,' she whispered. 'I can't go back there. You don't know what it's like ... whenever I hear them coming, I know they're looking for *me*.'

He began to say that everyone felt that way, that he had felt exactly the same when he was in prison, but she interrupted him, half mad with fear.

'It's different, don't you see? In your case, your instinct tells you they're looking for you, but your reason knows they're not – that they don't want to bomb you in particular at all, that you're not really their aim. But in my case, don't you understand, I *am* their aim! I'm a Jewish girl working at a munitions factory, and I'm *exactly* their aim, and if they don't hit me, it's only because they can't yet aim their bombs precisely enough.'

Paul knew that by the morning her panic would have passed. She would find an excuse for her absence and go back to making bullets, and when the next bombs fell she would flinch but force herself to stay at her work bench. Yet this did not make the slightest difference to her instinctive panic in this place at this moment. He understood so well that she wanted to be the stoically cheerful factory worker, but that a darker fear was with her all the time and would not cease until the war was over.

He took her in his arms and stroked her hair until she calmed down. Just then the walls of the room began to shake from a nearby explosion, and she pressed herself against him. He felt her warm skin and then her lips on his neck, his scarred ear, his face and finally his lips.

2

In the morning he went to his parents' home and pulled his old sketches of her from under his bed. He looked at them and at a couple of prison drawings he had kept for himself. The daylight would be changing her mood already; she would be walking up to her room now, and with every step the night would fade further into the past, would perhaps be recast as one of those blitz follies, as a way of snatching a fistful of life when death was very close. At Bentham College he had sometimes gazed at the sketches until he fell asleep and she stepped out of the picture, naked and alive. The idea of worshipping a piece of paper seemed pathetic to him now.

He walked down the street and thought: this cloud is for you, and that one over there, too. Those yellow flowers by the roadside are for you. The sky today, surprisingly blue between the clouds, that sky is for you. The siren is for you, and the all clear. This streetlamp is for you, even though they don't light it these days. The dark grass on the Heath is for you, and the red pigment in this tub of paint for you, and the silence in Silent Meeting is for you: it's all for you, my love; I made it just for you.

He tucked a note into the cardboard tube with all the drawings before he posted it.

These drawings are for you.

All my drawings are for you.

You, you, you: I can think of nothing else.

x

# Letters from the Isle of Man

## 1

Max sat on a wooden bench in the sun next to his new friend, a German wine merchant called Walter. Their internment camp on the Isle of Man had once been an ordinary town square surrounded by terraced houses. Only a barbed wire fence separated their bench from a shopping street.

How convenient this was going to be for the Nazis, Max thought. Once they invaded Britain, they would not even have to search the houses and forests for Jews from the Continent. Britain had done it all for them. Here they all sat, neatly trapped behind barbed wire.

Walter liked watching the shopping street because there was a wine shop similar to the one he had owned by the Rhine.

'Look at all those poor people,' he said now, and pointed at Manx housewives carrying baskets full of groceries. 'Imprisoned behind the barbed wire.'

They laughed and Max made a mental note to add the joke to his next letter.

He wrote two letters a week, one dutiful, the other more passionate. This might be a good joke for the dutiful letter: 'Dear Morningstars, here is a funny anecdote that will illustrate life in the camp for you ...'

He was careful to keep the tone jolly and optimistic.

Max left the wine merchant by the fence. First the dutiful letter. Very protestant, that. *Erst die Arbeit, dann das Vergnügen*, his father said somewhere between his right ear and his temple. Work first, then pleasure. Yet his father had never once helped them decorate the Christmas tree.

There was a bench by the square, private enough to write, public enough to half-listen to the rabbi from Berlin who was giving a lecture to a group of men sitting on the grass.

'Dear Morningstars ...'

It would be fairly easy: there was news. They counted thirty professors and a dozen rabbis among them, and this had given them the idea for a camp university. A Manx version of Plato's Academy.

'Dear Morningstars.'

Good start. Max rolled the fountain pen between his fingers. How many more letters were stored in that pen? He liked the idea of his future swimming in the ink, ready to flow out and be shaped into words. It made him think of all that had flowed out of it already. The teasing little line he had rephrased so many times before putting it in the card. 'In case you still want to practise (though it is not necessary). (It never was.)'

And that time he had crossed out her Sunday parade! The fury in her eyes! One eye had shot locusts at him, the other pestilence. That night he had rolled in his bed and laughed, and every time he finally calmed down he had thought of those furious eyes and burst out laughing again, until Mr Morningstar came in and asked if he was having nightmares.

The first words that had ever flowed out of the pen were '*Lieber Max ...*' in his father's handsome, slanted letters. 'Dear Max, I wish you much happiness for your thirteenth birthday.'

No, he thought, those were not actually the pen's first words. Its brown leather holder was shiny with the grease of many hands. His grandfather had owned it, then his father, then Max. Birth certificates must have been signed with that pen, a doctoral thesis, a will or two, love letters and a marriage contract before Max was even born.

'Dear Morningstars.'

He decided to take a little writing break. Rabbi Goldwater was talking about the concept of *gam zu letovah*, the idea that something good could be found in everything that happened. Max listened somewhat reluctantly. He had not seen much evidence of that.

Take America, the rabbi said. Remember how America was once our collective dustbin? The brother who gambled away the estate, the nephew who wanted to marry the village whore: had they not found themselves, one, two, three, aboard a ship sailing out of Bremen with the family waving relieved handkerchiefs from the dock?

This drew embarrassed laughter from the crowd, muffled by the shame of recognition. Max thought of his uncle Wilhelm, his father's brother, a compulsive roulette player who now made corsets in Brooklyn.

Gamblers, drunkards, good-for-nothings, the rabbi said. Yet are those gamblers, those drunkards, those good-for-nothings not the same people who are now busy writing affidavits for all of us to come and join them in America? *Gam zu letovah!*

No. Wilhelm had not written an affidavit. Neither for Max nor for his mother. So much for *gam zu letovah*.

And you, Max thought, looking at the rabbi behind his nodding audience, when you were scrubbing a pavement in Berlin with your toothbrush, surrounded by louts in uniform and your own laughing neighbours, is that really what you thought then: *gam zu letovah*?

Perhaps the rabbi did not quite believe his own words. Perhaps what the rabbi really thought was, it's been a while since I last spoke to God; I have this feeling he's forgotten about us.

'Dear Morningstars, apart from the university we now have a camp parliament, too. An upper house and a prime minister, elected in universal suffrage. In practice it is only male suffrage, because there are only men here!' Max wrote. 'But that is just an aside.'

He added the joke about the barbed wire.

What else ... oh, the elections! He had beaten the wine merchant, a professor of Greek mythology, two accountants

# Waterstones

11-17 Castle Street
Norwich
Norfolk
NR2 1PB
01603 767292
**SALE TRANSACTION**

| | | |
|---|---|---|
| FOLLOW THE MONEY | | £25.00 |
| 9781408714010 | | |
| LESSONS IN CHEMISTR | | £9.99 |
| 9781804990926 | | |
| MOTHER'S BOY | | £9.99 |
| 9781472257420 | | |
| **Multibuy** | 50.0% | -£5.00 |
| Balance to pay | | **£39.98** |
| Gift Card Tendered | | £39.98 |

- - - - - - - - - - - - - - - - - - - -

WATERSTONES PLUS CARD
CARD NUMBER: **** **** **** 7581
Your Current Balance          £0.00
Qualifying spend             £39.98
Starting Stamps total             0
Stamps earned in this transaction   3
Current Stamps total              3
Stamps collected so far on this card

Activate your card to redeem balance

## Waterstones
VAT Reg No. GB 108 2770 24

| STORE | TILL | OP NO. | TRANS. | DATE | TIME |
|---|---|---|---|---|---|
| 0672 | 2 | 762643 | 687174 | 22/03/2023 | 14:13 |

◻999020672002687174 6◻

and a psychoanalyst to become his house's representative to parliament.

'Between you and me, the professor would have won, but he and the analyst tumbled into a very unsavoury row over the true nature of Oedipus' relations with his family. I will spare you the unsavoury details, but by the end of it we all preferred to hear no more from either of them.'

Twenty lines: almost done. Something about herrings and the weather.

'Well, now I must "dash" off to the next leg of my Quest for Knowledge. Greek myths today! We vetoed Oedipus, the professor is going to do Odysseus instead.'

Thirty lines, and over.

He let out a deep sigh of relief and folded the letter.

On to a more pleasurable task.

Max took a bundle of letters from his bag and reread them carefully, one by one. He smiled. Maybe she, too, would enjoy the wine merchant's joke. But no – he liked to keep the two weekly letters separate. He would write to her about all the subjects he could not discuss with anyone else. About *gam zu letovah* and the Protestants, about how the air smelled of salt or grass, depending on which way the wind blew, about the dreams in which he glided through the barbed wire and swam in the sky, surrounded by herrings.

Thirty lines of duty, thirty lines of—

'Love,' he thought. 'That's a rather big word, isn't it, old friend? But why not? Why shouldn't our nice Mr Hoffnung fall in love?'

Greatly cheered by this thought, he whistled a tune, smoothed out the letter-writing form and picked up his fountain pen.

## 2

In November 1940, he climbed on a chair with six nails between his lips and began to decorate the windows with twigs and Christmas tree garlands cut from brown paper.

The camp university had lost its fizz. A mood of gloom and depression set in, of lives put on hold. The concentration of talent and learning that had entertained them at first now reinforced the bitter sense that despite their goodwill, despite all their efforts and their eagerness to serve society and be of use, they were men whom no one needed nor wanted.

Max grew to find the omnipresence of the rabbis oppressive. The bearded men in black gabardine who clustered together in the kosher houses seemed fierce and medieval to him, their rabbis like seers or sorcerers. Yet the reform rabbis, clean-shaven and smugly modern, made him equally uneasy, and it took him a while to realize why. With or without beards, they were continual reminders of a faith that was alien to him, that he had hardly been aware of until he was officially declared to belong to it. Initially he had enjoyed learning more about it, had particularly admired its emphasis on everything happening in this life rather than the afterlife. Yet as the weeks passed and then the months, and as the reform rabbis took to casting little asides and references his way as if he was one of them, he began to resist being drawn in. His mother had converted to Protestantism and raised him in that faith. Their year began with poached blue carp and lead-pouring: his father even let them use his Bunsen burner to melt the lead before they poured it into cold water and read their future in the shapes. It ended with Christmas carols, mulled wine and children in shepherd costumes stumbling over 'yonder star'. To begin the year now with fasting and atonement, to feel affinity with some tribe who got lost in the wilderness a very long time ago would be to accuse her indirectly of having withheld something important from him, of having failed to transmit to him some vital knowledge. She had refused to be one of the Chosen, and perhaps with good reason, for as far as he could see, being Chosen didn't exactly carry many benefits. Chosen, yes, he thought and picked a nail from between his lips. Chosen to be the first on the cattle train.

Rabbi Goldwater came in, cradling a mug of tea, and Max said through the nails without turning around: 'I know what you're going to say about my pretty twigs. Assimilation never got us anywhere. But I like it.'

'I was actually going to say that it looks rather jolly. As Hillel said, I walk, I fall, I get up; meanwhile, I keep dancing.'

'Well, here's what I say to Hillel.' Max took the last nail

from his mouth and drove it into the wall with a hammer. 'I get up, I walk, I dance: meanwhile, I keep falling.'

# 3

His boat sailed back to the mainland over the winter sea. The breeze stung his face. He sucked in the fresh, sharp air, air speckled with seawater that cleansed the mind of all that had been. Then he let his fist dangle over the railing. He had planned a grand gesture. He had planned to hurl the thing into the wind with a mighty cry, a survivor's cry, half triumph, half pain: the sort of cry Noah might have let out in the deluge. But when he stood at the railing he simply relaxed his fingers and let his father's pen and the shiny leather holder drop into the sea.

A new life washed in on the high tide. His glasses were blind with spray from the sea but he did not care.

They had escaped the school of the dead. Inge, Grace wrote, was enjoying life on the farm and had taken up horse-riding. Grace herself was training to be a nurse with the Friends' Ambulance Unit. And he, he would join the Pioneer Corps.

He took off his glasses and let the spray cool his eyelids. It seemed to him that Samhuinn had lain under a spell. Now they were free and, God, what adventures awaited them.

He arrived on the mainland in the evening, caught a train and spent the night at a cheap hotel near Russell Square. In the morning, he shaved in front of a dull chipped mirror and turned his face to make sure he hadn't missed a spot. He nicked his cheek, licked a piece of newspaper, slapped it over the cut.

At breakfast he considered ringing the Morningstars to tell them about his release. He ought to thank them for their work on his behalf, their letters to MPs, their insistence that despite his German origin, he was highly unlikely to lead the Nazis into Britain.

Then again, if he rang them later he might give them not just one piece of good news, but two.

The toast lay untouched on his plate. A sip of tea would have to do. All he wanted, really, was to grab his knapsack and be on his way. He took a quick gulp of tea and spluttered. In his distraction he had grabbed an old flower vase, empty but for an inch of stale water.

He laughed. The only other guests, two elderly men at separate tables, looked up from their newspapers and frowned. He laughed back at their frowns.

I will remember this for ever, he wanted to shout at them. I will for ever remember that on this morning, I was so nervous, so nervous that I drank from a flower vase.

Instead he nodded at them and picked up his knapsack. He left behind the untouched toast, the cooling tea, and the vase with its inch of stale water.


4


He saw her as soon as he entered the garden in Tavistock Square. She was sitting on a bench and reading a book. The

243

sunlight fell on her hair. And he stood there – simply stood – for five minutes, ten, just watched her turn the pages. He remembered how he had walked past her office five times, ten times, just to see her sit at her desk. How he had dropped a basket full of pine cones just to force her to stay there in the corridor with him for five, ten more minutes; as long as it took to collect them. How he had arrived at work early every morning during that cold winter to light the stove in her office because he wanted her to be warm.

And he suddenly thought that this was perhaps all his heart could hold, that this was the portion doled out to him. He thought that perhaps he ought not to be greedy, that he ought not to risk upsetting the fragile scaffolding that was his love for her, that he ought not ask for more than the apportioned share. Her sitting on this bench; her pouring pine cones into his cupped hands; her holding on tight to his arm on their last day at Samhuinn: those were small frail memories that a single wrong word, a single disappointed look could erase.

He turned round. And as he walked out of the garden he heard her frantic footsteps behind him, running, kicking up gravel, and heard her shout: 'Max! Max! Where do you think you're going? Max!'

5

They had a week together before she had to leave with the Friends' Ambulance Unit.

Once Grace said: 'I wish . . .' and Max placed a finger over her mouth.

'We are here now,' he said and traced her lips with his fingertip. 'There's nothing else.'

She closed her eyes and tried to register the precise sensation of his fingertip against her lip. He was right, there was nothing else. She must squeeze the juice out of every moment and store it away for when they were apart: like a bare-footed vintner treading grapes.

'Open your eyes.' His fingertips moved to her temples. 'The way your pupils suddenly contract when you open your eyes. The black and the grey. It's magnificent. I need to remember that.'

And she loved the way he said 'I need'. It was exactly what she felt: that she needed these memories, needed them as nourishment and sustenance.

Once she had thought of him as a shadow, as little more than a pair of sunken eyes behind horn-rimmed glasses. Now she was trying to build him afresh, to piece him together out of a thousand little elements, a thousand little tics and gestures, so that when they were apart she would be able to recreate his image faithfully. She thought, the way he stands by the bed in the morning, naked and talkative, and then he tugs at his penis in that thoughtful way, as if to prompt himself: I must never forget that. The way he reaches over his head with his right hand to scratch the top of his left ear. She wanted to notice everything about him that others failed to catch. During their first night together they couldn't sleep because they kept propping themselves up to look at each other. She asked him, with slight nervousness, whether he could imagine staying in England after the war.

'I think so,' he said, and smiled at her. 'I do feel at home here. In a way.'

'In what way?'

'Good question.' He thought for a moment. 'Sometimes I dream that I'm a giant with footprints as big as Hyde Park. I'm straddling the water with one foot squashing Hyde Park and the other on the Tiergarten. One foot is in London, and the other in Berlin. One hand dangles over Westminster; the other, over the Reichstag. With one ear I can hear spoons in teacups. And with the other, people arguing over a barrel of pickled gherkins.' He tugged at his earlobes. 'One eye on London, the other on Berlin. Exactly half of me is here, and the other half is over there. So really, I'm at home in two places.'

She nodded.

'And which way do you face?'

'Which way do I face?'

'Yes. When you're straddling the water.'

He pressed his eyes shut for a moment. 'South I think.'

'Ah.' She considered his reply for a while, and then she said: 'Then your heart's in Berlin.'

He rolled over to her.

'No, it isn't. I just turned round. Now I'm facing North and my heart is right here.' And he took her hand and placed it on his chest.

*

246

After they made love, he curled up against her back and she fitted exactly into the curve he made with his body. She thought, I must remember the exact coordinates of this, the head, the hand, the chin, the gentle snoring, the temperature of his skin, his heat against my body and my heat against him. I must remember it precisely and not let it slip away.

# 6

Usually everyone at Highgate Meeting would have had to give their approval, but half the members were evacuated or doing land work. Paul's father and another elder from Meeting dealt with the paperwork. On the Sunday before Grace's departure, a dozen people gathered at Highgate Meeting House.

Grace tried to calm her breathing, to sink into worshipful contemplation, but every time she looked up, she saw Max and had to giggle. He was trying to put on a most solemn and Quakerly face and she wanted to nudge him and tell him that it was fine, that he did not have to pretend to be anything, they were hardly going to throw him out.

She suppressed her giggles and gave him a questioning glance. He responded with a nod. They both stood up. She took his hand.

'Whither thou goest, I will go; and where thou lodgest, I will lodge; thy people shall be my people, and thy God my God,' she said in her clear, honest voice. 'Friends, I take this my Friend, Max Hoffnung, to be my husband, promising through divine assistance to be unto him a loving and faithful wife, so long as we both on earth shall live.'

She squeezed his hand and smiled at him.

'Friends …' He smiled. 'I take this my Friend, Grace Woolman as my wife, promising to be unto her a loving and faithful husband, so long as we both on earth shall live.'

Everyone in the room signed the marriage certificate.

Later, over tea and cake, not even her mother mentioned Max's omission of the divine assistance. It was a thoroughly happy day, though the best part of it, they agreed, was when they were on their own with the door locked behind them.

That night, she told him about her journey to Vienna.

'Where? Where? And did you see …? And did you go to …? And did you see …?'

'Max,' she finally said, 'I didn't see anything. I didn't see *The Kiss*. I didn't see the Burgtheater. I didn't eat the special chocolate cake. We'll go after the war and you'll have to show me everything. We'll pretend it's my first time.'

'You didn't even see *The Kiss*?'

She was chopping onions, he was peeling potatoes. They would have stew and boiled potatoes for their wedding dinner. Suddenly he rested his knife and said: 'Did you have any direct meetings with them?'

It took her a moment or two to catch the reference.

'I was more of a typist, really, so not really, no. Though I did sit by the door when one of the meetings took place, and

I could hear them talk inside. A Dutch lady, Christian, not a Quaker though. Gertruida, she was called. Known as Truus. And an official. And you know what, it was the strangest conversation I heard in my life.'

'Who was the official?'

'The head of the emigration office.'

'Eichmann?'

'Yes. I only saw him when Truus came out and left the door open. He was just one of those ordinary men. In uniform, of course, but without it, he might have been the janitor at our meeting house. Well, I don't know why I'd expected him to look different, but I had.'

'And why was it a strange conversation?'

'Because he asked her to show him her knees!' She had been wanting to tell this to someone for such a long time; and what a relief it was to have finally found someone who listened. 'See, I was just there in the corridor. So I sat down on a chair – I didn't spy through the keyhole or anything – but you could hear them clearly enough. Dr Eichmann. That was it. They told us he was very keen on being addressed as *Doktor*. So Truus piled it on: *Guten Tag, Dr Eichmann*, pleased to meet you, Dr Eichmann, and all that. Right away he told her he didn't talk to women and would she leave. She sat down and said she was sorry she hadn't brought her husband. And so on. Then she explained that she wanted to take Jewish children to England, and he listened for a bit and then ... Wait. First of all, he asked her to show him her hands. To take off her gloves and show him her hands. There was a bit of a pause and then I heard him say, now take off your shoes. Walk up and down in front of me, and lift your skirt so I can see your knees. There was another pause, and I could hear her rustle about in there. And eventually he said: Incredibly, a pure Aryan and yet so insane.'

Max had listened quietly. He picked up a potato and began to peel it.

'You see,' Grace continued, 'I haven't told anyone about that conversation, and I still don't know what to make of it. And I don't mean the fact that he was making these bizarre requests – I assume it was what he would call a bit of fun, or perhaps he really did believe in racial studies – but the fact that she went along with it, because she thought that would be the best way to reach a deal. And she did, she received permission to take out some five hundred children and that was only the start. But it doesn't make a very satisfying story, does it? I think that's what unsettles me about it. There's something very unsatisfying and irritating about it, not just sad and bizarre but unsatisfying, and for ages I couldn't figure out why. But I think I know now. You see, we went to Vienna to negotiate with these people, and we did negotiate with them, and even made a modest success of it, if you can call it that, given the circumstances. But when I heard him say, now take off your shoes, something in me bristled, and – and I was silently, you know, really furiously thinking to myself, sending her a silent message, sort of saying, Don't do it! Don't take off your shoes! Tell him to go to hell! But that wouldn't have been the prudent thing to do, would it? That

250

wouldn't have been of any use to those children. That's what makes me so terribly annoyed with our people sometimes, that we're so practical and sensible, and we never slap anyone or tell anyone to go to hell. We just send them Christmas cards saying, wouldn't it be wonderful to release all prisoners from the camps? And if someone asks us to take off our shoes, well, we take off our shoes. Every time I hear someone say, gosh, I'd never shake that man's hand, I think, well, we shake everyone's hands. And it does mean we can do good, in a very quiet, ordinary way, but it also means, frankly, that we go through life shaking an awful lot of dirty hands.'

'And I've peeled the entire potato.'

'Ha, well done.'

'No, I mean, look.' He held up a tiny naked potato, the size of a radish, then pointed at a whole pile of shavings. 'I was listening so hard I almost peeled it away.'

'Thank you. So what do you think?'

'It's interesting. Clean hands, dirty hands. But to be honest, I wasn't even really thinking about Eichmann. Or about the Quakers. I was thinking about my father.'

# A Trembling Bathtub

# 1

*You, you, you. I can think of nothing else.*

No one had ever written such a thing to Esther Morningstar, née Adler. No one had ever *said* such a thing. The closest was: 'I have never met anyone quite like you, young lady.' The moist stem of an old brown pipe tapping the back of her cold hand.

And: 'Esther . . .' Spoken with the desperate urgency of a sinking man.

Surely there must have been something a trifle more stirring. She thought back to her first encounter with her own husband, their early days of marriage. Nothing. 'Essie, old girl' was the best she could find in those draughty memories.

She turned the cardboard tube upside down and tapped it until the drawings edged out. Two flimsy pieces of paper fell out of the roll and sailed to the floor. She picked them up with two fingers, recognizing the waxy texture from so many institutional bathrooms. She laid out all the drawings on the kitchen table and stared at the six nude drawings of her daughter.

In Antwerp or in Hatton Garden, Mother would have burned the drawings and thrown the ashes in her face. That sort of reaction had no place in progressive Hampstead. She would roll up the paintings, leave the cardboard tube by the door and pretend nothing had happened.

*That's a very sensible idea, Esther,* her mother's voice said. *Turn a blind eye to it, and when the inevitable happens, well, you'll know how to fix it. Mind you, husbands like yours aren't easy to find any more. Modern young men have wised up to our ways.*

Surely it can't be my fault, she thought. Had she not given Miriam all she needed to live her life with dignity and a sense of purpose? Had she not married an awkward, clumsy man who collected old horse harnesses, because her sisters told her he was kind and a little gullible, and those were the exact qualities she needed? Had she not hidden her disappointment that Miriam should show no aptitude for natural sciences, and indeed still struggled to understand calculus at the age of twenty? Had she not sent her daughter to Samhuinn, a crank school where she was allowed to substitute experimental dance for maths? Had she not risked her own good name to secure Miriam a place at the Bentham College social sciences department, and had she not stoically accepted Miriam's choice to drop social sciences for Modern Print-Making: An Introduction to Linocuts?

She picked up the scrap of toilet paper with the most

obscene sketch of them all, opened the slatted door of the stove, tossed it in and banged the door shut.

It vanished into the flames with a barely audible rustle.

Esther stood very still and listened to the whispering fire. What an utterly foolish thing to do. Now Miriam would know she had discovered the drawings. With hectic guilt she rolled up the larger ones, only to find that there was soot on her fingers and she had smudged the paper. She tried to rub off the soot with her sleeve but that only made matters worse.

Well, all sorts of things got lost and dirtied in the post. She glanced at the clock. There was a colleague's paper on the kitchen worktop that she ought to be reading now. But she was stuck in the moment, stuck between the typed stack and the charcoal sketches, unable to decide which one should be dealt with first, which one was important. And she had never felt more of a failure than at this moment, when she knew that the sensible thing would be to ignore the drawings, when she knew that only a hysterical superstitious mind would interpret them as a symbol and a judgement and a curse.

She picked up the second piece of toilet paper, opened the slatted door but did not let go of the paper quickly enough. The corner caught fire and curled up, blackening and erasing the drawing and scorching her fingertips. It was the smell of accidents in the attic, of badly handled lead and temperamental gas flames. She was in the attic in Hatton Garden again and she was also in her kitchen in Hampstead, and that was perfectly possible because the path that connected the two was no longer a narrow straight line but a strange cursed road that twisted and doubled back beneath her feet as she walked.

As a girl, she had expected progress to be continuous and linear. There could be no other way. The past she saw as a collection of data that, if entered into a grid, would clot around a rising line. Her hungry, nameless ancestors she pictured crouching about in dark cottages and eating potatoes. They huddled on the cold fringes of Europe, somewhere close to the point where the y axis met the x axis. A knock on the patched-up door, a flicker of a fearful pair of eyes, a dying candle stump waxed to the table.

From there to Antwerp, which she pictured as one large garden under a blue sky with a washing line drawn through it. A clear white line travelling away from the potato-eaters, a line travelling out along the x axis that measured time, out along the y axis that measured . . .

What did the y axis measure, Esther? Look, even now you fail to label it accurately. How could you trust your model when you did not even know what the y axis measured?

Upwards, always upwards. Antwerp. There was that stifling workshop, but still, it was better than the cold Russian hut and the fearful ancestral eyes.

Ten years to the right on the x axis, and several unnamed units up on the y axis, and there was Hatton Garden, her own childhood home. The workshop was still stifling but their kitchen was clean and big. Ten people could fit around that table. Eight of them would fan out and continue the climb, always upwards, towards the sky, away from the roots and the dirt. She had *willed* it. Out of the darkness and into the light, eight bright new Adlers. She herself was the wonder girl, the promising scientist, the fifty-seven facet brilliant. But the others, she generously conceded, would do well enough too, as cutters, merchants and wives. Her seven brothers and sisters would sparkle with eight facets each.

A few more years to the right on the x axis, and then her careful model collapsed.

She could not understand it – why the line that traced their luck suddenly began to move in such a scraggly and unpredictable manner. It brought deep and sudden pain, but it brought success and good fortune too, and *that* was the most corrosive feeling. She tried to discern a clear pattern, at least a sequence of transgression and punishment, but there was none; the data was random and scattered.

Someone had given, someone had taken away, and left the pattern broken.

And yet she had pushed ahead, onwards along the time axis. She pushed ahead, she moved into the draughty house on Rose Walk and tried to will the line to rise again in progress. When her husband told her that prayer might help her calm down at bedtime and improve her somnambulism, she replied: I'd rather be a somnambulist than God's slave.

Upwards!

And it had worked, hadn't it? She had mastered the line.

She had set it on a rising path again. She had calculated the trajectory of bombs and in the process had corrected her own trajectory.

But when she pushed the remaining three drawings and the note deep into the stove with a black poker and shut the slatted door, she wondered whether she had quite risen to the challenge of the bold new century, and whether she quite fit into the model she used to map out her years; and she told herself that perhaps the model, that long positive line of progress, had been faulty all along.

She inspected all the dots between her y axis and her x axis, one after the other, and she realised then that there had been only one time in her life when she had been truly content, and that had been many years ago, when all the mirrors in Hatton Garden still reflected two old faces and eight young ones.

*You, you, you. I can think of nothing else.*

## 2

Three days passed and then Miriam came into the kitchen one morning after her night shift and found the cardboard tube, which had been too large to push into the stove. She recognized Paul's handwriting in the address field. She opened the stove door and poked around in the ashes. When she saw her mother that night, she asked her calmly why she had burned the drawings her artist friend had sent her.

'It wasn't the sort of thing I wanted in my home,' her mother said without looking up from the paper she was annotating.

Miriam went upstairs, fetched the suitcase she had packed in the morning and made for the front door.

'Are you going on a trip?' Her mother's voice was unnaturally shrill.

'Burning a work of art isn't the sort of thing I want to happen in my home,' Miriam said. 'So I've decided to find another.'

Her mother began to laugh in the same shrill register. 'Don't be silly. It was only a drawing, and not a particularly good one, frankly.'

'How would you know?'

'I may not know much about drawings, but I do know a thing or two about life. And the first thought that struck me was, what sort of young man would sit around in London and doodle when the rest of us are struggling to stay alive?'

'A conchie.' Miriam thoroughly enjoyed the look on her mother's face, so much that she added: 'He doesn't want to sign up, you see. He'd rather sit here and doodle.'

Her mother glanced at the suitcase and Miriam could see that she was taking in its size, estimating how many sets of clothes she had packed, whether the departure was a bluff and she would be back within a few days. All this infuriated her.

'I see.' Her mother smiled. 'I suppose that's a very wise decision of his. Your uncles had a friend who was a conchie, you know. A man called Leybesh. He made a very clever choice, survived the whole war without as much as a scratch. If only your uncles had been that clever.'

'Daddy never served, either.' Miriam, too, knew all about the precise spot that could cleave the entire crystal.

'Because of his health.'

'Is that so? He told me it was because of his age. Auntie Hannah told me it was because he didn't want to go and knew the right people.'

'Well, we're not discussing your father's war record now.' Her mother folded her hands and looked just past her face, into the middle distance, as she always did. 'I've experienced quite a few disappointments over the years, as you know. And it certainly hasn't been much fun watching you flit around between all your half-finished tasks and making very little of your life. But I have to say that it would never have occurred to me, not even when I most doubted that you would ever accomplish anything of lasting value, that when push came to shove, when a time came when we'd all be tested, my own daughter would be spending her time posing nude for a deserter.'

'He's a conchie, not a deserter.'

'I think you'll agree, when you put some thought into it, that the only difference is one of timing.'

Miriam had never seen her mother angry. She had never seen her overjoyed, either. Even when she was small, she had been very aware that her mother was not like other women; was not like her aunts, with their smothering embraces and

259

pots full of food; was not even like her father with his fondness for old knick-knacks and fairy tales. Her mother rarely praised and rarely scolded, rarely rewarded and rarely punished. She found satisfaction in solitude and dry equations, and Miriam had often imagined that somewhere in London there was a family as mismatched as hers, a family with a loud, round mother who loved bright colours and hated being alone, and a quiet, withdrawn daughter who found solace in numbers.

The woman who was now standing in the doorway with a face distorted by pain and rage was neither her own mother nor that imagined, ideal one, but a madwoman, a madwoman who must have been hiding inside that sensible crystallographer all along.

'If you are going to live with that man, you need not come back,' the madwoman cried and tightly gripped the door. 'I mean it, Miriam. When this door falls shut, it's shut for good.'

'You've forgotten one thing,' Miriam said with more weariness than anger, and turned towards the street, suitcase in hand. 'To be properly medieval, you ought to say Kaddish for me after I leave.'

## 3

'You're a hopeless old sentimentalist,' Miriam said. 'And every time you mention grey, it reminds me of that lady . . . Mrs Rye?'

'Mary Pye. She once told me I reminded her of Moses. Because of my slow tongue, you see.'

'Well, you don't have a slow tongue. And also, I'm named after Moses' sister, so I think we'd better ditch that comparison altogether.'

Miriam's friend at the munitions factory had an attic room not far from Embankment, which they borrowed for a while. The house stood near the railway tracks and every time a train passed, the entire bathtub trembled. Paul dipped the sponge into the cooling water, wrung it out, dipped it into the water again. A train passed and he washed Miriam's shivering wet back. Her hair hung down to her shoulder blades in thick black ropes. He gathered them in one hand and flipped them over her shoulder.

It was a white enamel tub and the glaze had cracked in patches to reveal the rusty metal underneath. The water felt too cold now to sit in. At any moment she would suggest they get out. Paul leaned forward and kissed her left shoulder, and then he washed her back again. Like a racoon, he thought: they wash their food not to make it clean, but to make it theirs.

He dropped the sponge and pulled her close so that her shoulder blades pressed into his chest. She had become so thin and brittle, and he wondered what had happened to the spirited girl with the saucepan on her head.

'There's this line I've had on my mind for so long,' he said. 'It comes to my mind every time I see you. "She wants to eat of the fruit of all the trees in the garden of the world."'

'Have you been reading Wilde?'

'No. I thought it was a line from a song.'

'It's a quote from Wilde. It's "I want to", though. "I want to eat . . ." and so on.'

'Well, I do. I want to eat of the fruit of all the trees, too.'

He kissed her.

'Urgh. The water's cold.' She stood up with much teetering and splashing, laughed and put one hand on the side of the tub to steady herself.

'Stay like that.'

'What? I'm about to fall over.'

'Stay like that . . . one second.' He jumped out of the tub and dribbled suds and water over the tiles, the linoleum floor, the beige rug. His hands left dark watermarks on the sketchbook but he was too caught up in the moment to dry them. He squatted by the door with his sketchbook and charcoal and captured her in one swift and strong line, her curved back, one hand on the rim of the bathtub, the other covering her breasts. The tub trembled again. He let her get out and rub herself dry with a towel, the smooth texture of her damp skin against the rough weave of the fabric.

'Stay like that.' With the corner of the towel against her cheek and one leg propped up on the wooden stool. 'You're not cold, are you?'

'Hardly,' she said with a brave smile.

He put aside the sketchbook and kissed her leg from the calf up.

*

Her drawings were much better than her paintings. He noticed that she was at her best when she had a limited range of materials to work with. A single colour, a single sheet of paper. It seemed to concentrate her skittish mind and bring out her verve and energy in the force of the line. He loved the drama of her confident shading and the expressiveness of her figures captured in motion.

He climbed onto the bed.

'That's not fair!' She playfully pushed him away. 'I sat for you for *ages*.'

He rolled her onto her back and kissed her.

The room trembled again, much harder this time, and he could hear the cold water sloshing in the tub next door. What a miracle it was to feel so alive, to feel all that hot blood pulsating through his body. How well their bodies fit together, his cheek against her warm cheek, his thigh between her thighs. They kissed again and with the next tremor she rolled on top of him. He held her tightly and let the tremor shake them.

'Crikey. Why would anyone buy a flat next to a train station?'

'That wasn't a train, you fool.' She shook her head in exasperation, but her face was soft and friendly. 'That was another bomb.'

She slipped into the room after her night shift. He was fast asleep. There was a pamphlet on the bedside table that he must have been reading just before he went to bed. She had made a pact with herself never to talk about his plans and beliefs, never to ask whether he intended to mop hospital floors until the end of the war. Once he had mentioned something about serving with an ambulance unit but she no longer knew whether he said these things to mollify her. It did not matter. He would not run off and join the army if it meant betraying his faith. His stance raised so many uncomfortable questions that she thought it better not to think about it at all, not to read any of his letters or newspapers, but this time she skipped her own rule. She picked up the pamphlet and read it, first with a sceptical smile, then with a frown.

# Three Hundred and Fifty-four Rats

## 1

It snowed every day. At five in the morning they rolled off their straw mattresses, scratched themselves extensively, then went into the bushes outside or the earth closet at the back of the overgrown garden. The well was frozen over, and by the time they had smashed the ice with shovels and cranked up a few buckets, their cheeks were red and their unkempt hair stood up in all directions: like a gang of Lost Boys.

The twins showed Charlie how to heat the water on the stove and take it to the stable to wash the cow's udder before milking. At first, he tried to squeeze the teats like a tube of toothpaste, but nothing came out. They showed him how to do it properly, squirt some milk on his palms and then massage the teats: it worked a treat.

'Why don't they keep this one with the other cows?' Charlie asked.

'It doesn't get on with the others,' said Jack, sullen on his low stool, smoking while he milked. 'It's a conchie cow.'

It was still dark when they split, Jack to work for a vegetable farmer on the other side of Ulverston, the twins and Charlie to milk the conformist cows at a farm down the road. He liked the cows. Friendly, tolerant beasts. Soon he looked like Jack and the twins, a Woodbine dangling from his lips, his capless head resting on the cow's side, squirting milk on his grubby palms before working the next udder. The farmer's wife brought them pints of cold tea and sandwiches. Then they would go off to work in the field, spreading manure with a fork, or they would scatter and repair drystone walls. Charlie was astonished to find just how many dry-stone walls there were around Ulverston. He tried to entertain himself with little fantasies, pretending to be a Chinese mason rebuilding the Great Wall, a foot soldier of Hadrian piling stone on stone, but in the end the monotony proved unconquerable.

At night, they trudged back to the hall, where they stripped off their soiled clothes and washed themselves as briskly and untenderly as they had washed the cows. With icy water instead of warm. How strange to think that water, such a harmless substance, could hurt. Charlie developed a technique of splashing and rubbing that made the process less painful. Their clothes hardened with grime and dried mud: all five of them were useless at laundry. One night Charlie, in a fit of exasperation, threw all his underclothes into an old pot and boiled them on the stove.

Once he tried to liven up the dinner conversation with his impersonation of the Elder of Snotsborough. No one responded, and he had the awkward feeling that the others thought that was in fact how he spoke at home, among his folk, among the peculiar people. In his dreams, he saw Quakers in thick dark coats walking over the moors towards Swarthmoor Hall. Nothing more, just those Quakers in wide-brimmed hats and cloaks walking silently through the storm and rain towards Swarthmoor Hall.

During the day, he thought of George Fox, the very first Quaker, who had roamed these hills and valleys as a wandering preacher, had crossed Morecambe Bay until he reached Swarthmoor Hall and the pious woman who lived there. Charlie tried to picture their early meetings for worship, which would have taken place in the draughty stone hall across the corridor, a gloomy place that made his teeth clatter when he thought about it. He still found it hard to understand why his parents clung to a faith that was so deeply odd, that valued silence and plainness when surely the greatest human accomplishments were speech and art. Yet even if he did not understand it, he began to like it a little more than before.

All this he thought while smashing the ice on a bucket of water; while writing Georgina's initials in the condensation on the kitchen window.

There were moments of beauty, too. Walking over the moors just as the sun began to rise. Watching snowflakes drift past the lattice-work windows. Taking pleasure in the one moment when he felt warm, genuinely warm: crouched on his milking stool, his forehead against the soft flank that rose and fell with the cow's snorting breath, his legs warmed by steaming manure, his hands massaging the warm teats until milk shot into the pail with a satisfying tinkle.

Every night, he heard the scratching, rippling sound of tiny claws scurrying past his ear. He borrowed poison from Georgina and laid it out according to her instructions.

For a night or two, there was silence.

Then they came back. Not two, not three, but dozens, *dozens*, he thought: dozens of rats racing along the rafters, tunnelling through the rotting walls, nesting and mating and ejecting naked pink litters under the floorboards.

Charlie developed a habit of giving his stew or soup a couple of vigorous stirs with his spoon before eating the first mouthful.

'Worried something's drowned in there?' asked Jack.

'Mind your own business.'

They had their meals by the fire, which gave off little heat but was comforting to look at.

'If you as much as touch Georgina,' Jack said one night while they were washing their clothes, 'I'll pin you to the barn door with a pitchfork.'

'Oh dear,' Charlie said, and tossed him the soap, 'that does sound unpleasant.'

'I'm serious.'

'So am I,' said Charlie. He walked around the house, took

a pitchfork from the barn, walked back to the courtyard and planted the pitchfork in the mud, right at Jack's feet.

The punch took him by surprise and knocked him over.

Jack was above him, ready to deliver another punch, but Charlie managed to grab his face with both hands and force him onto his back. They grappled in the mud, rolling into puddles and over crunchy sheets of ice, swearing at each other and rubbing each other's faces into the frozen ground, and then they were laughing but still went on beating each other, until they were exhausted, lay on their backs for a few breaths, then helped each other up.

'I'm going to put the kettle on for a hot bath,' said Jack, and they went to the kitchen, filled a tub with boiling and icy water and took turns bathing and chucking water over each other with tin buckets. Charlie decided that there was nothing more pleasurable in the world than sitting in a metal tub of scalding water with only his head sticking out.

That evening, Georgina tried to inspire Marx to another performance on the kitchen table, but the cold had numbed his revolutionary ardour. All he said was: 'Do you even know what Soviet means, Georgina dear? Do you even know?'

'Coffee, Marxy, darling. It means coffee.'

After dinner, Jack drew up behind Charlie and whispered in his ear: 'You do realize she's slept with all of us, don't you? Me, bonkers Marx, and even that quiet little Engels, who suddenly got rather loud when they were at it. I hope you don't mind.'

'I don't mind at all,' Charlie said loudly. 'It wouldn't make a difference to me if she'd slept with all of Ulverston, which admittedly has a fairly small population, so – I wouldn't mind if she'd slept with all of London. You see, I've freed myself from that sort of petit bourgeois constraint.' And he laughed right into Jack's furious face. A feeling of freedom and carelessness bubbled up in him that he had not experienced since he made love to Rosy, a barmaid, in a rented room in Holborn. He felt as if anything could happen, anything could be said, and he might as well make it happen himself, say it himself.

'Engels,' he shouted in the general direction of the kitchen, 'I hear there are times when you get rather loud?' And then he laughed again and slapped Jack's back.

## 2

Spring came and the frozen well behind Swarthmoor Hall thawed. The nights and early mornings were still cold but around midday they could feel the northern sun. Hard Red Winter, Western White and Northern Spring were the names of the farmer's wheat varieties, but Charlie read them as captions for his life at Swarthmoor.

Jack and the twins showed him the deep pool where the stream widened, just behind a stone bridge: the water was cold but they stripped off their clothes and jumped in, wrestling and dipping each other under the water. Jack was the strongest of the four. He challenged them to handstands, then challenged Charlie to a hand-walking race. Charlie collapsed before they reached the bridge, lay on the wilted grass and watched Jack walk on his hands to the stone bridge and back, stark naked, his cock and balls dangling limply over his toned stomach.

Quiet Engels let Charlie in on his secret, a miniature distillery made from an old pressure cooker and a rubber tube. He kept it in a closet next to the cow shed, concealing both the contraption itself and the ripe, sweet-sour smell of fermentation. Fed with molasses stolen from the farmer during the previous year's silage, the distillery yielded a steady trickle of spirit that they mixed with fruit and poured into the clerks and farmhands of Ulverston, until, through the alchemy of profitable transactions, they succeeded in converting their initial drum of molasses into a pedigree Wessex pig.

A neighbouring farmer showed them how to butcher it: messily, bloodily. Charlie fried the lungs in a cast-iron pan until they whistled. The kidneys went into a pungent pie. They took turns rubbing salt into the bacon and hams once a day. He had some idea that a stew could be made by boiling the feet with some carrots and onions; the leftovers cooled into a salty jelly that they ate with spoons. By the time it was sunny enough for Charlie to lie in the garden and press his cheek against the warm grass, not a bristle remained of the pedigree Wessex pig.

*

When the German bombers whined overhead, they sought shelter by the apple crates below the great hall, and hoped that the bombs would not blow up the house, especially since the cow was still in it.

And it was after one such night, when Charlie was washing himself in the stream, that Georgina chanced upon him. She waded into the water, fully dressed, with her hands over her eyes and said: 'I didn't see anything!'

'And anyway there isn't much to see,' Charlie said, remembering her comment from long ago, which still stung.

She lowered her hands.

'On the contrary, there's a *lot* to see.'

He was so taken aback that he slipped on a slimy rock and crashed into the water. She giggled, scooped up some river mud and flung it at him. He retaliated and his glob of mud hit her on the shoulder. She drew him into a slippery water-fight that left her soaked from her draggly blond hair to her blue utility dress, and then she told him to turn around as she would have to take off her dress and leave it to dry in the unreliable spring sun; and that was how one spring morning Charlie found himself on the riverbank, vigorously fucking the rat girl.

She seemed to know all the abandoned barns in the area, all the secret storage cupboards at Swarthmoor Hall, and Charlie could not help but wonder whether Jack, Marx and Engels knew them, too. She had read *Lady Chatterley*, she confided in Charlie as she guided his head towards her lap. Jack had given her a smuggled copy, and she had developed an irrepressible longing for the pleasures experienced by the heroine.

Charlie did his best to keep up with Georgina's requests for unusual positions, up to the point where, mid-coitus, looking back over her shoulder, she urged him to speak to her 'like a rough northern farm hand, just like a rough northern farm hand.'

She showed him how to lay out rashers of the pig's bacon for the rats: rasher, rasher, no rasher, poisoned rasher. At first they shunned the poisoned rasher. He thought of them sitting in their rat holes and scheming against him with twitching whiskers. They shunned the rasher, but they ate the jellied pig's feet. It was humiliating to be outmanoeuvred by a rodent. Only when Georgina gave him rashers that were just a little bit rotten did the rats finally yield, unable to resist this particular delicacy. They fed it to their young back in the rat hole, and the house went quiet.

Charlie was washing the cow's udder when he heard a rustling sound in the corner. He lifted a wooden crate to find the last remaining family: a rat and her new pink babies nestling in the straw. She was too drowsy or exhausted to move, so he whacked them with a spade, threw the bloody pulp out into the garden and went back in to finish milking the cow.

'I suppose my dream would be ... You may laugh, but my dream's actually very simple.' Charlie was lying between her thighs with his head on her stomach, listening to it rumble.

'My dream would be to get together with some chaps and buy a place just like this one, a bit smaller perhaps, a ramshackle old place where we can grow a few crops and fatten a few pigs and do whatever we please, because that's genuine freedom, isn't it, when you're not employed by anyone. There's real freedom in having your own farm, and I wish people would understand that.'

'Oh,' said Georgina, and played with his choppy, tousled hair. 'Tell me more about the farm.'

And he told her all about the farm. He told her about the old collapsing stone house in a secluded green valley that they would buy for a song, about the chimney breathing smoke over the treetops, about the overgrown fields they would turn into fertile land and meadows, about the pigs the size of cars and sheep so woolly you risked getting lost in them while shearing.

'And ponies,' Georgina said, and fell asleep with her hand on his head.

## 3

In June 1941, the weather was warm enough for them to bathe in the river every day, and Charlie decided it was time to tell the chaps about him and Georgina.

He found Jack in the kitchen with the wireless pressed to his ear.

'Jack . . .'

Jack scowled and motioned at Charlie to go away.

'Pin me to the barn door if you like, but what has to be said, has to be said.' Charlie crossed his arms. 'I love her and she—'

Jack let out a howl of frustration.

'She loves me. What can I say? Pin me to the barn door if you like.'

Jack threw the wireless at Charlie, who ducked just in time. 'You fucking idiot!'

'Well, what has to be said, has to be—'

'Will you shut up? I was trying to listen to the news! Will you shut up and listen?'

'I'm not explaining it well—'

'Shut up! Shut up and give me the wireless. Don't you know? Germany's invaded the Soviet Union. Oh, you broke it! You fucking, fucking idiot!'

Charlie picked up the wireless in panic and shook it, as if that would make it yield more information.

'But that can't be,' he said over and over.

'Listen, you idiot! Germany's invaded the Soviet Union.'

Charlie covered his face with his hands. When he looked up he saw that Marx and Engels had entered the kitchen, and Georgina too, and he realized then that it really had happened, Germany had invaded the Soviet Union, and the war would not be over any time soon. Now it would be a world war, he was suddenly quite sure of that. He shook the wireless once more and it sprung back on and blared into the silent room. An American journalist echoed his thought: 'As it becomes more and more clear that this war is going to be a world war ...'

He looked at the earnest faces of his comrades and knew that this was the last day of the Swarthmoor Hall community. The chaps would all enlist now. They were political conchies, and their political objection had become void. The war was no longer about capitalist and fascist empires fighting each other: it was about helping defend the worker state against the fascist aggressor. And had not Charlie told his friends on his very first day here that he was a political conchie, too? Had he not admired them for their stance and wished he had the courage to object on political rather than religious grounds? In London, Communism had been a game and a pastime to him, a rebellious ideology to fill his big mouth. Yet his friends believed in it so sincerely that they were willing to die for it.

Jack put an arm around his shoulder in silent comradeship and said: 'I'll tell you one thing that's satisfying. That farmer's never going to accuse us of being cowards and shirkers ever again.'

# Swell

The Germans were expected to arrive at 9 p.m. and Grace had no reason to question their punctuality. She drove up to the hospital in the second of ten ambulances and by the time they all jumped off their vehicles into deep brown puddles and splashed up the hospital stairs it was after 8 p.m. already. She feared Greek tardiness might clash with German precision and see them all taken prisoner – Quakers, patients and doctors – but when she pushed open the front door she saw that the reception was empty. They split and Grace ran down a corridor to her left and ripped open the doors as she passed them. The ward was empty. So was the staircase and the floor above.

'They're all gone!' one of the men called over, and they counted their own in the reception area and drove off through rain so thick they could not see the horizon.

The ambulance carrying Lance, who was in charge of the unit, drew up next to her and someone shouted: 'They were behind the hospital. Now they're in the village, huddled in the square, waiting for you to pick them up!'

Bugger. Why on earth had they not made themselves heard? They wrenched the ambulances around with much skidding and splashing and raced into the village. A quarter to nine. Drenched figures in bandages and on crutches hobbled across the small flooded square – 'They thought you were the Germans!' – only some twenty people, thank God, and they squashed into the ambulances and off they went again, pursued by the howl of the air raid. They swerved around the mountaintop and coiled their way down into the valley and then up again across a knife-edge pass with the Stukas behind. Up and down and up and down between the houses below and the enemy above.

'They thought we were soldiers! Serves us right for wearing khaki,' Grace said through the corner of her mouth, and leaned forward to make out the road in the rain. The young doctor who sat next to her nervously checked the sky.

They off-loaded the patients and doctors in a safer town further south and rested for a few hours; drank hot soup. Then they boarded their ambulances again for the second run. There was another hospital beyond the pass and over a bridge, where the patients were waiting to be evacuated. The rain stopped as if to collect its breath and then washed over them with renewed force. When the ambulances had crossed the pass and reached the bridge a British unit stopped them.

'You don't want to cross that one.' A soldier pointed his thumb back over his shoulder at the bridge. 'We're about to blow it up.'

They turned round, hid their vehicles in an olive grove and camped beside a stream. Lance went off to consult with the army in the chaos of a general retreat. They drove towards Athens and stopped by several hospitals to assist with the evacuation. When all communications had broken down they decided to continue to Athens and help where needed along the way. There was a village that had been strafed not more than an hour before they arrived, and either the bombs had been particularly efficient or anyone who was not wounded had fled. Dozens of bleeding men lay scattered in the village square and all the ambulance crews could do was carry them into a small church that stood unscathed, and bandage them up. When they left the village three men tottered after them and pleaded with them in Greek. They were Greek soldiers, fearful and exhausted, and they wanted a lift to the next town. One of them pulled away the tongue of his boot to show Grace the red open sore that was his foot.

She looked at the foot, looked at Lance.

'You said we wouldn't take soldiers.'

He squatted down to inspect the sore. Then he helped the men into his ambulance. He slapped Grace on her back. 'We won't tell the Elders.'

Lance went back up north to join the Australians, but Grace and six others were sent to Athens. They stayed in Kifissia, cool and leafy in the hills above the city, roads lined with jasmine bushes and orange trees. Some of the trees were still in bloom and others bore fruit. When Grace awoke from her first rest there, she closed her eyes again and inhaled the scent of jasmine and orange blossom, allowing herself one deep breath before evacuating the next hospital.

Their own evacuation began in the middle of the night. The scent of jasmine was at its heaviest and Grace thought that if she survived she would always remember that sweet dark smell and return to Greece one day to seek it out. They set out in a train that stopped every time a Stuka came near because the driver would jump out and hide in the bushes, until an RAMC officer climbed into the cabin with a revolver and then the journey went on smoothly to the end of the railway.

They changed into a lorry that tipped them into an olive grove near the beach, hid under the olive trees all day with the Stukas overhead and when night fell they marched down to the beach with RAMC chaps and soldiers and anyone in khaki who could make it. Grace had cut her hair and was taken for a boy in her baggy uniform. That suited her. They waded far into the sea to reach the landing craft that was waiting for them.

Just when she reached the ramp, it went up.

She stood hip-deep in the water with hundreds of soldiers around her and more on the beach: a jumble of Allied soldiers who had turned into frightened men trying to get on a boat. There was one more boat and she waded towards it. Already full. Still the men moved towards it, grabbed the ramp, hoisted themselves up, while the officers shouted at them to keep away.

Then three officers walked to the top of the ramp and drew their revolvers.

Grace spent hours in the hip-deep water. Eventually another boat took her out to the destroyer.

They drew guns against their own men, she thought. They drew guns against their own men. What animals we are.

'Did everyone get out?' she asked a fellow on the deck.

'Everyone?' He stared at her and she bit her tongue.

'I'm sorry. I meant the ambulance services.'

'How would I know?' He spat into the sea but then his voice softened. 'I heard some of your chaps in the north ran into the Germans. I suppose they were taken prisoner.'

Then to Crete and from there to Suez and from Suez to Alex.

There was a rocky outcrop near the *pension* where they stayed in Alexandria. While they waited for reinforcements Grace sometimes used it to go swimming. The others were more interested in ping pong and the wireless, but she did not mind swimming alone.

Rumour had it that the British-American ambulance corps was donating a dozen desert ambulances. Once they arrived in Alexandria Grace's unit would start to work again and carry casualties from ships to hospitals. It was a reduced unit. The Friends left behind in Greece had indeed been taken prisoner.

There would be no time for a ritual swim once work started again: all the more important to savour it now. Around three o'clock was the best time, when the noon heat gave way to a glow. Grace took off her sandals to grip the dry rocks underfoot. Someone had carved a path between the rocks that petered out half-way down to the water. It must have been a project conceived in the coolness of the early morning hours: *today I shall carve a path to the sea.* By ten o'clock, the anonymous mason would have been scorched and desiccated. Time to give the tools a rest and continue tomorrow, only tomorrow never turned into today. He must have been a foreigner, with a foreigner's hunger to improve what he found.

Up on the hill, on the road that led to her *pension*, a man and a donkey were locked in a tug of war. She would show him later how to move a donkey. Certainly not by pulling at the rope.

*Still so bossy, Grace!*

The sea was wild and whipped up by the spring winds, which brought seeds and cloudless skies. It foamed with rage and crashed against the cliffs. Grace had decided to go in, and once she had decided on something she did not like to change her course. She pushed herself off the rocks hard and fast to beat the waves and cut her toe on a barnacle. When she had swum far enough to escape the sucking currents she turned on her back and inspected the wound. It was deep and bleeding. She dipped it back in the water, determined not to let it spoil her swim. The next few years might well be spent rumbling over a dust track with her legs dangling over the back of the ambulance and one hand holding on to the canvas frame. A few days by the sea, ping pong and a rocky outcrop – what were the chances of that happening again?

The waves came high and strong. *Not like the Ladies' Pond, is it?*

When the war was over, she and Max would move to the seaside. Somewhere southern. In the best English tradition, she would be an eccentric lady who rode mules and sailed her own boats like a man. Nut brown and salt-cured. The Englishwoman and her husband in the cottage on the hill. A small hotel, a retreat for Friends and pensioners.

The water was inky blue in the shade, and green and golden where the sunlight hit the waves. Rising and falling with the waves was tiring, and when she tried to swim back to the cliffs the current kept pulling her away. She lunged at a rock and dug her fingers into a crevice. It was a stupid, risky manoeuvre: the next big wave almost dislocated her shoulder. She let it wash over her face and hair and clung to the rock. In the tiny pause between the sea crashing against the stone and sucking back its water in a vicious undertow she hoisted herself up onto the cliff.

This was the most delicious moment of the day: the salt and the short breath and the hammering heartbeat. Of course Max would like it.

It did not take more than fifteen, twenty minutes, her afternoon swim, but it was like starting the day afresh.

The fellow on the hill was still pulling at the donkey. Another tug and he would rip its head off. Poor creature. Grace dried herself, pulled her dress over her damp swimming costume and climbed up to see to the problem.

'Need a hand?'

The man turned round. A round face with a stub nose. You could mistake him for a Boy Scout. The freckles were covered by ferociously red sunburn. He was not as tall as she remembered. Max was far taller.

'Gee, thanks! This donkey is quite a handful.'

Gee. He must have picked that up from his wife. She helped him dislodge the animal with the help of a crust of bread she kept in her bag. They led it to headquarters and unloaded it, and only then did she tell him where they had met before.

'Of course!' He slapped his forehead. 'I knew you looked familiar.' And he laughed and rubbed the back of his neck. 'Swell.'

That, too, he must have learned from his wife.

She paused to give him time for a better and kinder reaction, but apparently he had nothing more to add. So she mentioned quickly that her husband was in London.

He could at least have showed a little disappointment, a hint of sadness at the lost opportunity, their lost opportunity. Instead he expressed sympathy. How hard it must be to be separated. He and his wife were lucky. They both worked for the American Friends and had come to Alexandria to handle the delivery of the twelve desert vans. Next destination,

China. Ambulances for the Burma road. The wear and tear there was terrible. He made an upside-down victory sign.

'That's the Chinese character for man.'

Swell.

That night she went to her room and after writing her daily letter to Max, she picked up her diary and noted the high waves and stormy weather. After a thought, she added: 'M. arrived today (with wife). The Lord moves in mysterious ways!'

She washed the salt off her skin and went to bed. How strange to think that something that had meant so much to her had, in fact, meant nothing at all. Had he come back to London and rushed back into her arms, then their one night on the fire escape would have been deeply significant. But because he merely passed through London on his way to America (with wife), the fire escape meant nothing, his bandit's beard in the morning meant nothing, and the fact that she had lied to him about being a big swimmer meant nothing, nothing at all.

She got up, lit a candle and added a line to her letter to Max: 'Today I learned the Chinese character for man: 人'

The sea was calm at sunrise and she decided on a quick dip in case the wind returned later. Her feet were already in the water when he appeared above her on the cliffs.

'May I join you?'

'Good morning.' She jumped in.

'I know you love to swim. You told me last time we met.'

It had taken him sixteen hours to remember it.

*M. joined me for a swim in the morning (without wife).*

He began unbuttoning his shirt. She stopped him with a wave of her hand.

'The sea can be quite wild, perhaps you should get used to this place first.'

He raised an eyebrow and turned his round red face towards the perfectly still water.

'As you wish. Come in, then.' Curiosity got the better of her. They held on to a protruding cliff and trod water like two old ladies in a thermal bath. He told her about Pennsylvania where, as you would expect from a place founded by Quakers, everything was swell.

'How did you manage to get to America?'

'I went to London with one of the children's trains and stayed behind. Then I caught a passage across. The Friends helped. And my wife.' He could at least have the manners to look a little guilty, she thought. It would only be polite. But his voice was frank and easy and his legs pedalled through the water.

'I heard. And I did wonder about that. You told me you couldn't stay behind, you couldn't stay in London because if you did, they might not let the next train leave.'

'I figured they wouldn't let out another train anyway. And they didn't.'

He was not as handsome as she remembered him. Sunburn never enhanced a person's looks and he was really very young. There was a smug grin on his face whenever he explained something; smugness at his superior knowledge.

It was on his face now as he gripped the cliff tight with one hand to free his other. He made the upside-down victory sign again and said: 'Can you guess what the Chinese character for big is?'

Oh, shut up, she thought.

'We should get out. My toes are all wrinkly and the others must be up by now.'

She scrambled up the cliff and showed him where to put his foot. 'You should bring your wife this afternoon. One last swim before you leave. I don't think we'll see another place like this before the war is over.'

He shook the drops out of his hair. 'She hates water.'

How could someone hate water? She might as well hate air.

Grace wondered how much longer the war would last, and where she and Max would be when it ended.

# Of Love and Other Wars

# 1

'It will kill Mother, of course,' Paul said.

Charlie said nothing.

'And Father.' Paul looked at his dry, chapped hands.

'Is there anything you would like to tell me other than that I'm going to turn us into orphans?'

'Think about it. Please.'

Charlie stood up. 'Look at me. Don't you think I've thought about it?' He lifted his blue-grey cap and put it back down on his head. He tugged at the collar of his blue-grey uniform. 'What do you think I'm wearing? This is the uniform our boys wore when they defended the sky over London and it's the uniform I'll be wearing one day when I defend the sky over Moscow and any other decent place where decent people live. This is the uniform some of our boys died in.' He grew loud. 'Chaps like you and me, Paul. But we didn't die, did we? We weren't up there. And you know why? Because we were sitting snugly in Highgate Meeting House and praising the Lord for keeping it safe and peaceful in there.'

'We weren't in Meeting House last summer,' Paul said quietly. 'You were at Swarthmoor Hall. I was in gaol.'

They sat at the back of a deserted pub. The landlord was polishing glasses with a stained old tea towel and now and then threw them a suspicious glance.

Charlie walked up to the counter and returned with a beer and a lemonade.

'I'd have preferred a pint,' Paul said, and took the lemonade. He rolled the glass between his hands. 'Look.' He put down the glass and fumbled around in his pockets. 'There's something I'd like you to consider.'

The card had softened around the edges, with small tears and dog-eared corners and a jagged boyish ink scrawl along the bottom. He drew it from his shirt pocket and put it on the table.

'Remember this?'

But Charlie was not looking at the card. He was looking over Paul's shoulder.

'It's our pledge card,' Paul said.

A hand pressed down on his shoulder.

'Pledge?' Miriam's voice was a little faded, a little tired. 'What pledge?'

She leaned over the table, picked up the card and read out: '"I renounce war, and never again, directly or indirectly, will I sanction or support another."'

With a curious expression on her face, she sighed and put it back on the table. There it lay like a leper's handkerchief.

It was like any old London pub. Dark wood panelling, a dulled brass rail around the counter, green tartan carpets. Windows latticed with blast-proof tape. And that made it all the more terrible, Paul thought: the fact that the props and backdrops that filled the stage of his life were like any old props and backdrops; and the stage itself was like three apple crates pushed together in the basement of a pub.

He had mumbled and shuffled at his tribunal as he had mumbled and shuffled a thousand times before, and he had sat at sticky stained wooden tables like this one a thousand times before. It was all so ordinary; the script, the lines, the props were perfectly ordinary. Yet the great screeching world insisted that he himself was different, was an outcast; not a brilliant and glamorous outcast, not a dashing bandit or revolutionary, but an odd little person whose wooden model must be feathered, whose mumbling must be ridiculed, and whose earnestly signed pledge card must be studied with pity and mild contempt.

Miriam was still standing next to the table. She hesitated, looked left and right, and eventually sat down next to Charlie, facing Paul.

'Paul.' Charlie spoke in a deep, fatherly tone, as to a child. 'Here are the facts. I've joined the RAF and expect to be shipped out to a training base next week. I would like you to come with me to Highgate and be there when I tell them.

That's all I'm asking of you. I'm not asking you to cheer me on, or pray for me, or advise me, or talk me out of it. I'm only asking you to be there when I tell them.'

Paul slid his hand across the table and placed it on the card.

'But you've got a card just like this one.'

'Somewhere between my old schoolbooks and those letters from my German pen friend. Probably, yes.'

'And you signed it. We signed it together. We said we wouldn't fight. You kept the card, you've said so yourself, and it's as valid as ever. It doesn't apply to a hypothetical war, it applies to *every* war. It applies to *this* war. If it was wrong to kill twenty years ago, then it can't be right to kill now. I knew this war would be a great test, and there are many reasons why men choose to break the pledge. But I, I cannot break that pledge. Our father and grandfathers and all the men in our family have honoured *their* pledge, they've all honoured the peace testimony, and every single one of them must have had a niggling doubt as to whether their particular war was different, whether their particular war was worth betraying the testimony for. But it wasn't, was it? The last war wasn't worth it, and none of the previous wars were worth it. What we're hearing now is the great noise of the war machine, but once it's fallen silent, once the guns have fallen silent, well, then we'll speak again. And we may find that when all is said and done, refusing to kill was not a bad choice after all.'

Paul leaned back, exhausted. Charlie and Miriam

exchanged tired glances. The pub landlord was still polishing the same pint glass.

And even though nothing had changed since Paul entered the pub, everything had changed. He had sat down at the table and waited for Charlie and Miriam: three accomplices united under the landlord's suspicious glare.

Paul stared at his pledge card that lay there like a leper's handkerchief.

Yes, there were three accomplices in the pub. But now it occurred to Paul that he was not one of them.

Miriam stood up. Just before straightening her back she hesitated and put one hand on her stomach in that dramatic way of hers, as if she felt physically upset by the argument. The same heightened emotion that he had once found so appealing now annoyed him.

'Go on then,' she said wearily. 'Go on covering your ears and debating it all in your own head and inventing a world of your own, while in the real world, my people are being murdered. What is it your brilliant Mr Gandhi wrote in that pamphlet of yours? "If I were a Jew ... I would claim Germany as my home even as the tallest gentile German may, and challenge him to shoot me or cast me in the dungeon." Well, that says it all. You and Mr Gandhi, you don't want to listen and you don't want to see.'

'I thought we'd agreed not to talk about all that,' Paul said.

'Well, we can try to ignore the world, but that doesn't mean the world will ignore us. And I'm not sure I *want* to ignore it. I grew up with three of my uncles in their uniforms looking down at me from the mantelpiece. There'd be no room for them on your mantelpiece, I suppose.'

'We could find pictures of them in civilian clothes.'

'And hide the military ones as if they were something shameful. Well, they're not shameful to me. When I have a mantelpiece I'm going to display all three of them because I'm proud of everything my family's done for this country. I'm proud to think that when the time came, our men always did their bit.'

She turned round and walked towards the door. Her slightly stooped back was covered in a shapeless wool coat. A faint smell of machine oil trailed her and mingled with the smoky air.

When she reached the door, she put her hand on the brass knob and paused. Charlie stared at Paul. Even the landlord stared at Paul. But Paul did not get up to hold her back, and she turned the brass knob and walked out.

When the door swung shut behind her, Charlie reached out and swiped their half-full glasses off the table.

'You bloody fool.' He grabbed Paul's pledge card. 'Look at you, with your martyr's face, with your self-pity, with your bloody steadfastness. Steadfastness! You'd rather let her walk away than concede an inch of ground. Oh, and I know what you're thinking. Martyrdom! A test of your sodding conscience! That's what you're thinking. You're looking at my uniform and her munitions job and you're feeling damn smug, aren't you, with your little pledge card and your little testimony and your pristine little Quaker brain? Well, I won't let you take the moral high ground here. We signed this when we were *boys*. And you think I ought to feel bound by it? You think I ought to pretend to be the Elder of Snotsborough for the rest of my life?'

He ripped up the card and flung it on the floor. 'You think this is a pledge? Well it isn't, Paul. It's just a postcard.'

## 2

By the time Paul and Charlie reached the little cottage in Highgate, Charlie was very calm. He wore his full Royal Air Force uniform. Curtains shuffled in the neighbouring houses and old Mr Boddington stood outside the grocery, next to his cabbages, grinning with satisfaction. The brothers ignored him.

'Shall I knock or do you ...?' Paul mumbled. Charlie simply stepped past him and knocked on the door.

Their father opened it. His face showed no surprise: perhaps he had been steeling himself for this.

'Charles.'

'Did you receive my letter?'

'Yes.'

'I'm not here to argue.'

'No one here has the slightest intention of arguing.' Their father's voice was as hoarse, as if he had been screaming all day.

'What I mean is, I've made up my mind.'

Their father looked over Charlie's uniform. 'I can see that.'

'Good.'

For a moment Paul thought it might all turn out acceptably well, that they might have one last cup of tea together. Then Charlie tried to walk through the door and their father blocked his way.

'I'm sorry, Charles,' he said. 'No man in uniform has ever stepped past this threshold and I would like it to remain that way.'

'I haven't come to stay. I've only come to see you and Mother before I head out.'

'You'll have to see us here, outside the door.'

'Like a dog.'

'Like someone who's unwilling to accept the rules of the house.'

'What about compassion?' Charlie's voice trembled. 'What about loving thy neighbour?'

'I do love my neighbour,' their father said in that strange hoarse voice.

'If you say so.'

'Oh, I love my neighbour. I love my neighbour even though he thinks I'm a spy. I love my neighbour even though he's put a brick through the window of my soap shop and called me a traitor. I love my neighbour even though he'd rather travel across town to a shop with a Union Jack out front than touch any of my soap. Yes, I love my neighbour who's given me white feathers and hounded me and almost driven me to bankruptcy, and stolen my son and put him in a uniform. I love my neighbour. But that doesn't mean I must allow him to take everything from me. My neighbour can have my food, my house, my business. But he cannot take away my faith. I can't allow that. And I love my sons, but I cannot let them take away my faith. This is a house of peace in a country at war and no man in uniform shall ever step over its threshold.'

In the dimly lit hallway, Paul saw their mother wringing her apron with both hands. Her face was very lined and grey and she closed her eyes and opened them again as if hoping that it was all an awful vision, that her husband would relent, her son become contrite.

Charlie lowered his voice. 'I want to say goodbye to Mother.'

Their mother stirred, but Charlie held up his hand. 'Not out here. I want to say goodbye to my mother in my childhood home. Father, surely you'll grant me that.'

Their father crossed his arms. 'You were the one who put on the uniform, Charles. It was not my choice. It was your choice.'

'Fine.' With deliberate, slow movements, Charlie took off his cap, unbuttoned the blue uniform jacket and slipped it off. He stepped out of his trousers, his shirt, his shoes and socks until he stood by the rubbish bins outside their door wearing nothing but a pair of grey briefs and a ribbed undershirt.

He pushed past their father, gave their mother a long hug and whispered in her ear.

Then he went out again, put on his uniform, and without another word to their father, left.

At the street corner, Paul stopped Charlie.

'I've been offered a place with an ambulance unit.'

'Well done. I'll be relying on you to patch me up then.'

'If you're very unlucky.' Paul opened his bag and took out a brown envelope sealed with tape. 'Since you ripped up my pledge card, I suppose you've thrown away your own card too. So I thought I'd give you this. You don't have to open it now, or indeed at all. It's just something Father gave to me, and I think you should have it. Think of it as a lucky charm.'

# The Triangle

When Max was seized by two uniformed men in a train station in northern Germany, he expected to be shot on the spot. The others in his intelligence unit had probably also been arrested, pulled out of flats and offices all over Europe, but they were Brits and at least had some protection as prisoners of war. He, however, was once again a German citizen, and as such, a traitor.

It doesn't matter which way I look, he thought: whether it's east or west, whether my heart is on this side or on that, my feet are always in the wrong place.

They did not shoot him. They took him to a camp. Behind barbed wire, once again; only this time there would be no university and no parliament. It occurred to him that this was what had happened to his mother, but the thought was too painful and he forced it into a deep trunk at the back of his mind and bolted down the lid.

On this first day, he thought he might survive. Then he noticed that everyone else was avoiding him. All the other inmates were avoiding him, even the weak and starving ones. What was it, he wondered. He wore the same clothes as everyone else, his head had been shaved like everyone's. What was it that marked him out as different?

In the queue for watery soup the others left a gap between them and him. Someone trod on his foot when the guard was looking: as if every inmate wanted to prove he was not his friend.

But what is it? Max thought, cowering under the glare of the guards, the glances of fear and pity from the other inmates. What is it that's different about me?

When he carried his full bowl along the queue, an inmate walking past him stopped and said: 'You don't know about your triangle, do you?'

No, Max replied, fearful that the guard would see them. What is it?

'The yellow triangle on your back. It marks you for death. At the next opportunity, they're going to get rid of you.' The inmate shrugged and walked on.

Max tried to look back over his shoulder, but it was impossible. No one can see his own back, he thought; no, no one can see his own back. I'll have to take this fellow's word for it.

Max had a shameful thought. It made him feel dirty every time his mind turned to it, yet he could not push it away. Soon it obsessively spun in his skull.

He might get them to remove the yellow triangle, he thought, if he told them about his father.

They would not release him, of course. But they might remove the triangle if he told them that while his mother was Jewish, by the race laws, if not by faith, his father was not. His father was an extensively certified, documented, proven Aryan (and how his father had painstakingly gathered those documents, hoarding them in his dark study like a ghoul). A physicist in Berlin, neither famous nor exceptionally brilliant, but respected within his circles. One whose career had dipped in 1933, but risen steadily after he divorced his Jewish wife and abandoned his half-Jewish son in 1935. Thanks to Mrs Morningstar's scientific journals, Max could recite a whole list of recent prizes and achievements.

In England, nobody but Grace knew this. Mrs Morningstar must have her theories, but she kept them to herself. He had even once overheard her telling someone that Max was the son of a distant cousin and that his father had died of a severe cold; and he had never felt more in awe of this neat practical woman who could lie as convincingly as any spy.

When he had first arrived in London with a note from his mother, he had assumed the Morningstars would eventually betray him. For a long time he could not shed this fear, and he kept a packed suitcase under his bed and another in his office.

He ought to have confided in Mrs Morningstar and told her everything. How his father had been the first to agitate against Jewish scientists, lest anyone suspect him of old loyalties to his discarded wife and son. How his father had time

300

and again proven himself as an ardent, dedicated party member, and yet succeeded in retaining the trust of old friends who thought that this was all for show, that he was a decent person underneath it all.

As young men, his father and Gottfried von der Weide had spent a summer selling shoes in Passau to save up for their studies. It was one of his father's favourite anecdotes. For a long time, he enjoyed telling his students that they both still knew how to measure a lady's foot. Of course it was also he who invited Gottfried to stay at his home when the faculty hounded him out for his opposition to the regime; and it was he who went to the authorities with recordings and neat transcripts of their confidential conversations.

If Max had told all this to Mrs Morningstar, she would not have destroyed the medal.

But why was he even letting that painful thought in? It was no use to him here.

The reason why he finally decided not to tell the guards was neither pride, nor loyalty to his mother, nor shame about his father's betrayal.

Whenever he pictured their faces as they picked up the receiver to ring Professor Hoffnung at his study in Berlin, he saw a mocking expression that quickly turned contemptuous: *Certainly, Herr Professor, we are sorry about the disturbance, Herr Professor*; for their enquiries would in all likelihood be met by stern denial, surprise that they would fall for such an easy fraud on the mere basis of a shared surname, and annoyed reassurance that he did not have a son, and certainly not one who was a prisoner.

Outside the showers was a pile of jackets.

'Theirs,' said one of the men, and pointed at a high smoking chimney to their right.

Another man in their line began to sway and weave from side to side like a drunkard. After two, three stumbling steps, he collapsed. There was a brief moment of disorder. The guards shouted, the procession paused. Max grabbed one of the jackets on the pile and shoved it under his own jacket with the triangle.

In the evening, in his bunk, he took off his old jacket and slipped on the new one.

He hoped the jacket had belonged to a dead man, not to a fellow inmate who would have to face his guards without a jacket.

Shivering on the wooden planks, he waited for dawn.

# PART THREE

## 1945
## When All London Sparkles
## with Illuminations

# Life Drawing

The young woman on the top floor mentioned her husband far too often, and her ring was a cheap thing she must have bought from a tinker. Before the war, Mrs Kosinsky would not have let the room to her, but these days the choice was between fallen women and prostitutes, and the former tended to have fewer visitors.

On the whole, the landlady had not much to reproach her for. There were occasional visits from a 'cousin'. She always left the little boy with a friend during these visits, and Mrs Kosinsky did not like what this implied. However, on most evenings her tenant was alone with the boy and sketched him on rough packing paper. The sketches covered the walls of their room and had begun to creep out into the corridor. Mrs Kosinsky decided she would wait until the New Year before pruning the excess. She blew her nose in her apron.

Her tenant cried breathlessly from the top of the stairs: 'Mrs Kosinsky! I couldn't ask you to look after him today, could I? I've got to go to the factory later.'

Shouting from the top of the stairs was against the house rules, but before the landlady could point this out, little Nathan emerged on the landing. He turned round, gripped the wooden baluster with both hands and lowered himself onto the next step. When his mother tried to pick him up, he swatted at her hands and returned to his task with frowning concentration.

Mrs Kosinsky's heart melted even before he completed his laborious descent and raised his fat little arms. She sat him on her hip, anchored him in the crook of her elbow and blew her nose in her apron again with her free arm.

'This morning they said the war was as good as over. Time for your husband to come home, I suppose?'

Her guest threw her head back and laughed too loudly. It was a nervous tic, this shouting and laughing: Mrs Kosinsky had noticed that the more nervous and agitated she was, the louder she became.

'He'd better!'

She picked up her bag and left, but seconds later she was back and pressed one last kiss on the boy's silky curls. She left again and came back once more, and by that time both she and Mrs Kosinsky were laughing at her infatuation, and Nathan gurgled happily because he thought it was all a game and that his mother wasn't really leaving for the night at all.

'I can't help it!' She shook her head, still laughing. 'I had such a wonderful dream last night, and it's left me in a very silly mood all day.'

Mrs Kosinsky liked hearing about dreams, especially when they were mystical, and was disappointed when it turned out to be a fairly ordinary one of a blue sky filled with white balloons.

'Barrage balloons?'

'No, not at all! They were simply white balloons. One of them popped and everyone thought it would crash to the ground, but it continued to float and that was a wonderful feeling, to watch that popped balloon float. I woke up feeling like a balloon myself, and if Nathan hadn't been there tugging at my hand, I might have floated away. And then, well, then something in my head sort of popped, too. Something I'd been thinking of for a long time suddenly made sense, and I knew exactly what I would do. I'm talking nonsense now, aren't I? It's like a cake that's barely set and needs to cook a bit longer, but when it stops quivering and the needle comes out clean I'll tell you all about it.'

Mrs Kosinsky smiled mischievously. 'Is it something to do with your cousin, perhaps?'

She threw her head back again. 'No, Mrs Kosinsky, but I'm very glad to see you're keeping an eye on me.'

The last sentence was uttered in a mocking tone Mrs Kosinsky knew and disliked, but she decided to forgive the peculiar Mrs Lamb for it.

She had been instructed to tuck the boy into bed upstairs and check on him only if she heard a noise. But Mrs Kosinsky had raised five children in a single room and did not believe in letting little ones sleep out of sight. She made a nest for herself on the floor and put her darling boy into her bed. If Mrs Lamb was going to tell her off in the morning, so be it.

In the middle of the night, she heard her bedroom door open a crack. She pretended to be asleep. Mrs Lamb peered in and gazed at her sleeping child for a long time. Then she slowly closed the door.

Mrs Kosinsky woke only once more that night. Her first, sleepily confused thought was that Mrs Lamb had kicked down the wall to fetch her son. The cold night air swept in through where the bedroom wall had been. Cursing and tripping over her long cotton nightgown, the landlady gathered up the bawling boy in her arms and ran to where the stairs used to be.

# Hardness Ten

'This paper is dedicated to my father, my brothers, and
all future generations of diamond-cutters in our family.'
*A Theory of Diamond-Cutting*

Esther Morningstar left Hatton Garden during one war and
returned during another. The street had been destroyed but
her parents still refused to move. They were frail and nervous,
and Esther and her husband had agreed to live with them for
a bit. Once again they were huddling together in their grief.
Once again all reflecting surfaces were covered.

The vast kitchen where Esther had stood on a lump of
coal had shrunk to a damp dark cubbyhole. Ten people used
to sit around that kitchen table and pray and eat and argue
and celebrate. The table was still there but these days no quick
little fingers folded tissue and paper envelopes for diamonds.
Nor did any soot-cheeked boys look up from their grinder
and dust with big bright eyes and cry: 'Is it fine enough,
Mother? Can I go out and play now? Surely it's fine enough?'

Outside, the grimy fog-shrouded café where merchants had tipped little mounds of diamonds onto the table and haggled and closed the deal with a 'Mazel und Broche' was gone. There was now a Diamond Club and a Diamond Bourse where her brothers had once dreamed of spending their days.

For there had been one single week when the lives of all ten people around the table were not silver, not golden, but blue-white like the most expensive stones.

Esther Adler had been offered a place at the Wizard's lab. The Wizard! Her own mother had heard of him, and she could not even read.

Nathan had recently married the daughter of an Antwerp diamond merchant and both Simon and Solly were engaged to daughters of equally good families. And her sisters were either about to be nicely settled or enjoyed picking their way through dozens of freshly delivered young men. They owed this great fortune to the war, which brought trainloads of refugees from Antwerp. Some of them wore their entire stock in leather wallets around their waists and in the great upheaval that ensued there were rich rewards for the bold.

Esther's father had spent a lifetime wishing he could shut the filthy attic for good, put on a pair of gloves and wander off to a café to trade diamonds. But how could a diamond cutter with eight children put aside enough money to buy even a couple of rough stones? They tried, but every time they had saved a little, one of the children fell ill or there was a dearth of jobs and the scaife stood still and they had to use their savings to buy food.

Then the war brought those merchants from Antwerp with their unmarried daughters and sons. At home they would never have looked at the children of a cutter, but here things were different!

Here the Adler children were real young Englishmen and Englishwomen who knew about fog and tea-drinking.

Here the Antwerp merchants told everyone who would listen about the glorious mansions and silver platters and mahogany desks they had left behind, but the Antwerp street vendors, beggars and shlemiels told everybody *exactly the same*! And when nobody listened, the Antwerp lot grabbed old Adler and his friends by their lapels, collars, beards and told them about the mahogany desks, and the London lot would shake themselves free and swear: 'Ach! Not that tale of the mahogany desk again!'

For in that foreign land, all refugees were the same. But a young English Jew like Nathan, fluent in the languages of all the diamond bourses of the world, who had handled so many stones that he hardly needed his loupe to tell good from bad: now there was a match.

Three quick merchants pledged their daughters to the Adler boys. The dowries were a splinter of what they would have been in Antwerp, but still enough to set the young couples up with a little capital, enough to give them a start in the trade.

Those blue-white days. Esther Morningstar sat down at the large empty table. Her husband was asleep and her father was asleep and her mother was asleep.

She touched the corner of the table where Nathan had sat with his young bride. It had been Rosh Hashanah and if the girl was disappointed by what must have been a modest meal compared to the luxurious feasts of Antwerp, she did not show it. Or she did show it and Esther had polished away any hint of discord that could have stained the memory. All she remembered was the taste of apples and honeycake and her father's sweet expectation of three fine young sons at the Diamond Club. Not one of them would have to take over the old attic. Not one of them. Esther had been the wonder girl but this, really, was her father's greatest achievement. A maths award that came with a student's bursary, that was all well and good, but three sons at the Diamond Bourse! Now that was something.

Nathan had sat by the corner. Simon had sat by the window. Solly had sat where Esther was sitting now. Nathan's young bride had tasted the honeycake and said with a little pout, *at home we used to add a whole jar of preserved ginger*.

Now why did Esther have to remember that! The way the girl had wrinkled her nose. And Esther's mother, who had never in her life tasted preserved ginger, was not entirely sure whether to take it as an insult.

It would have been irrelevant, that tiny complaint about the lack of sophistication in her family. The years would have passed, Nathan would have grown wealthy and bought his parents a new house and new clothes. His wife would have grated his modest background into his morning porridge and over his luncheon sandwiches and into his evening stew, but Nathan was Nathan, he would have laughed it off.

'... and if I hadn't married you I could have married the son of the richest man in Antwerp ...' the wife would have said and wrinkled her nose.

And Nathan would have laughed and run his long fingers through his beautiful thick hair and said: 'If I hadn't married you I would have forged emeralds for a living and I'd be rich anyway! But thanks for the dowry.'

If the wife nagged too much he would have gone off and had a wonderful affair with an actress. The entire Adler family would have been sent free tickets to the theatre and feasted on honeycake with ginger every day of the year. They would have come to Esther's inaugural lecture wrapped in fur coats and with a diamond on every finger, a whole row of sparkling and twinkling Adlers.

Esther Morningstar laid her cheek on the rough wooden surface of the kitchen table.

There was hardness three that was the hardness of a copper penny, and hardness five, which was the hardness of a steel knife, and then there was hardness ten, the hardest thing in the world, and that was a diamond.

Nathan and Simon and Solly went to war and three telegrams came back. Their parents would have sat at this table and read them, but Esther could not remember that.

All three had gone as soon as they could because they were like that. They were not the kind of family to wait around until they were dragged away from their dinner by the hair. She could see it in Miriam: the way she had flitted about and been ready to jump into any passing fighter plane.

*'Don't forget my souvenir!'* Was that herself, Esther, that young woman with the heavy braided hair who cupped her hands around her mouth and shouted after Nathan? All the sisters lined up in the doorway for the great farewell but none of them was as proud as Esther. Such an intelligent young woman, such a fine mind who thought that working for the Wizard was the height of human existence and that going to war must be jolly good fun. 'Don't forget my souvenir!' And to the other two, Simon and Solly: 'Remember to write!'

Oh, if only she'd never returned to Hatton Garden. Memories were spiderwebs wafting in the doorway. She had come home and walked right into them and now there was no disentangling herself.

Remember to write, she had said, as if they were Boy Scouts.

And was that really her, the sensible young crystallographer, who boasted to her friends and showed them photographs of her handsome brothers in uniform?

Esther closed her eyes and reached under the table. Her fingertips found the grooves where Nathan had scratched a tally into the wood with his pocket-knife. She counted four notches and one across, and then another three. Eight. Eight what? Nathan, what did you tally up with your pocket-knife under the table, and were you pleased with the count? She had a clear memory of spying on him, a grimly concentrated boy who crouched under the table with his face close to the wood and a knife in his hand.

She saw the same fire in Miriam the day war was declared, when she came home from her air-raid precautions round with flushed cheeks, and had she been a boy she would have signed up right away.

My darling girl, Esther thought. If you had been a boy I would have given you the names of all three of my brothers, but how glad I was that you were a girl. In my family a baby girl was never a cause for celebration, but oh, how I celebrated you, how I cried with relief.

And of all my many mistakes, that turned out to be the worst: because you were a girl, I thought I would have to worry about your suitors and your prospects, but not about the war. For if you had been a boy, I would rather have mutilated you than let you go to war. I would have starved you or slashed you the way some mothers did when the recruiters for the Tsar's army came through the old country, which was what my own mother should have done too.

What a brutal and strange idea! It came all the way from a brutal and strange continent and it did not at all fit into this cosy kitchen in London. Thank goodness no one could read Mrs Morningstar's thoughts as she sat there with her cheek on the wooden table.

# Boys, Girls and Soldiers

Grace was trying to light a cigarette when her detachment came under fire. The cigarette fell out of her hand and rolled along the road into a bomb crater. With the next crack of a mortar, she ducked into an abandoned house. Paul followed her.

It would be another long night. The Germans had left their tanks and were hiding in a thatched farmhouse on the far side of a field. There was nothing for her unit to do but wait until there was a lull in the fighting and they could tend to the wounded.

She sat against the wall and pushed all ten fingers hard into the skin on her forehead. Very slowly she drew them across her eyebrows towards her ears. It was a trick she had developed over the years. Somehow it concentrated all the sensations in her body into that one movement. It helped her suppress all those other urges, especially the one to jump to her feet and run.

Paul had his own trick. He interlaced his fingers and

squeezed them hard. Sometimes she wondered whether he was praying, but she never quite dared to ask. It was one of the things they never talked about. Like the fact that he carried a knife – for self-defence he said – and she did not. Like the fact that she had not heard from Max in years, had not the slightest proof that he might be alive, and yet looked for him in every godforsaken village they passed, in every convoy of refugees, in every hole and ditch.

The fighting went on for an hour or so. When it stopped, she peered through the window into the darkness. To the right was the farmhouse, silent and still in the distance. To the left was the road with the empty German tanks.

Somewhere far away, a wounded soldier was screaming for help.

She strained to make out the words. They sounded German. A muffled, pained appeal.

She listened harder. Not all that far away, perhaps. Strangely muffled, but closer than she had thought.

Far too close to come from the farmhouse.

She looked at the tanks again.

That was it: some poor devil had been left in there. Or perhaps he had been hit while running away from his tank, and crawled back into it for shelter. Either way, he was in there.

She tiptoed over to Paul, who was pressing his interlaced fingers from red to white to red again. The screaming became louder, delirious: '*Hilfe* . . .'

'There's a chap trapped in one of the tanks,' she whispered.

Paul shook his head. 'Can't do anything now. They might start firing again at any moment.' Squeeze.

'They've left the farmhouse. It's completely dead there.'

'Might be a trap. Let's wait until the morning.'

'Can't you hear him screaming?'

'How could I not?' Paul got to his feet and rubbed his face. 'I've been listening to him all bloody night. Jesus.'

Grace decided to go out and find their section leader. Some of their own might be wounded, too. Just then, the mortar fire returned. It boomed overhead and all around. She sat on the floor next to Paul and took his hand.

Between the shots, they could hear the German in the tank. She had been in the ambulance service for four years, and she had never heard anything so pitiful. The voice was high and frightened, a mere child's voice. And that ceaseless calling: '*Hilfe . . .*'

It was as if dawn would never come, as if they would be shut for ever in this darkness with the battle noise and that lonely boy's despair. Like Max: like Max calling for her in the dark.

Four knuckles pressed into her forehead. She must not think of Max. Yet she could think of nothing but Max. She heard him in the voice of every single refugee begging for bread. She saw him in the face of every freed prisoner, of every torn-up man in a ditch.

Now she heard him in the cries of that boy soldier. Max calling for her. She would give her own eyes to make it stop. Better to be dead than . . . but he *must* be alive. She would be turning a corner any day now and there he would be, in a camp with an open gate, in a cell with an unlocked door. He was there now, waiting for her, calling for her.

The gunfire stopped again. A pause, first, then a hopeful silence beyond a pause. Paul pulled his hand from her grip.

'I'm going out there,' he whispered. 'You stay here. Keep your eyes on that farmhouse.'

From the shattered window she saw him creep towards the road. No sound from the farmhouse. He straightened up and quickly glanced around. Then he climbed up the first destroyed tank and looked inside. His hand briefly covered his face and he climbed back down. She lost him for a moment, then spotted him coming up from behind the second tank. He paused. The screaming turned into a low moan, then rose again: *'Hilfe . . .'*

She listened out for any movements on the farm. Nothing. Nothing from their own side, either. No sound at all, except for that moan, muffled but persistent. When she looked back at the tank, Paul was half-way through the hole with only his head sticking out; and then he was completely gone.

She checked her watch. Half an hour until dawn. They should have asked their section leader. What were they thinking, climbing into German tanks like that, acting without an order?

Perhaps she should creep over and urge Paul to come back. But she could not leave her position by the window. She checked her watch again. Ten minutes already. How would he even get the chap out of the tank?

And then, all of a sudden, the wailing stopped.

Paul's head appeared above the hole.

Then his shoulders.

Finally his legs.

He ran back towards her without even looking around, desperately wiping his hands on his uniform as he ran.

When he came in, she put her hand on his shoulder but he shook it off.

'Water.'

She handed him her drinking bottle. He poured the water over his hands and wiped them on his uniform again. In the milky light of the new day, his face was cold and pale, his eyes locked into a numb stare.

He blinked, turned towards her and put down the water bottle. Several times he opened his mouth to say something, but in the end he simply looked at his bloody hands.

# Three Ships

They would all be freed. They would all be shot on the spot. Dragged out to sea. Left to starve.

'Handed over to the Swedes,' whispered Max's friend, Pivnik, a Silesian cobbler.

'Handed over to the fishes,' replied Max before a guard ordered him to shut up.

Max resisted rumours, even though the last one was tempting. When the guards had taken them to the bay, he had seen several Red Cross workers handing out parcels. Some of the younger men still gained great hope from the sight of that red cross. Max and Pivnik, however, did not expect anything from the nurses. Certainly not rescue, certainly not liberation.

They would all be freed, shot on the spot, shipped off to Sweden. Each rumour was as credible and ludicrous as the next. The war was almost over, that he could see from the frantic nervousness of the guards. But what this meant for him, he could not tell.

Max had learned not to speculate. In order to survive until the war was over, he needed to survive this night. In order to survive this night, he needed to survive this afternoon. In order to survive this afternoon, he needed to survive this minute. At this minute he was being herded onto a freighter. Surviving this minute meant not resisting orders.

The deck was piled high with goods under a tarpaulin. Below, two holds with floors made of metal plates were only slowly filling with cargo. The lower hold was fully loaded by the time Max and Pivnik were taken to the upper hold, where there were a few hundred, perhaps a thousand men.

They found a space near the metal steps that led to the deck. The floor was so cold that Max thought he could hear his shivering bones rattle against the metal plates.

'Good night, my friend,' said Pivnik, and closed his eyes.

'Good night.' Max folded his hands. The rabbis on the Isle of Man had taught him to pray in a group of standing men. But now he prayed the way he used to pray as a child at bedtime, lying on his back, alone in the dark, his hands folded over his chest. *Oh Lord, you freed me of the yellow triangle. You found me a place in Pivnik's workshop in the camp where I survived the years. You led me onto this ship. Do not abandon me now.*

During the night, the ship echoed with sighs and groans. Typhus spread with every sigh.

By dawn, the space between Max and the metal steps was stacked high with corpses. The metal floor had chilled further overnight. With clattering teeth, Max crawled on top of two corpses next to him.

They were still a little warm. Warm enough to shield Max and Pivnik from the icy metal. Not warm enough to fool the lice. Slow and heavy with blood, the lice abandoned the corpses and moved onto the live flesh that breathed on top of them.

Max and Pivnik stirred in their sleep. They brushed the drowsy lice from their stomachs by the handful.

Pivnik the Silesian cobbler died on the third morning.

Farewell, my friend, Max thought. Farewell, my dear friend.

*Oh Lord, you have . . . do not abandon . . .*

His mouth was very dry.

*Oh Lord, you took Pivnik.*

And already he saw Pivnik's lice crawl out from below his collar, along his scrawny neck and infected ear, and towards himself.

*Oh Lord, you took my friend Pivnik.*

There was a crust of bread in Pivnik's trouser pocket. Max touched it. Withdrew his hand. Touched it again. Soon the eyes around him would also spot it. He snatched the crust of bread and stuffed it into his own pocket.

He licked his salty lips.

A light appeared at the top of the metal steps. More prisoners were pushed down into the hold. Two young boys huddled behind the steps next to Max and Pivnik's body. They were withered like little old men, everything shrunk except their huge hungry eyes. Too small and withered to steal his bread. He took the crust from his pocket and furtively began to chew one corner. His mistrustful eyes flickered over to the boys. Their hungry stares were fixed on his jaw, and he chewed more quickly, swallowing the second half in great wolfish bites that rasped down his throat.

The younger boy began to cry. The older boy put his arms around him and said something in Polish.

The boat rolled slowly from side to side, and Max fell asleep again.

He woke because someone trod on his feet. People were running up the metal steps. Someone shouted that the ships in the bay were on fire. The guards had left – the ships were on fire – the guards had left, and they were free.

The boys – brothers, probably – were still there, sleeping. He woke them up and pointed up at the open square of sky.

The steps stopped just below the deck. From the top rung he had to reach up, grip an iron railing and hoist himself through the hole. He felt too weak, but one last push brought him over the edge.

When he looked back, he saw the boys. The younger boy kept slumping over while his brother tried to push him up the steps. Max reached down and hooked his hands under the boy's shoulders. Two other hands reached down beside him and grabbed the boy's arms, and the older brother pushed from below. They lifted the young boy through the opening and carried him across the deck.

Their own ship did not appear to be on fire. But there on the horizon was a large ship, a cruise liner engulfed in flames. Heads bobbed above the water wherever he looked. People

324

in boats circled the cruise liner, pulled some men out of the water, fired at others with machine guns.

The guards had disappeared from his ship. The large tarpaulin had been pulled back to reveal sacks and barrels bursting with food. Sugar and dried beans lay scattered across the deck. Two men were leaning over an open barrel and stuffing themselves with pickles. Another had collapsed on the deck, convulsed by stomach cramps.

He had stolen Pivnik's crust of bread, and two metres above him, all these riches. The older boy thrust his arm deep into one of the barrels until the brine reached his armpits. Max pulled him away and pointed at the chap with the stomach cramps.

They skidded over pools of pickle brine and rolling dried peas, climbed down the side of the boat and jumped into the icy water. After a short stretch, Max's feet found a sandy ledge. Shots rang through the air. There, on the promising shore, stood SS officers who fired at the crowd on the beach and the swimmers in the water.

Someone shouted orders: they must stand up and start marching. Max dragged the boys with him. They reached a grassy patch above the beach. The younger boy collapsed again, and Max was no longer strong enough to help him up. The SS officer next to them lowered his gun. He was short and stocky with a tired face, a kind face really.

*Lord ... do not abandon me now.*

*Praise praise praise praise the Lord.*

*Gam zu letovah.*

*Amen.*

The SS officer nodded at the younger brother, then told Max to prop him up against a tree. The older brother helped and they managed to sit him upright against the trunk.

The officer nodded, pointed his gun and shot him.

# Maurice

'Lastly . . .'
*A Theory of Diamond-Cutting*

# 1

By the end of the war Esther Morningstar had once again fallen from favour. Not dramatically this time, not with the violence of a hammer threatening to come down on a diamond, but slowly and quietly.

She had reached her high point in 1944 with 'A method for computing the weight of incendiary attack required against Japanese cities.'

Then the stranger's house where her own daughter slept was hit by a German bomb, and instead of a hunger for revenge, Mrs Morningstar felt only a definite and essential desire never to send any bombs to any country ever again, directly or indirectly.

She resigned from the lab the day her parents' home in

Hatton Garden was struck. Her parents were unharmed, but her father must have been more shaken than he admitted. He lost his appetite and no longer took pleasure in passing his loupe around the dinner table. During his final weeks they spoon-fed him like a child and he submitted to them with docile tenderness.

It was then that Esther attempted to tell her mother about those patterns she had watched her cut out in Hatton Garden decades ago, and how she felt they had influenced her own love of geometry. Her mother laughed awkwardly and wiped the spoon on her apron.

The continuing assault on German and Japanese cities seemed unnecessary, vindictive and cruel to her. She made this clear to the Wizard when she resigned.

He pointed at her wedding ring, which she now wore in the lab. 'That ring, that's not the gold from poor Mr von der Weide's medal, is it?' And he chuckled.

It was this chuckle that the younger men now imitated behind his back. For the Wizard's hard and feared rule had ended long ago; only Mrs Morningstar had never realized. She had been so obsessed with the lab's glorious past she had never thought to wonder about its present. The lab had been on the brink of bankruptcy before the war; only the bombing research had injected it with new life. The Wizard's best men had left his lab long ago and worked on developing radar systems during the war. The ones who remained with him were mid-calibre scientists, trusty workhorses who could estimate a load of explosives but would not be expected to generate brilliant new ideas. This was why he had invited her to return to the institute despite the awkward memories. There were simply not that many decent mathematicians, let alone crystallographers, who were eager to work with him. Other labs had enough Nobel medals to line a shelf.

It did not hurt Mrs Morningstar much that she was among the mid-calibre talents. She had achieved *something*; in her own small way she had counted. She would go back to Bentham College and teach first-year students, and watch the class with sharp eyes in case she spotted a young woman with the potential to be a fifty-seven-facet brilliant.

'Oh, I never destroyed that medal,' she said with delicious nonchalance. 'At least, not in the way you assume.'

The diamond cutter died, leaving most of his stock to Esther's mother. The remaining stock was divided among Esther's four sisters.

To Esther he left a few raw diamonds and the workshop in the attic.

She could not fathom his intention. Was this an insult, a terrible judgement from the grave? A reminder of the three sons he had lost, and for whom she could be no substitute? A reminder that no matter how high she had risen, no matter how free and educated she thought she was, she must never forget that this was her home; she had been raised in a dark attic and must never think she could escape it?

'Perhaps it was meant as a kind gesture, as a fond nod to

the family's only crystallographer,' said her husband. They were sitting by the Hampstead ponds, as they often did these days, and he was folding paper boats.

She did not believe him. He showed her how to fold a paper boat, and she said: 'I'm no good, and he prefers yours anyway. I'm no good with practical things like that.'

She put her boat on the water and watched it grow soggy until it sank.

'Will you show me the workshop?' Her husband stood up. 'I've only visited it once before, you know.'

The steep steps were difficult for him. He had to bend one knee and put that foot on the next step, then drag the bad leg after him. Twice she suggested he abandon the climb, but he insisted on continuing. She paused before the door. The key, the lock, the empty workshop. Any moment Nathan would pipe up behind her: 'Come on, lambchops, we haven't got all day.'

When she opened the door a breeze blew into the attic and stirred a pile of folded envelopes on the worktop. They fluttered to the floor and she stopped and picked them up one by one, thinking of her father folding them with his old stiff hands. The scaifes were covered with grey cloth. She took the raw diamonds out of the safe. Glassy pebbles. Her husband rolled them around in his palm, entranced.

'All these years I've been married to a diamond cutter's daughter, and I've never once touched a diamond.'

'I suppose we'll sell them as they are.'

'Can you?'

'Well, someone will take them. Of course we'll lose a packet. The best thing would be to cut them and then sell them, but . . .' She gestured at the covered scaifes.

'Someone in the family could cut them here, in this workshop.'

'There are no more cutters in the family.' She gathered up the empty envelopes, dropped them in a dustbin by the door and repeated: 'There are no more cutters in my family. Father, Nathan, Simon and Solly. They're all gone.'

She patted some dust off her dress. 'They're all gone. We'll sell the place as it is, someone will snap up the raw stones, and that'll be that.'

The expression on her husband's face unsettled her. He looked straight into her eyes as if wanting to draw out something.

She laughed sadly and shook her head. 'He never taught us girls. Whoever heard of a diamond cutter in a skirt?'

'I have.' He uncovered one of the scaifes.

'I told you, we didn't learn any of that.'

He swiped his finger over the scaife, picked up diamond dust, dabbed it on her forehead.

'I've seen you.'

'What do you mean?'

'I've seen you do it.'

She tensed, then pushed him away.

'That's not possible.' After a long pause, she said: 'It's not possible. Even if I *did* at some point learn to cut diamonds,

331

which I didn't, I certainly wouldn't have continued with it after we were married.'

'Not during the day. At night.'

'I don't want to hear it. We're leaving. I cannot bear this – I cannot bear being here. You don't understand what it is like for me to be here.' She tugged at her collar for air. 'It's suffocating, it's—'

'At first I was a bit worried, you know.'

'I told you, don't speak to me of that. It has nothing to do with my family. It's a medical condition, you've said so yourself, it'll get better once this awful war is over.'

She was using the terse, strict tone that always silenced him. But this time he held her gaze and continued in a calm and friendly voice, as if she had not spoken.

'You see, there I was, freshly married to this girl who seemed perfectly normal all day long, until she went to bed. She would fall asleep and about an hour or two after midnight, she would begin to toss and turn and then would sit up and begin the strangest ritual I'd ever seen.'

'I cannot understand why you're doing this.' Esther covered her ears.

'Once I shook you awake, but then you looked at me with such terror that I never dared try that again, so I let you just get on with it. It was every night, in the early days.'

'Yes, because I suffered from somnambulism. There is no use reading anything else into it.'

'Wait. I haven't told you about your ritual yet. I've never told you because I knew you didn't want to hear. But if I don't tell you now, I'm never going to tell you. And, Essie, dear, I need to tell you.' He sat down at one of the scaifes. 'I've needed to tell you for so long.'

She folded her hands and pressed them together. She did not want to hear what he had to say. She wanted to leave this attic and never hear it mentioned again. She wanted to pretend she had never entered a diamond-cutting workshop. Only it was the first time he had asked her for anything. Could this be true? She cast her mind back. There was not a single request she remembered, not a single demand. Not even a plea to have their cook replicate his favourite childhood dish; no, she did not even know what his favourite dish was.

'Well, then.' She sat down at the scaife next to him.

'You had your ritual. It was the same every night. First of all, you would mutter to yourself. Mathematical stuff usually, so I never had a clue what it was all about. And sometimes you'd talk to people and give them orders. And all the while, you'd be hunched over something, like this, one side of your face scrunched up like this, staring at something between your hands, and your right hand would be gripping some invisible stick or tool and moving it about. And there I was, a newlywed chap half terrified of his clever young bride, and I couldn't for the life of me understand what it was all about, until one day we dropped by your father's workshop, this workshop, to pick something up. And there he was. I'd only ever seen him at home, or in shul, but there he was sitting hunched over his scaife, and then I knew what my bride was doing every night.'

'Yet you didn't tell me.'

'You hated the subject of diamonds then, remember? You told me never to mention diamonds. I wanted to buy you a ring for our engagement, but you wouldn't let me. A pendant, earrings. You wouldn't let me. The only thing you ever allowed me to buy you was the wedding ring. You hated going to the workshop. You would have been mortified to hear that every night, when the world stopped watching you, you turned into a diamond cutter. It would have been unkind to tell you something that you would be ashamed of, and that in any case you couldn't change. Once Miriam was born, you did it less and less, until ... well, you know, until about a year before the war.'

'And now?'

'Less fretfully. You used to be very agitated and fretful, as if that blasted diamond was about to slip out of your fingers. It was terrible to watch. Now you just sit there like a contented old cutter at his scaife.' He paused. 'In the beginning I was worried that it would give you ... how shall I say? ... a nerve fever, you know. That it would harm the child. All that rocking back and forth and shouting orders and muttering formulas – it didn't seem a healthy thing for a woman who's expecting to do. But I didn't want to tell anyone about it. It would have felt disrespectful towards you. So ...' He scratched his cheek in embarrassment. 'Well, this will sound terribly daft, but I ... well, you know, we were very young, weren't we, and the young come up with all sorts of sentimental nonsense?' He scratched his cheek again. 'You see, in those early attacks, you were ... it was as if you were possessed. Or ill, even. And I would sit there in the dark and watch you and have no idea what to do. I didn't want to touch you for fear of waking you up and frightening you. I didn't want to call for help because, damn it, Essie, I thought if I told anyone about this they'd cart you off to an asylum. But I had to do something! So the only thing that came to mind was this. One night I was watching you and I remembered how you had walked around me seven times on our wedding day. Remember? To spin a protective web around me. Afterwards you said very loudly, and to everyone who would listen, that all these rites were of course hocus-pocus and future generations would laugh at them. But when you were walking around me, the truth is, Essie, I *did* feel protected. I was a nervous young chap, and there was this bright clever girl spinning her web around me. So that night, when your fits, or your sleep-walking, or whatever you want to call it, when it became truly terrible, and you were rocking back and forth, well, I got up and I moved the bed away from the wall a little, very carefully, with you on it, and then I walked around it once, slowly, because I didn't want to wake you, and you went on muttering and rocking, and then I walked around it again, and you took no notice at all, and again, and by the fourth or fifth time you seemed to have calmed down a little. I walked around you seven times. You'll say that it's not surprising that it had a calming effect. Everyone knows that children find it soothing when you walk up and down with them, so there might be a perfectly rational explanation, but in any case, the fact is that I walked around you and our child seven times, and when I was done you simply sat still for a bit, and then you lay down and went to sleep.' He sighed. 'And after that, whenever it was very bad, I would walk my circles around you.'

She slumped against the scaife and did not care that the sleeves of her dress were smudged with black diamond dust.

'Did I ever ... you know ... did I ever talk during those attacks?'

'I suppose you're asking whether you ever revealed in your sleep that Miriam was another man's child,' he said as calmly as if they were still talking about how to sell the raw diamonds. 'The answer is no.'

'You knew!'

'I may not be a mathematician, but I can count to nine.'

She wiped her eyes on the sleeve, and that was her face blackened, too.

'It was the most evil thing I ever did.' Her small, shaking voice was hardly audible. 'And I'm so sorry. My dear, I'm so very, very sorry.'

'She's our daughter in all the ways that matter. I've never cared about anything else but the fact that she's our daughter.'

'How you must have hated me when you found out.'

'I was too relieved to hate you.'

'Relieved?'

'I thought I was the only one with a hidden blemish, so to speak.' He pointed at his leg. 'It was never broken, you know. That cast, well, my mother advised me to put it on when I first went to meet you.'

'But you still walk with a limp.'

'I've always walked with a limp. I had polio as a child, and that leg was left crippled. Only I thought you wouldn't want me if you thought I was a cripple. My mother told me not to worry. She had an idea. I was to put on a cast and pretend I'd broken my leg. Then after the wedding, well, we never really thought about what I would tell you after the wedding.'

'But my relations must have known – Hannah – my sisters knew your family. Hannah knew all about you, she told me you were considered especially kind.' And gullible, she thought, especially kind and gullible; and she wanted nothing more than to cure all the wounds she had ever inflicted on him.

'Everyone knew, Esther. Hannah, the other girls, even your mother and father. Everyone knew that I was crippled for good and that you were expecting a child. They matchmade us. And what a match we were.' He looked sadly at his useless leg. 'There I was, limping around our bed seven times, one moment terrified that you would develop some nervous fever, the next moment terrified that you would see through the broken leg business. You were a scientist, for goodness' sake, the brightest person I'd ever met, and here I was trying to fool you with a mock plaster cast. Then when Miriam was born, and when I counted to nine and hit on a date well before we ever laid eyes on each other, well, I was relieved. I thought, thank goodness, she'll never mind about my leg now.'

'And I never did, but not because of Miriam. I wouldn't have minded anyway. Whereas I suppose you must have minded once your relief, as you call it, was over. You must have rather regretted your deal.'

'Never.'

'I suppose that makes you a saint.'

'Not a saint. Just a man who loves his wife and the little girl who's been his daughter from the moment she was born.'

Esther burst into sobs. She rolled the raw diamonds over the worktop with her fingers.

'It was our formula.' She was sobbing with the uninhibited pain of a child. 'The numbers and letters I was muttering, that was our formula. I had come up with a formula for cutting the perfect stone. It was going to make us rich.'

'Essie.' Mr Morningstar thumped the worktop. 'That man has brought us nothing but misfortune. You *must* let go of your obsession.'

Esther let out an angry cry. 'Not the Wizard! He had nothing to do with it, nothing! It was *our* formula, do you understand? Mine and Simon's and Solly's and ...' her shoulders were heaving with sobs, '... and Nathan's.'

All week the scaifes turned, but on the seventh day they stood still. The shop was locked. The hissing flames and humming wheels fell into respectful silence before the sound of songs and prayers. Esther's father did not touch his diamonds. Her mother did not sew. Shabbat folded its thick warm blanket around them and they sat swaddled in it until nightfall. Nathan had a duplicate of her father's keys, so it was not stealing exactly. They were going to see Leybesh, he said, and it was not a lie since they did go to see Leybesh, only then they all went to the workshop: Nathan, Simon, Solly, Esther and Leybesh, though Leybesh always grew bored and left early. Esther, the wonder girl. She measured and calculated and knew all about refraction. And her brothers, well, Nathan liked to say that he could cut a stone just by looking at it. She explained her calculations to them. They taught her to cut a stone. They would develop the perfect cut together, and it would make them rich, so fabulously rich and famous. That old lump of coal would finally have transformed itself into a gem, and no one in their family would ever have to make diamond dust again.

*Remember to write! And when you come back, we'll finish the perfect cut. Adler & Sons & Daughter.*

She slid her hands over the cold scaife.

'We were going to cut them together, don't you understand?' Her palms were black with dust. She touched the bench. This was the bench where Nathan would have sat. She touched the scaife to her left, Simon's scaife, and then the one to her right, where her husband now sat. Solly's scaife. Solly, whom they had called the rabbi because he was so studious.

And then, with a delay of almost thirty years, she screamed. She screamed and clawed at her own face, and when her husband tried to pull her towards him and calm her, she screamed even louder and clawed at his face, until they were both smeared with black dust and grease.

'I killed them,' she screamed. 'Don't you understand? I made them leave, when I should have held them back. Do you know what I said to my brothers? "Remember to write!" And I couldn't wait to see them in uniform so I could boast to my friends!'

'Bullets killed them, Essie, not you. Other men killed them.'

'And I killed her too. I told her to get out of the house and she moved into those grimy factory dorms and then that awful shabby flat . . .'

'The bomb killed her.'

'I made her sleep there. I made her leave. And I made them leave, too.' She beat on his chest with both hands. 'So now you've been warned, and what can I say, save yourself while you can. I have the touch of death, you know. Everyone near me must die, so save yourself or you'll be next.'

'That's nonsense, and you know it. That's pure superstition. There's no such thing as a curse, Essie. There's no deeper meaning to a bomb. If you want to know why our daughter died, I can tell you. She died because a high-explosive bomb hit her flat. If you want to know why your brothers died, I can tell you that, too. They died because other men fired at them with machine guns. They died because the human skin is not bullet-proof. If you want to know why we are still alive when they are dead, well, the reason is that our bedroom was not hit, and I was never called up for military service because of my leg. Everything else is nonsense and superstition.'

She collapsed into his arms, and cried until she was spent.

They sat on the bench together, her head on his shoulder, his thick strong arms around her shivering body.

'Maurice, dear.' She smoothed back her hair, blackening the grey, and stared at the scaife with such hatred as if her brothers had been ground up on it. 'I suppose we ought to light that gas flame.'

He arranged the tools for her and passed her a loupe. She wedged it into her eye socket, softened the lead dop, pressed one of the raw stones into it. The formula was in her head, adjusted and perfected over thousands of nights. With the tired routine of someone who had done this countless times before, she sat down at the scaife and began cutting her stone.

The perfect cut: it would not make them fabulously rich, but it would bring in enough money to fix the roof, to paint the walls, to build a swing in the garden for their grandson. She had thought that the house in Hampstead was too old and dangerous for a toddler, as old and dangerous as herself. She had meant to look after the little boy until the first sharp shock had worn off, and then pass him on to a cousin or a niece, where he would be safe from her curse. A spring child for a new beginning, saved from the rubble of a block of flats.

No, she thought now, no one else was her grandson's

keeper. No one else would fold paper boats for him with such dedication. No one else would love him as much as she and her husband did. They were old, flawed, and had been mended many times over, but they would look after him and keep him safe. She felt her husband's hand on her back. With her eyes on the spinning scaife she dreamed of the new roof, and the pale green walls, and the swings in the garden for little Nathan.

# Death Vomit

Charlie adjusted his goggles with one hand. He had never seen a German vessel before, but now the sea was swarming with them. Submarines, freighters, warships, patrol boats moved about frantically like insects in a burning house. His squadron attacked three submarines in the bay of Lübeck. Then he and another pilot, Archie Hayes, flew west and looked for more ships. The insects had cleared the water for now. They attacked an airstrip near Schleswig instead. Charlie shot down one Dornier, Hayes another. The flak was heavier than anything Charlie had ever experienced. What a day.

'Good work,' said Hayes when they were back at the airstrip.

'That flak. Unbelievable.'

Hayes nodded and pushed back his goggles. 'Haven't seen anything like it since the Battle of Britain. It's a sort of death vomit.'

'A what?'

'A death vomit. When your dog has a tick, if you're not

careful when you twist it out, it's easy to sort of squash it. And what they do then is, they vomit into the dog. And all the disease that's in the tick ...' Hayes cupped his gloved hands, '... it gets vomited into your dog. So you've got to be careful to get the tick out alive. And that's what this flak fire is. A dying tick.'

On 3 May 1945, at four o'clock in the morning, a chap brought Charlie a cup of tea. Briefing: plenty of movement on the water again. Nazis leaving the burning house, possibly to Norway.

'Told you,' Hayes said, and slapped Charlie on the back. 'Death vomit.'

'They ought to have surrendered when Hitler killed himself.' Charlie scratched his chin. 'Saved us some trouble.'

'Can't be long now ...'

'Yes, yes, I know. Death vomit.'

Another cup of tea. He climbed into his Typhoon. Bad weather. Cloudy, rain. Could have stayed in old Blighty for that.

He destroyed a locomotive and a couple of lorries. The weather was still too bad to attack the bay. Back to base for some breakfast. More tea. And up again. Another locomotive. He'd fired at so many locomotives he didn't care if he never saw another train.

He looked over his shoulder. Hayes's plane was on fire. Bugger. Charlie saw him sail towards the ground, dangling from his parachute.

After lunch the weather was still rotten. They chased some Junkers. Charlie hit one and it burst into flames. This was shaping up to be a good day. Below the formation of eight Typhoons, lorries scurried like ants across the land. And then the bay, the ships bound for Norway. The order came and Charlie pressed the salvo button. Eight rockets. Nice. Each of the other Typhoons launched eight rockets. Crikey! The largest ship looked as if it was lifted out of the water by the impact. Then it burst into flames. Bad flak from one of the smaller vessels.

*Death vomit*, Charlie thought.

The chaps were celebrating. Charlie blocked the offered drink with a raised palm. It would do him good to cut down a bit.

'Didn't think I'd see you again this soon,' he said, and knocked his empty glass against Hayes's full one. Hayes and his parachute had landed in a tree behind a primary school. The children escorted him to a local policeman, who briefly arrested him, then released him when he heard a rumour that the Americans might be about to roll into town.

'This war is over,' Hayes said, and laughed. 'I don't care if it's official or not. You should have seen the policeman's face! And the children were so disappointed, the little bastards – they couldn't wait to see me strung up on the nearest lamppost.'

'All right then.' Charlie held out his glass. 'But only a small one. Hang on. Not *that* small.'

He looked around. Hayes was still talking about the bloodthirsty children. A crowd of men pushed in through the doors. He knew only about half of them. The doors swung back and hit the face of a limping chap who trailed behind the others, struggling to keep up. A clerk of some sort: he was carrying a folder under his right arm.

Charlie went over.

'Need help?'

'I can still just about open a door, cheers.' He rubbed his scarred face where the door had hit him. The nose was crooked from an old fracture and coarse knobbly tissue welded together the left side of his face from his temple to his cheek. The scarring pulled at his left eye and lips and it looked as if he was sneering. Or perhaps he *was* sneering.

'I remember you,' he said. 'Charles.'

'Jack. Good to see you.'

'Don't lie.'

'Let me get you a drink.'

'I'll come with you.' He dumped his folder on the table and confidently selected two, three bottles. 'Will you have one? I invented this one myself. The Flaming Gladiator. The key is not to go overboard with the ingredients.' He shook spirits into a tall glass. 'Watch the flambé effect right at the end. I used to torture my wife with this. She winced every time I set another one on fire. Evil of me, but what can I do? I'm very fond of it.'

'You're married?'

'Sort of. They sent me home after I crashed, but the wife

and I didn't get on too well once I was there all the time. She loved me better when I was in the desert. We got married when I was on home leave, you see, so she thought that was the deal she was getting. Then a friend got me a job at a paper, and here I am.' He mixed a second cocktail and handed it to Charlie. Then he struck a match and watched the flames dance over the surface of their drinks. 'Satisfying.'

'Cheers.'

'Cheers.' Jack downed his drink and mixed himself another. 'So here we are, the cripple and the fighter ace. Who would have thought. Have you heard from any of the others?'

'I saw Marx in Rhodesia, of all places. He was playing the great agitator at some mine or other ... No, thanks. I think I'll switch back to beer.'

'Well, it's easy to lose touch. You may have noticed, for example, that my right leg has vanished. Or perhaps you haven't noticed. They did a nice job with the peg leg, though I still miss the real thing. My big toe is believed to be in Abu Sueir, and the knee, somewhere behind enemy lines. I hope the Italians appreciated it. It was a good knee. *Un bel ginocchio.*'

'I'm sorry.'

'Don't be. It wasn't your fault. Or your *ginocchio*, for that matter.' Jack's glass was empty again. 'If that's the price for never having to fly again, I'd pay it twice over. I'd throw in my arms as well. Anything to never get into another bloody Gladiator, flaming or otherwise.'

Charlie glanced over his shoulder. The other chaps were out of earshot.

'I know what you mean,' he said.

'You do?'

'Oh, in the beginning it was all right. I threw up every time I flew a loop, but then I'd see an impala or a herd of elephant or one of those snowy mountains and I'd tell myself I was the luckiest chap in the world. Now I just want it to be over.' He glanced over his shoulder again. 'To be honest, these last few days have felt like ... well, one of the chaps called it a death vomit.'

'But you've done pretty well. I've heard all about you.'

'Well, I loathe it. Even in the beginning I loathed it. You know what happened the very first time I climbed into a Tiger Moth? I'm there on an airfield in Bulawayo, kites roaring overhead, and the instructor shows me how to take her up, and all I can think is, oh fuck.' He poured himself another beer. 'Those were my exact thoughts. Oh fuck. And that feeling's pretty much remained with me. If anything, it's got worse.'

'Well, good luck for tomorrow.' Jack grinned and slapped him on the shoulder. 'If you crash, I know a good plastic surgeon in Alexandria. He used to do all the society belles.'

'Perfect. I'll come out of the war with better cheekbones than before.'

He wrote a letter to Georgina and told her about Jack. Then he went to bed. At midnight he woke up and could not fall asleep again. He tossed and turned, and eventually got up and made his way over to Hayes's room.

'Hayes.'

'Huh?'

'Sorry. I've got to ask you something.'

'What time is it?'

'Late. Early. Sorry. I'll let you get back to sleep in a minute. It's just ... listen. When they send you home, do they send you home in uniform?'

'Not if you take it off.'

'I mean, when they send you home in a box.'

'Hmm. Yeah, I suppose they do.'

He kneeled down and put his hand on Hayes's shoulder. 'Would you do me a favour?'

Hayes grunted vague assent.

'If they send me home ... in a box ... do you think you could switch my uniform for civilian clothes? Not all of it, just the jacket and the trousers.'

'Jesus!' Hayes sat up.

'Only the jacket and the trousers. It's for my old man. It would make an awfully big difference to him.'

'But he won't see you. It's not as if they go and show your body to your parents. At least I don't think they do.'

'Still. It would make a difference to me, I suppose.'

'You don't want to be buried in your uniform?'

Charlie looked away. 'Sorry, it must sound odd. But that's how it is. And also – if you don't mind – if you could give them this.' He placed a wooden box at the foot of the bed.

'What's gone into you? This is about to be over. Even if they hit you, you'll be fine. Look at me, I was shot down and here I am.'

'It's just a feeling I have.' Charlie didn't want to tell him about Jack, about what it had been like to see Jack and see himself in Jack. He lifted the lid off the box. 'If you want to know what's in it . . .'

'No need to tell me.'

'Well, I've got nothing to hide. It's just some bits and bobs, pictures and things. There's an envelope with a white feather in it, if you could give that to my old man. And an old sort of postcard, that one's for my brother. Or just give the whole wooden box to my parents.' He carefully replaced the lid. 'And if they ask, or even if they don't ask, if you could tell them about the uniform, that would be good.'

'Hang on, they wouldn't send us home in a box, though. They'd bury us here. Jesus! Now you've made me think about it too. Go back to bed, will you? We'll be fine. The war's over.'

Hayes was right. The war was as good as over. A few more days in his Typhoon. Then home. But still, better to be safe. In all likelihood, he'd take the wooden box to Highgate himself. But there was nothing wrong with a bit of precaution. It made him feel safer to have given all that stuff to Hayes, as if he'd tricked fate. Like carrying an umbrella to make sure it stayed dry.

He went back to bed, lay on his back and pressed his palms to his face. To be alive. Unlike the poor buggers in the lorries, the locomotive, the ships. To be alive. To have all of life before him. All the poems he would write. All the cities he would see. All the mountains, all the jungles.

And perhaps, perhaps he and Georgina would even buy a farm.

# My Own

It was almost over: Grace could smell it. Every day now stretched out painfully, to be endured with her last ounce of strength, for when the war was over, she could finally start looking for Max. She would find Max, and together they would find Max's mother.

In Holland, in the deep winter, she had built a snowman with some local children. They ran around looking for sticks to turn into arms. 'Here, here!' the smallest boy cried, and pulled a branch out of the snow. A long, straight branch, with a shorter branch laid across and tied into place with wilted grass. 'And there's another one – wait – and over there . . . and there—'

'Let's put them back,' Grace said as calmly as she could. She took the crosses from the boys and drove them back into the snow. Three neat lines. They walked back to the camp and built another snowman closer to the barracks.

Now she pictured all those crosses amid the molten snow. Pools of muddy water. That would be the end of the war: pools of muddy water divided by brittle brown crosses.

Grace and Paul sat in the back of their ambulance. Paul kept his back against the metal frame and a sketchbook on his knees, his pencil jumping about because of the potholes. Children spotted them from afar and came racing across the fields. They crowded around the back and drummed on the metal platform with begging hands. Barefoot, picking at scabs, scratching arms red with scabies. The dull blond hair so thin he could see lice crawl between the follicles.

One evening Grace gathered the men in her unit around for Silent Meeting. She looked up to see Paul standing there. He did not join in their worship but stood outside the circle until it was over, as if he wanted to tell her something. When she asked him what was up, he shook his head and slouched off to his unit.

She would have asked him again the next day, for she was sure that something was eating away at him. But the following day brought strange rumours, the strangest she had yet heard during her service. They were driving through northern Germany, on their way to a newly liberated concentration camp near the bay of Lübeck. The war was not yet over and they heard gunfire every night, crossed pontoon bridges, bomb craters hastily filled with rubble. Then a rumour reached them that the RAF had sunk two ships in a nearby bay. The pilots had apparently thought the ships were carrying fleeing SS officers. In truth, the passengers were thousands of prisoners being transferred from several camps to an unknown destination. It was mayhem in the bay, utter chaos: survivors and bodies, and far too few ambulances to deal with them all.

She ran over to Paul and told him the news.

'I'm going to try and get them to send me there.' She seized the collar of his uniform and dragged him closer. 'Do you understand? Thousands!'

'Terrible.'

'That's not what I mean. Thousands. That means there's a possibility that Max might be there.'

'If he is in a camp.'

'Well, if he's still alive, he's in a camp.'

'He could be in the one we're heading towards. The one they just liberated.'

She could see that he did not want her to go to the bay. He had heard the same rumours, and he did not want her to stand before a thousand drowned men and look for Max's face. She was still holding on to his collar.

'He could be. But I'm going to go to the bay and help those men there, and I'm going to stay until I've seen every single victim. The drowned ones, too. If it's thousands, well, I'm going to look at thousands. And you, you're going to the liberated camp. And when you enter it, I want you to look at every single man in there, dead or alive, no matter how ill, no matter how ...' she let go of the collar '... repulsive. Even if it's horrible in there and you don't want to go near them. Just throw on more de-lousing powder and get close enough to see their faces. Or to let them see yours, because, well, Max might look different now. Will you do that for me? Please. Don't let them chuck Max into a mass grave.'

He looked at her with the sympathy and kindness reserved for the slightly unhinged.

'I'll do my best,' he said.

She gave him a quick pat on the back and ran back to her unit.

There were hundreds of bodies on the beach and in the sea. Blood had dyed the water red. Striped jackets floated up and ballooned in the waves. She bent over and checked for a breath, a pulse, but they were all dead. She walked on, stepping over bodies, trying to find signs of life. She began talking to them, nonsensical nothings in a friendly voice, just in case there was one who heard her voice and answered.

The sea crashed in and brought more bodies. She checked them too, then went back to those on the beach. When she straightened up she saw that she had hardly advanced ten yards, and there was still the entire beach stretching out before her, covered with bodies.

There was some movement ahead. A group of survivors clustered around a shop front on the promenade above the beach. One of them was wrapped in a sheet. She spotted ordinary townspeople, too. Women dressed in cotton dresses with buttons down the front. Boys in short trousers. Grace shouted up to them to come and help, but the

355

women hurried away and ushered the boys into low brick houses with washing lines strung across the front.

Grace wished then that she had a gun and could force them to assist her.

A couple of survivors came out of the shop carrying loaves of bread. The one in the sheet was now wrapped in a large coat. Grace walked up to them. They had deep red burn marks on their limbs and faces. She opened her bag, applied some cream and bandaged their wounds. She told them more ambulances were on the way. They should rest by the shop.

Two, three more groups of survivors staggered towards her. Soon her supplies were used up and she had to fetch more.

She paused and surveyed the beach. An emaciated figure with a shaved, scarred head moved towards her. The gaunt wizened face bore no burn marks, but he moved with a heavy limp. Broken ankle, probably. She took a step towards him and offered him her arm. He stopped. Licked his cracked lips. He mumbled something, the pitiful creature. She looked up from his broken ankle and tried to focus on his mouth, which moved helplessly until the tongue found enough strength to shape the sound. His eyes met hers. She held his gaze and could do nothing but nod, and nod again, and again, and nod through the tears, and keep nodding, before she even made out the word he was trying to form.

'Grace,' he said at last. 'Grace.'

# When All London Sparkles

In the dark damp hall of a medieval convent in Holland, a tiny withered nun had approached Paul with a boil up her nose that needed to be lanced. *I've had it since before the war, dear, and there was never a chance to have it seen to. God bless.* By the time he was done, the cup of camomile tea another nun served him had frozen over.

So much of his service had been spent either uselessly waiting, or patching up men so they could be sent into battle again. And then there was the German soldier who haunted his dreams. In his dreams he saw a tank in the night and a creature inside that was reaching through the hole at the top and trying to climb out and towards him.

When he sat in the back of his ambulance with his pencil jumping up and down on the pages of his notebook, it seemed to him that the only genuine good he had done during the war, or in his life, was lancing that old nun's boil.

They reached a stretch of heathland. Sandy paths curled through the heather. There was a large compound surrounded by barbed wire, and a gate with a sign that said, 'Danger: Typhus'.

They put up their tents and spoke to the men who were already there.

'Go on in,' one of them said, and pointed his thumb over his shoulder. 'Just make sure you get a good dusting of delousing powder first. And whatever you do, don't let them touch you.'

Paul covered his nose and mouth, and then he entered the camp.

The smell hit Paul as soon as he walked through the gate. He pushed his collar over his mouth and followed the straight sand road past a series of empty huts, as low and wide as barns, to the end of the camp.

The first bodies he saw lay close to the pools, as if they had tried to claw their way to the water; half-naked, with limbs contorted by rigor mortis.

He paused and entered one of the huts. Three silent creatures crouched in the dark, ape-like, with hollow eyes and bared teeth. There was no expression of joy or relief at his presence. Only this cowering, snarling, diseased, hungry watchfulness.

A kind of hysteria gripped him. He heard a noise behind him and whipped around. Something shuffled in the dark. If it tried to touch him, he would kill it. When he turned back to the cowering group, he thought they had edged closer.

He went outside to calm himself.

In the next hut, two inmates huddled in a corner with their emaciated arms around each other. One opened his mouth in a gargle. The other slowly stood up and staggered towards Paul, held out his skeletal hand. Paul raised his own hand and forced himself to smile. The man moved his hand up and down, still making that awful gargling sound. Paul hesitated. Then he took the man's hand and shook it. The bones felt loose under the papery skin.

When he left the camp and walked back to the ambulance, he noticed a small red bite on his right hand, between his index finger and his thumb.

He squatted down and washed his hands in a puddle.

There was a system they called the human laundry. It allowed Paul to carry out his tasks mechanically without having to pause and reflect. An inmate was brought in at one end of the human laundry tent, stripped and shaved of the hair on his head, his chest, in his armpits, his groin, carried to the next station where he was washed, dried, dusted with DDT, wrapped in a blanket, carried out to the hospital tent.

In the hospital tent, every bed shook with ceaseless cries for water. However much the helpers filled and refilled the cups, they could not quench the cries.

Paul was carrying a stretcher in from the human laundry when he saw one man get up from his bed. He tottered over to his neighbour, who was being fed intravenously with saline solution. The man unhooked the bottle with the saline solution, drank the contents and put it back on the hook.

Paul thought then that they might as well all give up. Ask God to wipe them all out and start afresh.

It was not retribution exactly, roping in local girls to bury the dead and help run the human laundry, more of a practical decision. There were thousands of inmates who had to be washed and fed, and only a hundred or so soldiers and the ambulance crew. At first the girls were sullen. They knew about the typhus risk. They reported for work every morning, leaning on their shovels while they waited to be de-loused. Some joker insisted on spraying powder down their blouses.

The German nurses slept in a tent that Paul entered once when he was looking for the sister. The space was extraordinarily neat and cool, a white cube lined with parallel white camp beds and white sheets folded into squares. It was because of this white sparseness that the photographs stood out. One over every bed. There they all were, smiling out of their studio portraits. Wehrmacht, Luftwaffe, SS. Side partings and shaved necks. Blond and handsome, blond and ugly, boyfriends, brothers, sons and husbands ... Paul thought, what on earth do you do with a country like this one?

It was around that time that he noticed a certain numbness in his right hand, between the index finger and the thumb, where the bite had been. He would massage it reflexively every now and then, but it did not go away. Instead it slowly spread to his fingers. He could still use it for the rough jobs around the camp, the feeding and washing, but he wondered what would happen if he tried to pick up a pencil or a carving knife. A hand had to be really rather strong to handle a carving knife, and rather calm to guide a pencil.

He asked the doctor about typhus symptoms. Numbness in the hand was not one of them.

He trained his left hand to hook up the bottles with the saline solution and to guide spoons towards the patients' mouths.

It was only when recovery set in, when the inmates had enough life in them to express something other than a cease-less demand for food and water, that pity recovered, too.

As the spoon-fed sugar water turned into tubs of steam-ing soup and finally, bowls of stew and potatoes, the products of the human laundry slowly became men again.

One afternoon the sister brought a vase of wildflowers and leaves into the hospital tent and placed it on a wooden crate in the centre for everyone to see.

The next morning Paul entered the tent and noticed that the cornflowers and yellow gorse were still there, but the green leaves had been stripped off their branches.

He cautiously asked what had happened. The men tended to hoard bread and potatoes under their pillows. His initial fear was that they had crawled out of their beds at night and eaten the leaves. Then he noticed that some of them had placed the leaves beside them on the pillows.

'Why did you do that?' he asked the man in the next bed.

'It is so pretty,' the man said. 'I wanted to have it close to me.'

The pyjamas were delivered two days later, on 7 May. Until the delivery, the inmates had worn their camp clothes. Then, the pyjamas. Paul handed them out with practised efficiency, ticking off names, quantities, walking through the tent with his clipboard. He came to the end and handed the last pair to a man who sat on his bed. He ticked off his name and then stood going over the list, making sure no one had been left out. He had been living through lists for weeks. This many bodies washed, this many mouths filled with soup.

After a minute or so he noticed that the man still sat on his bed in the same position, holding the folded pyjamas in his lap. Paul nodded at him, as if to say, yes, they're yours, put them on. But the man did not move.

It took Paul another moment to realize that the man was waiting for him to go away. He wanted to put on his new pyjamas, and he did not want to undress in front of another person. He was displaying a very natural, a very human sense of modesty, of modesty and shame.

Paul left the tent, walked past the ambulance where an old woman from the village was reading someone's palm, crouched down behind a hut and rested his forehead on the clipboard. He sat like that for a while. When he looked up, he spotted one of the nurses across the path, a stocky local woman with a round freckled face and blond hair she

362

wore in a coiled braid at the back of her head. She was unloading another delivery of pyjamas. He went to help her.

'They make such a difference, don't they, those pyjamas,' he said. It was not at all what he had wanted to say. He wanted to tell her something about what he had seen. About how a pair of pyjamas could make someone human again, and how terrible that was. But he could not find the words, and he knew he would never find them; that there would always be this image of the man with his pyjamas, that there would never be the words to match it.

'I noticed that, too,' she said. Then she stood up, and as she stood up she bent over slightly and put her hands on her stomach.

It was a mere moment; she straightened up and walked away before he could even convey that he had noticed the gentle roundness.

The truth was that he had noticed it that time at the pub with Charlie and Miriam, too. When she had stood up and paused ever so briefly midway with that hand on her stomach, some hidden part of him had known the gesture. Some part of him had known that her recurring nausea had nothing to do with her exhaustion from the night shifts.

The nurse had reached the hospital tent. She parted the canvas and weak voices drifted out still praising the new pyjamas.

That evening, there was a tremendous noise outside the Lambs' cottage in Highgate, as if the four winds had come together and blown upon the dead. Mr Lamb put his finger between the chapters of Ezekiel he had been reading and pushed back the curtain. Instead of an army of bones, he saw only a brass band trailed by cheering women and children.

His wife called from the hallway and he shuffled towards her, still holding his Bible with the index finger between the pages. In the bright rectangle of the doorway there stood a young man, an airman. His feet were respectfully planted outside the threshold, which no uniformed man had ever crossed.

The Bible slipped from Mr Lamb's grasp. It landed on the carpet with a soft thud. Then he realised the man in the doorway was not Charlie. He was some young man in an RAF uniform, but he was not Charlie.

His visitor stepped inside, reached out, steadied him with a strong arm just as the brass band passed their front garden. Mr Lamb tried to say something, but the drums and tubas drowned him out with their triumphant song.

He shook off the airman's arm and stared past him, at the open doorway where for a split second he had so clearly seen Charlie.

They were talking now, his wife and the young man: he was handing her a wooden box, murmuring condolences. Mr Lamb stood with his back to them, still staring out. The brass band was already disappearing round a corner. One of the children, a little boy, stopped to kneel down and tie his shoelaces. Mr Lamb waved at him. The boy smiled, waved back, then ran to catch up with his friends.

*

364

Mrs Morningstar watched the green fireworks from her office at Bentham College in Bloomsbury. She switched on the Anglepoise, tore the old blackout paper away, and leaned out of the single illuminated window in the vast black façade. Cheers and shouts drifted up from the streets.

It was time, then. She pulled back into the room and walked to a shelf crammed with lab tools. From the back of the shelf, she carefully retrieved an opaque jar containing 23-carat gold dissolved in aqua regia. The trajectory of human life was irreversible: the blue-white days were gone for ever. Neither her daughter nor her brothers would come back to life.

However, there were other travel paths that could be retraced. A Nobel medal, for example, could be smuggled from Heidelberg to London, could be dissolved in a jar of aqua regia to hide it, could be precipitated from the solution and sent to Sweden to be reminted, could be handed back to Professor von der Weide when he was restored to his teaching post. Yes, she decided, that was how it would be. She carried the jar down to the chemistry lab, carefully poured sodium bisulphite into the solution and waited until the gold mud settled at the bottom of the jar.

In a hospital in northern Germany, a British Army medic drew aside a curtain and asked: 'Mrs Hoffnung, are you quite sure this is your husband?'

She nodded.

'Well, he's lucky you recognized him. Under the circumstances.'

She cupped her hands around the brittle fingers. Out in the corridor, some of the soldiers broke into song.

'I didn't,' she said. 'He recognized me.'

He had lost consciousness and they both knew he would not make it through the night. Grace sat down on his left side, the heart side, and held his hand. When the medic was gone, she carefully laid down on the bed next to him, her hand on his skeletal shoulder, her head next to his on the pillow. She would stay with him. She would talk and sing to him as long as his heart was beating. And even then she would stay with him. She would not let them throw him in one of the group graves, six to a hole. No, she would rather bury him herself, if that's what it took. With her sensible strong hands, she would dig his grave herself.

'Max,' she whispered, 'we've never talked about this, but the one thing that I would ask you, well, if there's some way you could let me know where you are, once you're there. Because I'm really rather ignorant about these things, and we never had much time to talk about them, so I'm not quite sure if the Jewish place and the place for Quakers is the same. But I thought, if you could let me know somehow ... because you see, I don't really mind which place I go to. I'd just like to make sure it's the place where you are. I couldn't bear to be in any other place.'

The boys in Paul Lamb's unit were peeling potatoes and singing. There was going to be a feast. A bottle was going round and Paul already felt slightly drunk.

Men in a tent, celebrating their victory with wine and song: the ritual was ancient and eternal. They could have been camping by the town of Issus or indeed the river Euphrates, drinking wine out of animal skins and rams' horns. King David would have celebrated like this after smiting the Philistines. Paul thought of Miriam again, of what she would say if she could see him now, celebrating like King David: would she still think him unfit to be a father? To think he was a father! To think he had a child! Well, he would show her that he was not unfit. Stranger lives than theirs had been broken up and put back together.

He took another sip. King David rose to be a mighty warrior because the Lord was on his side. But towards the end of his life, the king wanted to thank God by building a temple: and God said no. He did not want David's temple, because David had shed too much blood.

Paul would tell Miriam that when he saw her again. He had not been completely wrong, or at least not more wrong than David. He and Miriam would sit on the Heath with their child and laugh and argue and laugh again, because that was how it was in peacetime, one could argue about these things and then laugh them off because they did not really matter very much.

He picked up another potato. The sergeant cook was chopping onions to the rhythm of the song. When they got to the end the cook punctuated it by driving his knife into a whole bulb.

Paul put down his peeling knife and mumbled that he was going out for air.

Outside the tent, with the hoarse singing voices behind him, he kneeled down and wiped his hands on the damp grass. He reached into his front pocket, scooped out the torn-up remains of his pledge card, pictured Miriam's face for a moment while he held the bits of paper in his fist, then scattered them over the grass.

# ACKNOWLEDGEMENTS

I would like to thank Jessica Leeke and Mark Stanton for their unwavering support, brilliant editing and sense of fun. A special thank-you goes to the Bensimon-Lerner family, without whose warm hospitality the early research for this book would not have been possible.

I am very grateful to Edwin Wrigley, Noel Makin and Clifford Barnard for telling me about their experiences as conscientious objectors, and to Rosemary Pearse for talking about her father, Dick Sheppard, a hugely influential pacifist. It was a privilege to hear their stories.

Staff and fellow researchers at Friends House Library, University College London, the British Library, the Imperial War Museum, Swarthmoor Hall and the Peace Pledge Union (especially Bill Hetherington) have been immensely helpful, knowledgeable and welcoming. It's wonderful that so many archives and libraries are still open to the public, offering free access to our shared heritage. Sion Dayson and Stephanie Ramamurthy offered excellent comments on the final draft.

Finally, I am very lucky to have Dan Lerner as my first reader. Thank you for laughing at the funny bits, commiserating over the sad ones, and quoting my favourite lines back at me when I temporarily lost the plot.